The Best of Philadelphia Stories
10th Anniversary Edition

Edited by
Mitchell Sommers, Courtney Bambrick, and
Julia MacDonnell Chang

PS Books Editors
Carla Spataro and Tara Smith

PS
BOOKS

Regional Publishing, National Voice
A division of Philadelphia Stories

Masthead

Publisher/Editorial Director
Carla Spataro

Publisher/Executive Director
Christine Weiser

Fiction Editor
Mitchell Sommers

Assistant Fiction Editor
Amy Luginbuhl

Poetry Editor
Courtney Bambrick

Nonfiction Editor
Julia MacDonnell Chang

Art Editor
Melissa Tevere

Director of Development
Sharon Sood

Production Manager
Derek Carnegie

Web Design
Loic Duros

Board of Directors
Kerri Schuster
Alison Hicks
Mitchell Sommers
Polia Tzvetanova

Contest Coordinator
Nicole Marie Pasquarello

Editorial Boards
fiction
Melinda Clemmer
Brian Ellis
Kathleen Furin
Elizabeth Green
Aimee LaBrie
Nathan Long
Ally Evans
Chelsea Covington Maass
Carla Spataro
Lena Van
Darrah M. Hewlett
Daniel Huppman
Andrew Linton
Brianna Garber
Meredith Hritz
Walt Maguire
Aidan O'Brien

nonfiction
Sam Dodge
Rachel Mamola
Deborah Off
Tracey M. Romero
Cassandra Visceglia
Sarah Wecht

poetry
Peter Baroth
Deb Burnham
Liz Chang
Margot Douaihy
Pat Green
George McDermott
Liz Dolan
Donna Wolf-Palacio
Aimee Penna
John Shea
Maria Thiaw
Valeria Tsygankova
Glenna Walsh
Liz Gray
Charlie O'Hay
Luke Stromberg

The Best of Philadelphia Stories
10th Anniversary Edition

© 2014 by Philadelphia Stories, Inc.
Published by PS Books, a division of Philadelphia Stories, Inc.
ISBN 978-0-9904715-0-9

Cover Image: "Aged" by Vincent Natale, acrylic on canvas, 24" x 18"
Cover Design: Sarah Eldridge
Book Design: Sarah Eldridge

PS Books
93 Old York Road
Ste. 1-753
Jenkintown, PA 19046
www.psbookspublishing.org

Correspondence and submissions to Philadelphia Stories should be
sent via our website at www.philadelphiastories.org. We invite submissions of short stories, poetry, essays, and artwork. Please see the
website for submission guidelines.

Contents

*Winner, Marguerite McGlinn Prize for Fiction
**Winner, Sandy Crimmins National Prize for Poetry

Introduction

This anthology is the result of ten years of publishing the best and brightest of the greater Philadelphia writing community. We're proud to have been able, over the years, to introduce you, the reader, to these wonderful poets, essayists, and fiction writers. *Philadelphia Stories* was the first to publish some of these writers. Others have found an audience in *Philadelphia Stories* in a long line of published work. We celebrate all of these writers because we can't imagine living in a community where creative writing isn't celebrated. We call our journal *Philadelphia Stories* because stories come in all forms and because Philadelphia isn't just where we live—it's who we are. Philadelphia is a city with heart and is defined by its passion. We are no different.

Philadelphia Stories has come a long way since our launch at Brasserie Perrier in 2004. Our early fundraisers were at times overwhelming but always satisfying. What still makes me the happiest is to walk into an event and see new faces. Of course I'm always happy to see old friends and supporters—who isn't? But meeting new writers and artists—people who are just now learning about *Philadelphia Stories*—is incredibly exciting. A community such as ours is a living, breathing thing, and we work hard to cultivate that community. We need everyone to thrive, and we only succeed because of you—our contributors and our readers.

In addition to *Philadelphia Stories*, we also publish a magazine featuring the work of young writers, *Philadelphia Stories, Jr.* Our books division, PS Books, is flourishing with the release of four titles, including this one, in 2014. We also offer many professional development opportunities for area writers, including our annual Push to Publish conference every October.

The writing collected in this anthology was carefully selected by the genre editors and myself. Since we've published two previous anthologies, we tried hard not to duplicate much. For me, the choices were tough. I love all the work we've published over the years. Some of my personal favorites did not make it into this anthology—either because they'd been anthologized before or because there simply wasn't enough room. The good news is that every story, poem, and essay we've ever published is archived on our website so you (and I) can read them anytime we want for free.

Thanks to all of you who've helped make this tenth anniversary possible.

Sincerely,

Carla Spataro
Editorial Director, PS Books
Co-Publisher, *Philadelphia Stories*

Acknowledgements

It would be impossible to thank everyone who has helped us reach our tenth year of publication. Our contributors make us who we are, and so we offer our heartfelt thanks to every poet, essayist, short story writer, fine artist, photographer, and reviewer whom we've had the privilege to publish. We would not exist without the tireless work and dedication of our various editorial boards led by Courtney Bambrick, Julia MacDonnell Chang, Mitchell Sommers, and our art editor, Melissa Tevere. The magazine always looks great because of Derek Carnegie, who has been designing it since 2004. *Philadelphia Stories, Jr.* owes a great big thanks to director Stephanie Scordia, who recently stepped down, and to Aileen Bachant, who has agreed to take up the helm. PS Books is in the dedicated hands of director Tara Smith and designer Sarah Eldridge. On this volume, we're grateful for the eagle eyes of proofreaders Elizabeth Cosgriff and Darrah M. Hewlett. The distribution of *Philadelphia Stories* is handled quarterly by Vincent Natale and Mario Sbraglia. We also want to thank the legion of editorial board members (on two magazines now), interns, and volunteers who help tirelessly with the many logistics involved in publishing one free magazine every quarter and another twice a year: reading mountains of submissions, working events, distributing magazines, organizing event details, blogging, Twittering, Facebooking, sticking thousands of snail mail labels, and so much more. The endless commitment and passion of these individuals make every issue and book the best it can be.

Without our members and our business sponsors, there would be no *Philadelphia Stories*. This is due almost entirely to the hard work of our development director, Sharon Sood. We'd also like to thank some of our longtime contributors, in particular the McGlinn and Hansma families for their continued support of the Marguerite McGlinn Prize for Fiction; Joseph Sullivan for his support of the Sandy Crimmins National Prize for Poetry; Tom Peters (Monks

Café); the folks at Writer's Relief; Alison Hicks (Greater Philadelphia Wordshop Studio); and Rosemont College.

We'd also like to thank our board of directors: Mitchell Sommers, Kerri Schuster, Alison Hicks, Polia Tzvetanova, and Alex Husted. Thanks to these volunteers for help with our strategic planning this year: Louise Turan, Barbara Bloom, and Stephanie Boudwin.

Finally, we'd like to thank the spouses, families, friends, and supporters of writers and artists everywhere, ours especially.

The Sphinx
Marguerite McGlinn

*Philadelphia Stories published Marguerite McGlinn's
story "The Sphinx" in the Fall 2007 issue. Marguerite
was a dedicated essayist, short story writer, and novelist.
She was also a teacher, wife, mother, and great friend.
Following in the footsteps of other great writers like J.F.
Powers and Flannery O'Connor, Marguerite addressed
themes of Catholicism and her Irish ancestry in her work.
She served as our nonfiction editor from 2005 until her
death in 2008. She and her family were dedicated supporters of Philadelphia Stories during her lifetime, and
her family continues to support the magazine by sponsor-
ing the prize named in her honor. Each year we are hum-
bled to award the Marguerite McGlinn Prize for Fiction
to a deserving short story writer. Several of the stories in
this anthology are winners of this national prize.*

Our Lady of the Angels Grammar School was a brick
building without artifice—not a tree or a shrub broke the
solid flank it presented to Felton Street. I was walking back
to Angels with my two best friends, Joyce Wotowski and
Rosemarie DeLullo. The school had no cafeteria, so most
kids went home for lunch. The walks back and forth were
the best part of the day anyway.

We crossed Market Street, walked up Hirst, and followed the bend around Arch. Midday clouds had taken
away the familiar pattern of sun and shadow. Joyce had an
umbrella, which her mother made her carry. I didn't care
about getting wet, but Joyce always had swollen glands,

so her mother made her carry an umbrella on cloudy days. We were on the first block of Felton Street between Arch and Race when a pack of boys raced around us. They jostled Rosemarie and tried to make her drop the soap sphinx she was carrying.

"Leave me alone. I'm gonna tell," she shouted as they ran off. Joyce and I closed in to protect her and began fussing over the awkward package she held in front of her like a take-out pizza.

"It's all right, Rosemarie. See, it's all right," I said.

I could see she was starting to cry, but she cried a lot. The sphinx was glued onto heavy cardboard and then wrapped in a cut-up brown bag. With the wrappings all you could see was a flat thing with a lumpy middle. Underneath the paper, though, was a miracle. Twelve bars of Ivory soap had been sculpted and glued into a towering monument to Sister Francis Xavier's Egypt display. Rosemarie had the most important piece and had special permission to bring it to school after lunch since she couldn't carry it with her schoolbag. My mother wouldn't let me make a special project. "A waste of good soap," she said. She felt the same way about using bed sheets for costumes in the Christmas pageant. "The good sisters, God bless them, don't know the value of money."

The boys had moved onto other mischief. Since it was trash day, metal cans lay on the scrubby patches of lawn that lined the curb. Some eighth-grade boys were jumping on the lids to flatten the handle against the corrugated metal. Soon, a screen door banged, and a woman with tight hair shouted at the rampaging boys. "Look what you've done. You should be ashamed!" The boys made a defiant line across the street but broke and ran when she marched down the porch steps. Robert DiGiordano lingered behind the other boys. Once in the street, he grabbed a trash can lid, threw it onto the nearest lawn and walked slowly away.

We watched from across the street. Robert DiGiordano was taller than the other boys. He had dark hair combed into a slick pompadour and had enough of a waist to keep his white shirt tucked into his navy blue school pants. His angle-striped tie sat at a cocky slant, making him look like an Italian Elvis Presley in a Mercy School uniform.

I thought about Robert a lot. In my room I listened to Elvis singing, *"Is your heart filled with pain, shall I come back again?"* and thrilled with despair. I would lie on the floor in the dark and moan with unrequited love. I told no one. I knew the odds were against me, and I didn't want to be teased. In the schoolyard he would lean against the chain link fence in an insouciant pose which the other boys tried to mimic with their graceless, lanky bodies.

"I think Robert DiGiordano likes you, Rosemarie," Joyce said.

Rosemarie sniffled a response. She was still shedding tears over the near-demise of the sphinx.

"Did you see him looking at you? And he came over to us at recess. Remember—the other day?"

"So what?" Rosemarie said. "We were all there. Maybe he likes you."

Rosemarie didn't like attention from boys. She wanted to go into the convent, to be a Sister of Saint Ann like the nuns at Our Lady of Angels School. All the girls wanted to be nuns at one time or another, but with Rosemarie it had stuck a long time. Boys liked her, though. She was tall and skinny. We both were. But Rosemarie was skinny in a better way— she already had breasts and real hips, not so straight up and down like me. She wore her long, black hair in braids. My mother made me get a perm.

"He likes you," Joyce kept saying.

She was probably right. A hot and bitter jealousy mixed into the boiling cauldron of unrequited love, but I had no choice. I had to join in.

"He does, Rosemarie. Remember he was on Hirst Street when we walked home yesterday. That's out of his way."

Joyce kept chanting in the background, "He likes you. He likes you."

Rosemarie clutched the sphinx tighter. "Stop it, Joyce. Stop saying that."

"He does. I can tell. Kathleen just said the same thing." Joyce skipped a little ahead of us, chanting, "He likes you. He likes you."

"I don't like boys. I'm not boy-crazy like you, Joyce Wotowski."

That was a low blow. Joyce was fat. She used to be the tallest girl in class, but we had caught up, and she started moving outward. Maybe it was her glands. Besides, everyone liked boys, except for Rosemarie.

"That's a mean thing to say, Rosemarie. Why did you say I'm boy-crazy?"

"I didn't say it. My mother said you were boy-crazy. She doesn't want me to act like that."

We reached the schoolyard right before the bell rang. I maneuvered myself into the row next to the eighth-grade boys. Sometimes Robert DiGiordano was in the very next row, and I could stand just an arm's length away.

Today, he was there, right ahead of me, so I could look at him all I wanted. He was looking at Rosemarie who was close to the front of the line. She always either led the line or held one of the doors open because she was a safety. The boys around Robert were smacking each other while staring ahead, but he just stood there. No one smacked him.

When we got into the classroom, everyone fussed over Rosemarie as she carried the sphinx-package to the back of the room. Since I was Rosemarie's best friend, I had to be part of the procession that formed around the sphinx.

"Rosemarie, put it down here on my desk, and I'll help you take the paper off," I said. She began moving in my direction.

"Kathleen will help Rosemarie. Everyone else, take your seat," Sister said.

I got scissors from Sister's desk and began cutting away the paper.

"Be careful," Rosemarie said. "Don't poke it with the scissors."

"I won't. I can cut paper."

"Girls," Sister's warning voice. "Work quietly and quickly. Everyone else, take out your arithmetic books."

Rosemarie looked wounded that Sister had to speak to us, and she gave me a look as if it were my fault. I angled my head in a "so what" gesture. I finished cutting the paper, and we lifted it off together. The sphinx was intact. Rosemarie had coated the soap with sand from the playground, and her mother had hair-sprayed the sand in place. The sand clumped a little around the face, but Rosemarie's sculpture was a Rodin among the clumsy pyramids and half-hearted obelisks already in the exhibit.

"Oh, Rosemarie, that's so nice," Sally Moore said later that afternoon when the class gathered around the Egypt project. "It's the best thing there."

"Rosemarie did a good job, as she always does," Sister joined in.

Behind her back, Francis Glennon was mouthing Sister's words.

Other classes came to visit our Egypt display, but we knew they really came to see Rosemarie's sphinx. Sister Francis Xavier tried to hide her pride as the other nuns clucked over the good work that her class had done. Sister Rosa Mystica even brought the eighth grade, and they rarely made classroom visits. The eighth-grade boys and girls filled all the spaces in our room. We eyed them with envy as they claimed the pride of place that was theirs. Robert DiGiordano was among the final few entering the room. The boys smirked at the exhibit. "Kid's stuff," Philip Tibault said. Robert didn't smirk. He looked right at Rosemarie. He held her eyes in a long stare and then said, "Nice sphinx." She blushed and looked down.

Three weeks later, the school heat came on, threatening the wax sculptures. On Friday afternoon, we packed up our Egyptian icons for the trip home.

We had to stay in line until we crossed Vine Street. Once we had crossed, the lines broke into disorderly masses of kids. Boys took off their jackets and loosened their ties. Girls clustered into groups. I joined Joyce and Rosemarie as she carried the sphinx home with the same care she had used in bringing it to school.

When we crossed Arch Street, Robert DiGiordano was there with two other boys. They gave him a push, and he walked over to us alone.

"Hi, Rosemarie," he said.

We all answered, "Hi, Robert." He ignored me and Joyce.

"Want me to help you carry that home?" he said to Rosemarie.

Rosemarie didn't answer, and Robert reached for the sphinx. His buddies started to cross the street, and then they broke into a run and jostled Robert as he reached for the sculpture. He lurched forward, and it fell to the ground. The boys stopped in horror.

"Fuck," one of them said.

"Hey, watch your mouth," Robert said.

"We didn't mean to do that," the other one said. "Sorry, Rosemarie."

Rosemarie dropped her book bag and fell to her knees. She ripped open the paper and peered inside. The sphinx was in pieces. The delicate head was flattened, and the wings lay in a twisted jumble. Bits of soap clung to the paper wrapping. Rosemarie leaned back on her heels and started to cry.

"We'll help you," I said getting down on my knees. "We'll help you put it together."

"Leave me alone," she said. She was really crying now, big lurches in her chest and snot coming out her nose. "Everyone leave me alone." She used the back of her hand to wipe her nose. Then she grabbed her school bag, stood up and ran. The rest of us stood in a circle around the fallen sphinx.

"Geez, it's just a few pieces of soap," one of the boys said.

Robert looked embarrassed. "Yah, no big deal."

I looked over at Joyce and smiled.

"What should we do with it?" Joyce asked and looked around the circle.

Robert picked up the largest piece of soap and threw it at a lamppost across the street. I grinned and scooped up the head and wings. I tossed them at Robert.

He caught my hand. "Watch it, Kathleen."

By now the other boys and Joyce were squashing the soap pieces with their feet. Robert and I started laughing and joined them.

On Monday morning, Rosemarie told us that she and her brother Tommy had gone back to rescue the sphinx. They found it broken-up and pieces of soap all over the sidewalk.

"Dogs," I said, and Joyce nodded in agreement.

Spring

Sandy Crimmins

*Sandy Crimmins' poem "Spring" appeared in the first is-
sue of* Philadelphia Stories *in 2004. Sandy was a unique
artist who not only pushed the boundaries of her own art
but was also a good friend to other poets and performers.
After her publication in* Philadelphia Stories *she became
a good friend to us as well by serving on our editorial
board and always supporting our fundraising efforts
and events. Her unexpected death was shocking, but we
are grateful to be able to support other poets, as she did,
through the annual poetry contest named in her honor
and supported by her family.*

Aunt Ginny is up in her Cessna
Navigating circles and dips
Swooping in the sun
Uncle Jack is on the porch
Smoking dope and thinking
This getting old's a bitch
When you're sick
He faces the sky and
Looks for Aunt Ginny
They had a tough winter with his cancer
And weather so bad she couldn't fly
But it's spring now
And things are good
Uncle Jack rocks
Smokes dope
And plans

Thinking:
The sun is strong
The flowers are sweet
Maybe I'll eat lunch today
If that's stronger than the chemo
He rocks
And watches
While his beautiful white hair
Dead at the root
Blows off his head
Strand by strand
Sprinkling new flowers like snow
Up in the sky
Aunt Ginny does another loop de loop

Richard the Third, the Second

James W. Morris

The sofa or the bed?

Richard opens the door and finds Vickie on the sofa, watching TV. Disappointing.

"I aced the final," he says.

He waits for her to say something. She doesn't; she keeps both eyes on the TV. It's a cable movie that she's watching, one of those ones in which every five minutes the hero comes running toward the camera and then you see a big explosion behind him. Vickie hates them.

"Why are you watching this?" he asks.

"Why not?"

Vickie is cute, with long black hair, big green eyes, and nice hands. Since losing his position as King of England, Richard has learned many things, and one of them is that he is really very attracted to women with nice hands.

But Vickie's best feature is her voice. It has a rich, warm, clear tone, deep and sexy. If she is standing behind him and speaks unexpectedly, he'll shiver. Vickie doesn't know it, but Richard once enjoyed a reputation as being hard-hearted— back in the old days he sent half of his extended family to their deaths so that he could be king—but one phrase from Vickie and he's all tears, overwhelmed by beauty. On several occasions he has suggested that she exploit her gift by auditioning to narrate car commercials.

"I think I aced the final," he repeats.

"Swell," she says. She uses the remote to change channels.

"Nineteenth-Century American Humor. Remember? Not that funny, actually. Lots of drinking and cruelty to animals."

"Uh huh." She changes channels again.

He gives up, sits down next to her with his hands on his knees. In the past, he was mean and charming. Famous for it. He once dispatched several members of a woman's family and then made a pass at her while she was tending to the coffins. Her name was Anne. Back then he had a hump, a limp, and a withered arm. He talked to Anne in such a crazy and insistent way that she agreed to meet him secretly. (Charming.) Later, he and Anne were married, but he soon found he needed to get rid of her for political reasons. Richard tried to let her down easy, giving her the "It's not you, it's me" speech, the "We've grown in different directions" talk, and promising they could still be friends. Then he executed her. (Mean.)

He looks at Vickie. She knows nothing about his past. She doesn't even know he's English—he's worked hard to learn contemporary American diction and a flat, from-no-where-in-particular kind of accent. His day job is selling paint and wallpaper. She's a manicurist.

He takes the remote from her and mutes the sound on the TV.

"Am I mean?" he asks.

She looks at him steadily. "No."

"How about charming?" He puts his head on her shoulder. "Am I charming?"

"No."

When he comes home from the final exam for his other class later in the week, Vickie is again on the sofa, watching TV. Vickie doesn't live with Richard—she lives with her mom—but she likes to be at his house when he comes home from night school. He gave her a key. Vickie says people Shouldn't live together Before Marriage, that it represents a Half-Assed commitment to the relationship (Vickie tries to capitalize certain words when she's talking, you can tell). She insists that he walk her home, no matter how late it is. It's Only Two Blocks.

When Vickie started the habit of letting herself into his apartment, Richard didn't mind—most of the time he'd find her naked on the bed when he returned. It has now been nineteen days since Richard has seen Vickie naked.

"It's been nineteen days since I've seen you naked," he says. (Mean.)

"You'll Live."

He throws down his textbook—*The Experience of Poetry*—near her feet. "Look. What's wrong?"

She turns slowly towards the textbook. "I hope for your sake that that was not Aimed At Me."

His immediate reaction is to apologize, but he hates it when she overdoes the capitalization, so he bites his tongue. Let her wonder.

She clicks off the TV. She stands. She puts her hands on her hips.

"I've Decided," she says.

"Yes?"

"I've decided I'm Not going to Waste My Life with someone who just works as a Clerk In A Paint Store."

Time passes without anyone saying anything. Then Vickie turns and heads for the front door. She'll walk home by herself.

Richard gets the last word: "It's a Home Improvement Center."

Mead. That's the stuff. Hard to get nowadays, special order. The looks he gets at the liquor store. But he wants a sweet wine to get drunk on, and there's nothing sweeter. Spiked honey.

His king days were long ago, but he hasn't forgotten.

He takes another drink, this time straight from the bottle.

When you're the king, even your enemies—men enemies, that is—treat you with respect. But not the women. No. Even the ones he charmed into bed ended up hating him. Possibly something to do with all the murders. Hey, he was God's chosen representative, blah, blah, blah. Still, a propensity for the ruthless execution of innocents makes a guy hard to warm up to on a personal level.

What would he do without Vickie? The voice, the hands. He drinks a swig as a toast to Vickie's hands, then changes his mind and drinks nine more swigs so that each of her fingers is honored separately.

When he stands to make his way to the bathroom, Richard wobbles and falls headfirst into the piano. The piano lid is up, and his head plays an ugly chord, which reverberates disagreeably in the air. Lying on his back beneath the keyboard, drunk and in pain, he feels an aside coming on:

Richard: At Bosworth I fell.
Laid at last upon the ground,
Undone, uncrowned, and unloved,
I bade Death drop her veil.
But even Hell would not have me;
Stabbed to death, I died not.

Mead hangover: not recommended. Richard awakes in the morning still under the piano, his head cradled by the sustain pedal. The underside of the keyboard when he opens his eyes looks to him like the dark wooden ceiling of the cell in which he slept for many decades, and for a minute he is fooled into thinking he's back there, in the monastery, where he rose every morning to live his life happily unchanged while generations of monks around him aged and died.

He rolls over onto his face. The floor beneath him gyrates. He burps and tastes honey-flavored vomit.

"Good morning, Your Majesty," Richard says aloud.

After a minute, he manages to lift his head and survey the living room. It's amazing how much damage one lovesick drunk can do. He should be careful—the furniture is not his. It came with the apartment. The piano, which Richard is learning to play now that his arms have become the same length, was included.

"Richard of Gloucester shall rise again," he says, and pulls himself to his feet using the piano for support. Then he runs to the bathroom and throws up.

After his stomach settles down, Richard checks the clock: five-thirty. Still plenty of time before he has to go to work, so he decides to take a bath. Although an innately adaptable creature, Richard is not yet able to warm up to a few modern inventions, including DVDs, ball-point pens, and digital clocks, but he has grown to like the ease of simply turning a knob to run a bath—Americans clean themselves almost continuously, it seems, and Richard has taken up the habit.

Lying in the tub, he begins to feel the effects of the hangover lifting. He looks down at himself. His body is, well, beautiful. It's still surprising to see it this way; he was misshapen for centuries. Not that he's had any surgeries or anything—no, he couldn't risk that. When Richard finally made it to America, it was his intention to keep a low profile, and simply live the exalted life of an average American citizen. Soon after landing here, however, almost from the first moment, he was wracked with various terrible pains in the ugly parts of himself—his withered arm, humped back, and spindly leg. An illegal immigrant, Richard lived on his savings for weeks in a cheap motel, writhing in agony, unsure what to do. Then he realized that his small, twisted arm was hurting so much because it was actually growing and untwisting. And his back was straightening, his weak leg getting stronger. From that moment, he welcomed the pain as a friend.

America was his cure.

His King of England days are long past, and his burning ambition to ruthlessly rule the entire civilized world ebbed away centuries ago. So the question now is: does he have enough drive left to achieve a more modest goal, say, becoming manager of the Home Improvement Center? And would that be enough to induce Vickie to stay with him?

Changing jobs is too risky to consider. As an illegal, Richard was fortunate to have been hired by Baron Paint and Wallpaper. The Human Resource Department (one semi-retired guy named Mel) just assumed Richard was American and forgot to ask him for the paperwork required to prove it.

He thinks about how he got ahead in the old days. Back then, Richard had two brothers: Edward, who was king, and Clarence (called George—don't ask why), who was next in line. What Richard did when he decided to usurp the throne was tell Edward, who was never, as they say, the sharpest knife in the drawer, that he, Richard, had had a dream, a dream in which Edward's reign was to be ended by someone with the initial "G." Technically, this was not a lie, since Richard was also called "Gloucester." But Edward, superstitious, predictable Edward, made the leap Richard wanted him to, and had George drowned in a vat of wine. Richard moved one step closer to the throne.

The manager of the Home Improvement Center is named Paul Saddell. The assistant manager is named George (coincidence?) Krauth. When Richard arrives at work that morning, he immediately goes to Paul's office and tells him he's had an important dream.

"What?" the manager says, blinking rapidly, looking at Richard as if he's crazy.

The day has just started and Paul already seems exhausted. He's a big old guy who doesn't take wallpaper orders or mix paint colors or put away deliveries or wait on customers anymore. He just sits in his office and drinks coffee and talks on the telephone. At lunchtime, he opens one of the right-hand drawers of his desk and takes out takes a brown bag containing a tuna or peanut butter sandwich that his wife has made for him.

"I said I had a dream last night, Paul. A dream in which your position is usurped by someone with the initial 'G.'"

Paul stares, uncomprehendingly.

"What does 'surped" mean?"

"Usurped. It means 'taken away,' you know, 'stolen.' I dreamt someone whose name begins with the letter 'G' is after your job."

Richard lifts his eyebrows empathetically.

"So?" Paul says. "I'm retiring next week anyway."

OK, the ouster of Paul was effected in an unintended way; that is, it wasn't effected by Richard at all, but the result is the same—Paul is out, and Richard possibly one step closer to ascending the glorious throne of paint store—home improvement store—management. The logical person to replace Paul—provided no one is hired from outside the store—is, of course, George, the assistant manager. The remaining employees, Richard's rivals for George's soon-to-be-vacated assistant manager position, are Marshall, a jovial young man from the Cayman Islands, Vince, a college student more interested in flirting with the female customers than in selling them paint, and Sandra, a brassy lady who runs the wallpaper department.

Richard thinks he should be chosen over these other contenders, although they all, except for Vince, have about the same amount of experience. But Marshall is too laid-back, and Sandra too female—paint stores are one of the last places to hide if you're a male chauvinist. The problem is that George will get to pick his new assistant, and George hates Richard.

George is a short, stout, doughy-looking man who suffers from that disease that makes people hairless. He has not one hair on his head, not even where his eyebrows should be. He's in his late thirties, but still lives at home with his parents and older sister, and sleeps in the same bed he used as a kid. His resentment of Richard began the day six months ago when he returned to work after a family trip to Europe. George was showing the vacation pictures—twelve rolls worth—to his co-workers when Richard noticed that the photos were bereft of people. There were seventeen pictures of the outside of the gift shop at the Tower of London (Ah, memories!) but none showing a person going in or out. Richard made this observation out loud, meaning no harm, but everyone laughed, and George, deeply embarrassed, flushed a deep red and never forgave Richard, whom he seemed to half-like previously.

The following week, on his last day of employment, Paul is given a little party on the loading dock. Everyone sits around on five-gallon paint cans and drinks ginger ale out of Styrofoam cups. There's a cake. There's a picture of a paint can on the cake and the paint can has a little face and the little face has a speech balloon coming out of it that says, Good Luck, Paul!

The regional manager is there and he gives a speech. He talks about how Paul joined the company before he, the regional manager, was even born. He says that when he was first hired he used to see Paul throwing five-gallon cans of joint compound (62 pounds each) up on a loading dock one after another, for hours at a time.

Richard looks over at Paul, perched uncomfortably on a bulging plastic container of Latex Interior Primer, and tries to imagine him lifting something heavy. The regional manager has given Paul a gold watch, which he's wearing; he took off the one he normally uses and put it in his pocket. In his right hand, pinched between two fat fingers, he holds the ornate crimson box the new watch came in. He doesn't know what to do with it.

The regional manager continues his speech by pretending he wishes he could retire too, like Paul. He mentions golf. Richard looks at Paul again and tries to imagine him playing golf, and that picture seems even stranger than the one in which he lifts something heavy, and sad too.

At the very end of his speech, the regional manager announces that George will be the new store manager. Marshall will be the Assistant.

At the beginning of the following week, Paul is gone and George calls Richard into what is now his office. Richard does not feel well. Knowing Vickie's mother was out of town—on a cruise—he tried to contact Vickie last night. He dialed her number repeatedly and listened to her shapely recorded voice tell him that she was currently Unable to Take his Call. The extravagant beauty of these vocalizations did not quite fully compensate for the ugliness of the fact they implied: Vickie was not, and continued not to be, at home. All night.

After Richard enters the office, George closes the door behind him. An awkward silence follows.

"Congratulations on your promotion," Richard says at last.

"You're fired," George replies.

Richard knows he's beaten. He rises, makes his way to the door, then stops when a thought occurs. Unlike most former kings of England, Richard of Gloucester is a member of the United Food and Commercial Workers Union.

"Wait a minute, George," Richard says. "You can't just fire me like that. You have to have provable cause for the union."

George sighs. "You're right. I'll work on that."

He puts his face close to Richard's face. "In the meantime," he says, "I want you to know you have no future here. I'll get you out one way or another."

Richard has spent centuries trying to eradicate every ounce of competitiveness and violence from his nature, partly to atone for the harm he caused earlier, and partly because it was a way to keep a low profile once he realized that—for whatever perverse reason—he was going to live an artificially long time. Now with George's fat hairless face pressed within inches of his own, and the man's hot yeasty breath fouling the air between them, Richard feels the return of his old impulses.

He looks around the office for a rapier.

Never one around when you need it.

"Get back to work," George says.

Richard knows he bought some time with his threat to go to the union, but also knows George will find a way to fire him if he really wants to; Richard will have to act quickly.

To achieve his kingly objective in the past (after Edward conveniently died), Richard and his pal Buckingham (his temporary pal—he had to kill Buckingham later) together engineered a stunt to have the Lord Mayor of London offer Richard the crown while behind the scenes Richard and Buckingham were discrediting some of the other candidates and beheading the rest. Well, in this case, Marshall was the next person in his way, but beheading Marshall wasn't an option—it was too messy and hard to get away with in America's "politically correct" climate. And he liked the fellow—liking the person you're beheading, Richard found, always made it less fun. (Though it was true that Marshall had taken to his Assistant Manager duties with more crack-the-whip enthusiasm than Richard would have preferred or predicted.)

Lying in bed that night, unable to sleep because of back pain, Richard has an idea. Marshall speaks a suspicious amount of French for someone supposedly born in the Cayman Islands, which is, after all, a British colony. Speaking French is, or course, not uncommon in the Caribbean, but Richard has a feeling Marshall is not who he says he is. He's probably another illegal hired by Mel.

Richard gets up, logs on his computer, and, after checking for email from Vickie (without finding any), accesses the website for Homeland Security. There he gets an idea what the department's letterhead looks like, and within a few hours he's printed out a fairly persuasive-looking document addressed to the Baron Paint Store manager, containing such phrases as "Marshall Bodden, a person in your employ," "investigation into illegal immigration," "deportation," and "prison sentence." These phrases were meant for Marshall's eyes alone; one of his new duties as Assistant Manager is to open the store mail.

Two days later, Richard looks up from mixing custom colors for a customer and sees the postman handing Marshall the mail. Richard thinks he spots the letter he sent—with its colorful stamp—in the stack.

"Oops," Richard says. He was so intent on watching Marshall that he accidentally squirted four ounces of green colorant into the pink paint he was supposed to be making.

This gets the customer's attention; people don't like to hear the person making their expensive, non-returnable custom colors say "Oops." Richard hammers the paint can lid closed, puts the can with the store's other "Oops" paint, and starts over with a fresh can, the customer now hovering over his shoulder. After the cans are shaken, the customer insists that Richard open them and paint out samples to be certain all the colors match.

After the customer is finally satisfied and leaves, Richard goes over and peers into the store office to see if he can watch Marshall open the envelope he sent. But Marshall is not there. Richard enters and examines the stack of mail, which was left on the desk. About half the envelopes are opened; the one he sent is missing.

Richard surreptitiously searches the store premises. Marshall is not on the loading dock, not in the bathroom, not in the ladder room.

He's gone.

•••••••••••

Two days later, George approaches Richard as he is putting away stock and says, "I guess Marshall's never coming back, so I'm making you my Assistant Manager. On an interim basis. Understood?" He walks away before Richard can reply.

That night, Richard dials Vickie's number again. Normally, he just listens to her lovely, lovely recorded voice telling him I'm out screwing someone else (not literally—it's implied) and then hangs up without saying a word. Tonight, at the tone, he speaks: "I got promoted," Richard says.

The machine declines to respond.

Richard took pleasure in forcing George to promote him right after threatening to fire him, but knows he isn't out of danger yet. His elevation was the result of there being no other credible candidate—Vincent was simply too young and Sandra wouldn't have taken the job even if it were offered, as she liked being, as they called her, "The Queen of Wallpaper."

Richard waits two days to hear Vickie's reaction to his promotion. Then he waits one more day. Then he walks over to her house at night and peers through the blinds. No one is home.

As he walks slowly back to his apartment, Richard again tries to think of a way to get rid of George. It is enjoyable to have such a specific goal once more, to again revel in the ecstasy of good hate, but he is paying a price: within the last fortnight all of his famously bad parts began aching anew, his strong back bending, his flawless arm furling, his thick leg shriveling. He'd better eliminate George before it is too late. *If it were done when 'tis done, then 'twere well it were done quickly,* he tells himself, knowing well he is thinking of the wrong play.

Two nights later, Richard dials Vickie's number and someone answers. It's her mother, back from the cruise.

"Is Vickie home?" he asks.

"You know she isn't."

"Where is she?"

"On her honeymoon," Vickie's mother says, and hangs up. Her honeymoon?

Richard looks for the mead.

An hour later, the ghosts appear. These are same ghosts who appeared to him before he fought at Bosworth, and periodically after that for the last five hundred years. They've pretty much lost their power to frighten over that span, but they haven't given up.

Enter the ghost of Prince Edward.

Richard: Here we go.

Prince Edward: Let me sit heavy on thy soul!

Richard: Sez you.

Enter the ghost of Henry the Sixth.

Henry the Sixth: My anointed body by thee was punched full of deadly holes!

Richard: Yeah, and?

Enter the ghost of Clarence.

Clarence: Let me sit heavy on thy soul!

Richard: Can't. Edward's already sitting there.

Enter the ghosts of Rivers, Grey, and Vaughn.

Ghosts: Despair and die!

Richard: Who are you, the Three Stooges?

Enter the ghost of Lord Hastings.

Lord Hastings: Bloody and guilty, guiltily awake!

Richard: Not really. I was watching Conan O'Brien.

Enter the ghosts of the two young princes.

Ghosts: Let us be lead within thy bosom Richard, and weigh thee down to ruin, shame, and death!

Richard: You and what army?

Enter the ghost of Marshall.

Marshall: Yo, Rich! Why'd you do me like that?

Richard: Marshall?

Marshall: I never did you no harm.

Richard: But...you're not dead.

Marshall: Yes, I am. I was fleeing 'cause of your phony letter and blew out a tire on I-95 while going eighty.

Richard reaches for the bottle.

•••••••••••

Richard awakes under the piano again. This time he is not fooled into thinking he's back at the monastery—no happy feeling asserts itself, even for a second. Marshall's death, as Clarence would have it, sits heavy on his soul.

Five hundred years. Five hundred years he's lived virtuously, hoping to redeem his place in heaven, but now he's ruined it, fallen back into his old ways. For the love of a manicurist.

Richard sits up. He feels awful, and not just because of the sick, dehydrating mead hangover. His arm, his leg, his spine: all have reverted to their original twisted state.

The army surplus store.

"Do you have a rapier?"

"What? A rapier?" the man says.

"Yes. You know, a slender, two-edged sword with a cup-like hilt."

"Well...we have some swords in the case over there. Look, you're not planning to stab anybody, are you?"

"Just my boss," Richard says. "Through the eye. Out the back of his fat skull."

"Uh..."

"I'm kidding," Richard says. "It's for a play I'm performing. Richard the Third. Do you know it?"

In the end, Richard chooses not to purchase a sword. Too conspicuous to walk around with these days. Instead, he buys a more easily concealed blade called a tanto, a foot-long Japanese knife used—as the clerk cheerfully explains—in the disemboweling suicide ritual called *seppuku*. That's the advantage of multiculturalism—weapons from all over the world.

Richard, blade secreted beneath his coat, limps into his workplace. Sandra is there.

"Rich. What happened? You're all bent over."

"I was sent before my time into this breathing world, scarce half made up."

"What?"

"Back spasms. I took an Advil. Is George in yet?"

"In the office."

When Richard reaches the doorway of the office, he finds George on his knees, paying homage to the bottom drawer of the filing cabinet, his precious fat hairless bulging neck rather obligingly displayed for beheading.

George is oblivious to the presence of Richard, who draws his knife, wishing he had gone for a full sword instead of the shorter blade. The tanto is for stabbing.

Richard raises the blade high, preparing to bring it down on George's neck with all the force he can muster. He pictures the manager's noggin severing cleanly, spinning for a moment in the air, then dropping—a surprised look still on the face—into the open cabinet drawer, which, impelled by the momentum of the head, slams shut with a satisfying thunk. Richard imagined leaving it there, filed under "W," for "Who ain't got no head?"

Richard's brief reign as King of England ended when his army was defeated by Richmond's at Bosworth. The main problem was motivation. Richmond's army was willing to lay down their lives for what they saw as a just cause; Richard's army was comprised largely of mercenaries. Money and glory are no match for righteousness.

Richard walked away from the office and hid the tanto, unused, behind a display of extension poles. His current quest for paint store power was over. There would be no beheadings, no poisonings, no drownings in vats of wine. His motivation was gone.

"Richard?"

That voice. Nearly a year has passed since he heard it.

Richard turns to find Vickie behind him in a movie line. She's with her mother, who gives Richard a dirty look. No husband in sight.

"Vickie. How are you? I heard you got married."

She says nothing, but waves a hand under his nose. The ring is nice; the hand is nicer. Richard nods.

"Here alone?" Vickie's mother asks.

"No. She went back to get something from the car." This is a lie. He is alone.

"You look well," Vickie says. This is true—Richard's body returned to its ideal shape once he let his ambition die.

"You too," he says, and this is also true. In fact, Vickie is fairly glowing with health, beauty, and happiness.

When Richard's turn comes, he buys two tickets, then steps aside as if waiting for his date to re-appear. Vickie and her mother take their turn and Vickie forces her mother to go inside without her so she can talk to Richard some more.

"I never properly explained," she says. "Steve was someone I knew for a long time. When he came back into my life, I felt I had to make a choice."

Richard nods.

"Are you all right?" she asks.

"I'll survive," he says. "I always do."

She kisses him on the cheek, then goes inside.

He watches her go, watches the door glimmer as it settles into place. Soon he feels another aside coming on:

Richard: Wed new to another, made beautiful by bliss,

Her voice singing his name, her hands entwined with his!

Was ever a woman in this humor wooed?

Was ever a woman in this humor won?

Nah.

The Decade I Longed to Be Grown

Penny Dickerson

I wanted to talk jive.
I wanted to be funky
like the white boy who sang
psychedelic slang
& give birth
to a new dance trend
called disco.

I wanted to be
a kaleidoscope
big as an afro-shaped-globe,
spinning my own tempo
under black light dust.
I'd be a lava-lamp chick
—stone-cold bumping
my have-mercy hips—
& do the hustle
in mommy's platform heels.

I wanted to be cool.
I wanted to cruise
with my own fly-dude
& steer
the turntable wheels.
We'd groove
What's Going On?
in daddy's brown El Camino,
pose mean gangsta leans
in neon-fur-smothered-bucket-seats,
& watch

Lucy's Sky Diamonds
dangle & dance
like brilliant erotic dice.

Not Tony and Tina

Denise Gess

My mother wishes for me: I wish you'd cut your hair short. I wish you had some security. I wish you'd write about real Italians. That wish came on a rainy spring Sunday after she and my father had spent the previous evening attending the decade-old play-in-a-restaurant, "Tony and Tina's Wedding."

"Your cousin didn't like it either. And your father —" she batted the air, "Well, nothing bothers your father."

Not true, of course. Wool bothers my father, wool and the entire sad history of mankind and any and all humiliations to the human spirit big or small. Earlier, he'd stood in my living room contemplating the rose window in the church across the street. Then he turned toward us slowly, looking as though he'd just had a long talk with God, and announced that he wasn't coming with us to the annual Philadelphia Flower Show.

He wanted to watch a golf tournament. We left him in the company of Tiger Woods. By then it was raining heavily. I kept my eyes on the streets, trying to avoid the potholes, while she, waiting for my corroborating outrage, continued to describe the play.

"It's a satire, Mom."

"It was mean," she said. I let that one pass. Given her exasperation, it was not the time to lecture her on the properties of satire.

"When did you ever go to a wedding in our family where they served meatballs hard as a rock—instead of salmon or even just a nice chicken? And when was the last time you ever saw anybody dance on a table with her—all of her top was hanging out! The clothes were awful and the language. This we paid seventy-five dollars for? No one in our family acts like that."

No one in our family acts like that. My mother had been seduced into believing that those characters were badly-behaved members of our own family. She loved being an Italian-American. Tony and Tina had embarrassed her.

"And you," she said.

"Me? What me?"

"You should do something about it."

The parking attendant was waving and flailing at me. Lot full. I backed out onto the street. "Like what?"

"Write something good."

"Aren't I writing a novel?"

"Is it Italian?"

I had been keeping my own counsel with this third novel because there were Italian-Americans in the work. Until now, I'd never mined the depths of my Italian-American experience, mostly because I didn't think there was one.

My mother was already convinced she was the mother in two previous novels (women to whom she bears no resemblance, both of whom I'd killed off in violent ways). How could I tell her that I planned to showcase her in the new book? So far the writing had made me sleepy with guilt. Each time I shot an arrow aimed at the bull's eye authentic, I hit caricature.

We found a parking space two blocks away, then linked arms under a single umbrella and ran to the convention center, where we were cast into yet another ethnic wonderland: France. Amid the lush floral displays stood a mini Eiffel Tower; a Parisian cafe; a repro Tuileries. Geraniums, blistering red and swollen, spilled out of glazed pottery. There was even a reconstructed Japanese bridge against a canvas backdrop of Monet's garden at Giverney. Years before, I'd been to Giverney and had stood on the real bridge looking out over Monet's pond.

My father was stationed in France after World War II. For decades I've been running with the joke that my parents named me Denise because my father—who chose the name—was secretly fascinated with a French chanteuse named Denise. I've invented his French experience as romantic, clothed him in fluid gabardine instead of army fatigues, added an unrequited love to his post-war France. I wanted to account for being a Denise in a family of Joes and Marys. I wanted a reason. So I made one up.

That day at the flower show I said, "It doesn't look like this."

But my mother was thrilled, believing she was a guest at Monet's home. Should it matter then that the play had depicted Italians as lewd, gauche, dumb? Wasn't it all invention? This garden in a convention center? Those actors in a wedding? My mother didn't think so.

She believed that somewhere between depictions of Italians exerting brute force, wearing bad clothes, and making wisecracks, there had to be another portrait.

As we sampled bistro food under a striped cafe awning I began to feel shame—not for what I was, but for my obsessive efforts to banish all traces of it. I hid my maiden name: Piccoli. Gess, my married name, was short, sweet. What I'd barely admitted to myself was how much I loved its Anglo-Saxon-ness. I was a coward. I never wanted anyone confusing me with those other Italians.

"Where are the Italian-American writers?" Gay Talese had asked in an essay for *The Times*. Why so mute? Well, Italians don't grow up with books in their houses, he pointed out. There were books in my home and magazines, yet nothing that resembled a library. I wasn't read to as a child—I was talked to. I grew up in a family where everyone thought it was their obligation to articulate their raw emotions as if they were splinters that needed to be tended to immediately. The entire range of emotion was accessible by asking, "How do you feel?"

"Sit down and I'll tell you."

Seated around a table with relatives is how I learned story. Sometimes the stories were funny and sometimes they were somber, but my mother was right: they were not stupid, brutish, or lewd.

After we'd had our fill of croissants and espresso, we linked arms and left the convention center. The rain and wind had died out. The sky was opaque gray.

"Italians bleed together like cheap madras," I said.

"That's true," my mother said. She shrugged. I watched the sharp planes of her face shifting. "I'm not educated like you and your brother and your sister, but I know when somebody's making fun of me."

On the subject of my intense family ties I've been from A to Z and back again, as torn up as a dirt road after a drag race when I examine their blunders, their open-hearted messiness.

"Be funny," she said, "but tell a whole story."

Hadn't she, my first reader, always offered herself up for scrutiny? That day she was asking me to give something back, something more complex than stereotypes: real Italians.

"I'll give it a shot," I told her.

2005

How Is This My Story
Kathleen Donnelly

It's very hot here. Hotter than I've ever liked. Even
when I was a kid. Growing up, summer was only good for
me because school was out. Swimming's OK but I don't go
crazy for it. I like camping, to get out into the woods where
it's a little bit cool, 'cause those nights when you can't sleep
for being all sticky sweaty, that's not for me.

What I especially don't appreciate is being able to see
the heat. Sure, back at home we had hot summer days
when you could sometimes see it rising off the road—notice
I said sometimes. Here, everything's distorted by the heat
every day. Yeah, there's sand everywhere, but that's not
what gets you. It's the asphalt. Asphalt and concrete. You
go outside around here and it's the roads that pack a real
wallop. All they do is soak it up then throw it right back at
you. They're long and wide, and they melt away into heat
waves long before they ever reach the horizon. And they are
waves, really. The roads, the farther out you look, it's like
they move, swells at sea, rolling up and down, just a little
bit, and then they're gone. After that, it's all desert.

This is what I think about lying on my cot every night.
And every day. Not much else to do. That and pray. Yesterday, I knew something was up. Abdul—I have no idea what
his name really is, we're not on a first- or last-name basis.
I just call him that 'cause it's better than thinking, "that
guy with the fucked-up eye." He should wear a patch but he
doesn't. It's not good to look at. It's like he was burned or
something, and some of his eyelid got shriveled off and can't
quite close the whole way. And then there's always something seeping out of it. As I said, it's not good, so I call him

Abdul. I figure that's better than tying up his whole identity with something that probably happened in a split second and wasn't one of his best moments.

But anyhow, Abdul, when he came to drop off my bread and water, didn't smack me across the head as hard as he usually does. When he barked out some orders—or insults—at me, I thought I noticed a little touch of hesitancy, almost like a look of sympathy in his good eye. I tried to grab its focus for just a second. I said, "Hey, can you tell me what's going on in the world?"

He said something then pointed at the food. That's when I noticed a small dish of peaches—canned, in syrup. I hoped it was extra heavy. I wanted him to know I was grateful. I put my hands together in front of me, prayer-like, and gave a quick bow of my head. I thought I might have seen him give just a little nod back. Then, I couldn't believe it, he took out a cigarette, put this down on the tray, and threw a matchbook down along with it, after showing me its one remaining match. He spoke again and this time it came out sort of like a mumble, maybe even an apology. That gave me hope. I wanted to speak with him, have him speak back to me.

"*Tatakalm Alingli'zia? Sadik.* Me *sadik*—friend. *Kobry. Kobry.* I build *kobry.*" I gestured wide with my hands trying to demonstrate a bridge, cars zooming over top of it.

Abdul looked nervously out the hallway, again said something that I didn't understand, then began to leave. "Telephone?" I said, louder than I had intended. I knew I sounded like I was begging, and thought maybe it was time for that. "My family—can I call my family? *Usra, usra,*" I yelled. That reached him.

He stepped away from the doorway, walked right up to me and shoved his face in front of mine, his bad eye an inch away from my good two. His voice, rapid but contained and intense. Well, seemingly more intense than usual—he always sounded intense to me. Then he smacked me good. The hardest one yet. I fell back against the wall and didn't see anything for a while.

The fall. My favorite season here. Joey—that's my best friend, since second grade we go back. Him and me and the other kids on our road, we're up on Shaeffer's farm field. It's perfect for football and so's the weather. Cool, not cold. Sunny, but not blinding. Today, we cut to the field through the cow pasture. Joey has to be home early for some special dinner so we don't go through the woods that come up on the one side. It's longer that way but that's how you avoid the patties. Today, though, we take the pasture because we want to get a full game in.

We do. My side wins by 16 points—two touchdowns and one safety. The safety's courtesy of Joe. He's almost always good for at least one per game.

We're twelve years old. Seventh grade. Joe's five foot eight, weighs at least 190. He always plays the line—offense or defense, because he don't have speed but he has power. We're winning too good to quit with the sun, so Joe has to make it home quick as possible through the pasture.

We fly down the hill. I tell him good game before I split off right up the road toward my house. Lucky for him, his is right there because he's lumbering and puffing just from rolling down the hill. I'm still sprinting but pause a minute to yell back, "Hey, don't forget to kick off your shoes." He waves his hand like he hears me.

Joe's late, by over two hours. He goes in through the back door, into the kitchen. He doesn't turn on any lights but still sees that the dinner dishes have already been washed and put away. The only signs of life are coming from the living room, voices from the TV set. He figures he just has to make it down the hallway, past the living room, where his mom and dad are sitting, probably steaming, get up the stairs to his bedroom and he'll be safe. Well, remember Joe's stats—chances were pretty good he wasn't sneaking anywhere past anyone, besides he's still breathing hard from his downhill flight. So there he is in the hallway. He takes just a couple steps past the living room archway, and his mom's on him, yelling, "Joe, is that you? That better not be you. I told you be home by five."

Does Joe stop and take his punishment? No, that's not Joe. He still thinks there's a way out of it. So he takes off down the hall trying to get to his room as fast as he can, as if that's some kind of sanctuary or something. He gets to the steps, does this quick pivot to launch himself up the stairs, but all of a sudden his feet fly out from under him and he goes into this massive slide. Like, what? There's something on the floor or something? And wham! He goes down, slams his mouth against the first step, big time.

Pop! His mom turns on the lights, and there's Joe bleeding from his mouth real bad, one of his front teeth is hanging by a thread. He starts crying. His mom, she's ready to start yelling, but there's blood everywhere, so she's all worried instead. By now his dad's up, too, all grouchy 'cause something's interrupting his *Wheel*. His dad rounds into the hallway and you hear this, "What the—" and he takes a slide too, but doesn't go down, thankfully. That would have been real bad if he'd gone down, too. But anyhow, that's when his mom sees it. First, right there beside Joe and then all the way down the hall. She marches into the kitchen and there it is, beginning at the back door. A trail of cow poop right through the house. Idiot Joe, it was all over his shoes and he didn't kick them off outside the door, like I reminded him to. Yeah, he's still bleeding and all but the trail of cow you-know-what is too much for Mrs. Zupanic to handle. She's mad, real mad. She's there yelling at him about the cow crap. His Dad's all moaning that his back's gone out. He's slapping Joe upside his head, his mom's ranting up a storm while she's trying to get the dentist on the phone. Buster, their dog, he's sniffing all over the place and then starts licking it up.

Next day at lunch, kids fight to get a seat at our table, all morning whispering and wondering what happened to Joey and his front tooth, knowing that him telling about it at lunch time will be the highlight of the day, probably the week. This is one of the things that makes Joe real popular at school. He can make one story last through a whole lunch period, in between bites of sloppy joe and tater tots and the extra desserts kids give him. And it doesn't matter he's been grounded for a month, and that he's going to miss that tooth until he's old enough to get a permanent implant. He looks at anything happening—good or bad—as just another chance to be the center of attention.

So now we're at lunch and Joe's telling us all about it, every cow-poop covered step of the way. We howl. Me sitting on Joe's right, Jerry on the other side, Rob and Stanley across the table from us. When he gets to the slide, I laugh so hard my chocolate milk comes squirting out my nose. I'm laughing so hard I wake up, uncomfortable for some moments with the sensation that these memories are really only a story, figments of someone else's imagination that have somehow played themselves into my head without having any real connection to me.

I could tell it was coming on evening. Not because I had a window in my room but because I could see through the bars at the door the failing light in the hallway. My neck ached. I'd passed out crumpled against the wall, my head at a bad angle to my body. It took a few minutes to get a sense of where I was. The ache in my neck and shoulders resonated down to my empty stomach. I hadn't had the chance to eat yet that day. The tray was still there. But not the cigarette or the single match. Then I saw the peaches, too, but they'd been thrown across the room, lay scattered about the floor. I ate them, anyway. What's a little dirt gonna do you? The syrup was all gone, though.

As I was crawling over to the peaches, I tried to pull back those memories of Joe. I wondered why that cow poop story had come to my dreaming mind. Then I realized it was always the cow poop story that came to mind when I thought about Joe. I was reminded of it for years, every time he took out his false tooth, which he liked to do a lot especially when there were girls around.

Joe was plenty of things to me. My best friend, since the second grade. A teammate. Partner for a while when we thought we'd have a try at selling insurance. He's plenty of things to a lot of people. A husband now, a father, businessman—he works in a car dealership, makes good money.

And I'd bet he's up to three hundred. A real Santa. There're few people I'm as close to and shared as many laughs and worries with as him. In fact, he's the guy I talked to most seriously about whether or not I should come over here. He tried to tell me that if it weren't for his family he might have come too—the money was real good, what's the chance something would happen? Yeah, he's a lot to me—we go back twenty years. So why is the cow poop story the first thing I tell you about Joe? Then it occurs to me that in a person's life, it seems like there are some stories that get attached to them more than others, and for me, that one will always be a part of Joe. I always wanted to be there for that one, 'cause I really wish I'd seen that slide.

The peaches were good, if dry and dusty. The syrup, I guessed, had been extra heavy. I wished there'd been some left. They tasted especially good after a couple of weeks of just bread or rice and water. It didn't give me a good feeling, though, to be eating them. With every bite, I kept getting a deepening sinking feeling that peaches and a cigarette weren't a good sign. Why would they show kindness now? I didn't like it. Panic started rising up off my body like the heat from the roads, but I couldn't allow it. I knew if once I let it go, that'd be the end. If I had any self-control left, I'd have to put it to work now.

The hotter it got in the room, the more visions of Shaeffer's farm came to me. I'd close my eyes and sometimes could almost feel the breeze coming over the field. I'd see Joe, and Jerry, Stanley, Rob. Nine years old. Then ten, twelve, into our teens. Running around up on the field, or in the woods.

Growing up in my—I can't really say hometown, because it was so spread out, just a whole bunch of roads, and houses along roads, and then farms, acres and acres of farms, so I guess neighborhood is better. So, anyhow, growing up here, you tended to hang out with the guys you lived closest to. I was lucky that Joe lived right down the street. And Jerry Miller, Stanley Kukovich, Rob Belaski. We all lived on Pleasant Valley Road. In elementary school, we were walkers. Our school was just up at the far end of the road, at the top of a big hill. Sunrise Knoll Elementary School. When I found out later on in high school, or whenever it was, that "knoll" was another way of saying "small hill," I was kind of pissed off. I mean, who came up with that name? Our school was not at the top of a small hill—it was a full-fledged mountain; at least it was to a seven-year-old. I guess the guys who named it weren't the ones who had to climb it every day. Four years of trudging up that hill—the school didn't open until we were in the second grade—and I never once got to the top without puffing, at least a bit. At the bottom, you would get just the slightest feeling of queasiness looking up, you know, like that twinge you get at the bottom of the first hill of a rollercoaster. So there'd be like this pause and a gulp, a squaring up of your shoulders to get inside what you'd need to make it all the way to the top, then you take that first step.

That's when Joe, Jerry, Rob and Stanley and me got to be good friends. It was funny how some days we'd do nothing but complain the whole way, but on other days—without a word between us—we'd decided that we wouldn't show if we were having a tough time. It was always hardest for Joey—he was fat even in the second grade. You know, when I saw that Harry Potter movie with my nieces, the brother or the cousin kid, that character, he reminded me of Joe—not because Joe was ever mean like that or because he was spoiled, not by any means, but because he was fat like that and just couldn't not eat. Especially the sweets. That kind of skewed my take on the movie. I knew I wasn't supposed to like this fat kid, but I felt bad for him, because he reminded me of Joey.

Being heavy got Joe teased when we were younger. But once we got past gym class's scooter soccer and tumbling and building pyramids, which Joe couldn't stand because he was always at the bottom getting someone's knee right in the middle of his back, once we got past that kind of stuff and got down to playing real sports, especially football, Joe was the best. All he had to do was stand there and he'd knock you down. Starting from about fifth grade on, our football games got going up on Shaeffer's farm field. It was kind of magical how they came together. No one ever planned a thing. But after school, kids would just show up. Some of them we didn't even know. They'd come in through the woods or over the pasture. And always enough to pull together a game, almost never too many—just the right number for a couple of teams. Everybody got a chance to play.

Joe, Jerry, Stanley and Rob and me, we stayed tight right through middle school. We survived our first bouts with girls and all that stuff. And that probably came a little later for us, 'cause we were such good friends, we didn't need girls around.

Once we got to high school, yeah, there were some changes. Stanley, he didn't want to be called that anymore. We were only allowed to call him Stan. He joined the band, played alto sax, and he started getting pretty weird, dying his hair and all that. You know, whenever it was just the two of us it was OK, but our crowds didn't fit together any-more and it's hard to get past that in high school. By junior year, all we did was say "hey" to each other; sometimes not even that. At a reunion today, I bet we'd still be friends. But we drifted apart back then. It was OK, I didn't mope about it or anything, it's just looking back you feel bad when a friendship kind of dies.

But then something real bad happened. Rob's dad kind of wigged out and he shot his mom and then himself. He died, but Rob's mom lived. They say it was a miracle. But Rob...I know this is a terrible thing to say but sometimes I thought it might have been better if she had died too, 'cause then maybe he would have gone away and started over somewhere—things were never right for him again at our school. Nobody could look at him without thinking, "there's the kid whose dad went crazy." And even us, me and Joey and Jerry, we tried to stay tight with Rob, but what had happened to him, that was always somewhere in our minds. You couldn't shake it off. Even now, no matter what I remember of Rob in all the years we spent together—all

the games, the camping, just walking to school every day—
when I think of him, the first thing that pops into my head
is when his dad shot his mom and then killed himself. The
face I see of Rob is him at the funeral—dead blank, like he'd
been killed, too. We went for Rob, my mom said, "because
no earthly prayers could ever forgive his dad for what he'd
done." But we went to show our support for Rob, she said.
He did move away a couple of years later, once his mom got
back on her feet. That was a good thing, because it was never right again for him at home. He knew it, we all knew it.
And it hurt him, I know, that this stood between us. So they
left and started life somewhere new. I never heard from
him again. I hope things worked out for him. And I guess I
hope he kind of knows now how we felt back then, because
of what's happened here. He'll have heard about it and I
don't think he'll ever be able to think of me without this
popping up in his head. Maybe he'll know now how hard it
is to put some things out of your mind.

    That was the last thing I remembered thinking before
falling asleep. No dreams or memories came to me that
night, but still I woke up feeling good, if a little bit empty.
Was it a trick of my wishful mind or had the air turned
cooler? There was a quiet all around me, too, but whether
this was coming from my insides or the outside, I wasn't
sure. The sun was up, as usual, making its rounds, its light
slowly finding its way into my cell. I pushed my brain to recall Joe, Mom and Dad, my sister Jill and her kids. Forced
myself to see their faces, remember their stories.
    My self-control had won. I was calm and at peace when
Abdul and two other guards came to get me. They took me,
not to a courtyard or somewhere outside, but to a place that
seemed more like a conference room. OK—so it's not a firing
squad. OK, I thought, OK. There was a raised platform at
the far end of the room—a stage. Lights, a camera. A podi-
um off to the side. A dozen or so men, outfitted as soldiers,
were preparing for something, looking so serious about it
all—putting a microphone first here then there, moving the
camera around. I half expected to see a director calling out

shots, carrying a megaphone, wearing those old-style puffy pants, what are they called, jodhpurs? This suddenly struck me as funny and a short snort of laughter escaped from me. That earned me the sharp butt of a gun in my back. They were leading me up to the front of the room, to the stage, and I thought how I wished I had a report prepared, something to talk about. After all, maybe they were just finally giving a nod to my expertise on bridge building, wanted to hear my thoughts on the plans for reconstruction. Slowly, though, an old but familiar queasiness came to me. I was looking up the hill leading to Sunrise Knoll Elementary School. That one step—just that one step up onto the platform was as hard as that climb had ever been.

Microphones, the camera, the panel of speakers. It's a press conference, I thought. They're sending a message. I'll have to say something for them, I guessed. Lay out their demands. That's what this is, I said to myself. And as much as that idea made sense and me trying to hold onto it as being what was really going on, my stomach knew otherwise.

It was when they pulled my hands behind my back and bound them together that I could admit to myself what was happening. A guard I had only seen a couple of times pushed me down so that I was kneeling. Then Abdul waved him aside and knelt down to meet my eyes, my two good eyes. For once, I wanted him to really see me. I hoped that something of who I was would get through to him, through that good eye as blind to me as the other one. It could have been a lifetime that we stared at each other, but it probably wasn't even ten seconds. I remembered the last time I had uttered the word for family, what it had got me, but I didn't care. I said it again. "Usra," I whispered, just to him. That was the closest Abdul and me ever came, when I dared to say the word for family one more time. His mouth relaxed a bit and he nodded—just the slightest motion, barely perceptible, but to me it felt for a brief second like a blessing. But from somewhere in the background another word was said and his eye got hard. He spat something out in Arabic, then spat on the ground in front of me. Someone else jerked a blindfold down over my eyes, tied it tight. I could feel the light of the camera, hear its quiet whirring. Words, many words, were said. I knew none of them but felt their meaning. I tried to will myself back up to Shaeffer's farm, feel the cool fall breezes, smell wood fires, see trees and rolling grass-covered fields. Hands grabbed my head and shoved down. Then something sharp and cold and silent.

I was gone, really, before I could have told you what had happened. The next thing I see is the look of anguish on Mom's face when she finds out. Dad looks like he's about to be sick but he keeps it together and holds Mom up, her legs giving out she's about to fall down. Jill walks into the girls' bedroom. They're giggling, flipping through a teen magazine but stop cold when they look up and see her face. And Joe—he sits alone in his garage with the door closed, on a stool in the back corner and he lets it go, cries for hours, mopping his face, shaking his head no and no and no. I hear the news play in their heads. How they find out. I hear it told over and over again for days and days to friends, to strangers, to people who will never know me any other way, and all I can wonder is, how is this my story? And was it told from the very beginning, even when my mother brought me into this world, held me in her arms for the first time, me all pink and defenseless? Was this always the end, mocking everything good and right that ever happened in my life? Because how will anyone ever be able to think about me and not think about this? Joe, will you ever again be able to talk about me with a laugh and a joke? Because, really, that's what I would like you to do. No matter how hard it is for you, that's what I'm asking. Don't let this be what pops up first in your mind. Dig down hard and deep and remember something else. Don't let this be my story.

Called
Kelley White

as if pale doves lit
my kitchen with their wings
beating smoke
as if a shell sang
silver coins
into my bed
and your answer
turned to sapphire
and stayed spoken
as if the water
in my bath
turned to wine

The Prettiest Lie

Curtis Smith

Your life is going to change—how many times was that
prediction offered in one form or another during my wife's
pregnancy? Mothers often spoke with a bliss-touched smile;
fathers, with a smirk that was both sardonic and conspir-
atorial, and a distinct, cross-gendered handful uttered the
words with an unblinking intensity that rattled me more
than any of the bloody videos we watched in our childbirth
classes.

In the months before my son's arrival, my focus turned
inward to the lightless, floating world where he spent his
days. I say 'inward' in the truest sense, for I felt as if my
wife's watermelon belly had become an extension of my own
body. Amazing, our doctor's visits, the underwater *slurp-
slurp* of our child's buried heart, the ultrasound's cloudy
visions, the brief glimpses of his face, fingers and toes,
then deeper, into his bones, his air-awaiting lungs, more…
My wife and I adjusted our diet, took long, twilight walks,
our pace slowing as summer eased into fall. We developed
rituals—the Sunday Polaroids we shot to document her
budding growth, the jokes about turning the photos into
a flipbook, and the nightly conversations with my son as
I placed my lips to the curved, taut dome of her belly and
spoke words of encouragement and love, hope and strength.
Everything's OK, baby. Everything's OK.

He was placed in my arms in the delivery room,
cleansed and swaddled, his skin the pink of well-chewed
bubble gum. *He looks wonderful*, the doctor said, grinning
from behind her mask. I gazed upon him, this solid, warm
mass, his birthing cries short-lived and a single, curious fin-

ger worming its way out of the blanket, and when I began to speak, his unseeing eyes fluttered open, and I wanted to believe he recognized my voice, the words incomprehensible but the sound a welcoming bridge to this bustling, confusing world. *Don't be scared, little man.*

The next forty hours passed in a blur of interrupted sleep, doctors' consultations, orderlies bringing cafeteria trays, nurses jotting their notes. I took walks to stretch my legs, aimless wanderings that usually ended with my standing outside the nursery's long window. Fourteen had been delivered on the same day, a near-record that had the nurses counting back nine months and dubbing the batch "Super Bowl Babies." There was always a handful of infants in that room of blazing white lights and pinging machines, each wearing a beige knit cap topped with a Halloween-colored pom-pom, and when the door swung open, out poured the chorus of their collective breathing, a hum moist and tenacious and unlike any I'd ever heard before.

Back in our room, the muted TV heralded the arrest of the beltway snipers—a man and a boy, their smiling pictures leaving the rest of us to consider again the always incongruous face of evil. In between pokings and tests, our boy was wheeled into our room, his sleeping form nestled in a glass-sided shoebox, his high-pitched rasping already unique to my ear, a singular, unmistakable note I swore I'd be able to discern from the others.

Late October, and the rain fell long and steady, and the chilled gray crouched outside the concourse's floor-to-ceiling windows. The weight of my son's carrier threw an unexpected hitch in my stride, and my wife rolled alongside us in a hospital-mandated wheelchair. The nurse who pushed her told us the latest on the beltway snipers, the hard news of their capture giving way to speculating psychologists and retired attorneys, the case's undertones of seduction and brainwashing and cold malevolence oozing to the surface. I looked down at my sleeping son. How sad, the ease with which some of us lose our way; how sad, the fate of the oblivious victim, the lightning-strike violence of this world. Past us filed the sick and those who loved them, the workaday faces of the nurses and cafeteria workers and the maintenance men, and I smiled at them all, suddenly seeing them not as strangers, but as bundles once placed in their parents' arms, innocent and blank and incredibly fragile, and for a brief moment, I wanted to embrace them all and whisper in each ear the prettiest lie—Everything was going to be OK.

2006

Housemates

Eric Thurschwell

He told me about his war wounds. I recounted my masturbation injuries. We bonded.

Then came winter.

"See here, Klugstein," he said. "There's no need to raise
the thermostat above 45. If the pipes won't freeze, then
neither will you."

Inspired, I replied, "Righty-O!" and reached for the Echi-
nacea.

The New Year brought the worst ice storm on record.
The roads were impassable. The supermarkets closed. He
ate my cat.

"Sorry about little Priscilla, Klugstein," he said when
I objected, "but this is no time for sentimentality. There's
work to be done." Undaunted by gale-force winds and tem-
peratures below the freezing point of blood, he climbed onto
the roof to remove a fallen tree. I boiled water for herbal
tea. He returned shortly with his face encased in ice and
poured the kettle over his head.

"Good show, Klugstein! Keep the home fires burning!"
he exclaimed while disemboweling my puppy. He grinned
sheepishly. "All apologies, old chap, but I'm a bit short of
rope, and catgut simply will not do for this job." He went
out again with two hammers in one hand, a saw and a drill
in the other, and Bowser's intestines between his teeth. I
boiled more water.

He came back an hour later with an armload of chopped
wood, which he put in the fireplace. "Home is where the
hearth is," he chortled, and in one motion struck a match
against his mustache and flicked it into the kindling, which

ignited immediately. "Who needs natural gas?" he said. "The tree is gone, the roof is patched, and I save a trip to the lumber yard." He went to the garage to do something complicated to his car.

The next day, while I tried to open a stapler, he used the remains of the fallen tree to build a deck, a dining room table set, and a life-sized replica of Tensing Norgay. He stepped back to admire his handiwork. "Sherpas are a stout-hearted and industrious people," he said. "A model minority, if ever there were one. Our immigrants would do well to emulate them. Are you Jewish, Klugstein?"

I threw out the stapler and entertained myself with the puppets he had made for me from Priscilla and Bowser.

I knew little of his politics. He loathed all welfare hand-outs, including Halloween candy, and would toss fake choc-olate bars made of scrap wood into Trick-or-Treaters' bags. Around each splintery Hershey's simulacrum he wrapped a brief lecture on self-reliance and dental health.

On Mischief Night our mailbox was firebombed.

The next year he placed a trap of his own design in the mailbox, and we awoke to the screams of a nine-year old boy whose arm had been caught and permanently mangled by the device. The parents sued, but expert testimony that shifted blame to their child-rearing practices made certain their defeat. In a countersuit, he recovered all legal costs plus an undisclosed sum. The Judge sent the boy to a foster home in a remote part of the state.

He was an excellent housekeeper, but not given to so-cializing, so I was rather surprised when I returned home one evening to discover much of the furniture occupied by cadavers, including two in my bed. "Have you taken up grave robbing?" I joked.

"No indeed, by the time they're buried they're no good to anyone." He explained that he and several like-minded individuals in the medical and funereal professions would seize the deceased at opportune moments and donate them to Third World medical schools and to a few amusement parks in the less developed regions of Canada. "Waste not, want not, ay? Pardon my use of your boudoir, Klugstein, but if we leave them on the floor, they'll likely be stepped on, and we can't have that, can we? By-the-by, have you dusted in there recently?"

I tried to emulate him but lacked the will. Though he almost never criticized me, my self-esteem plummeted as I repeatedly failed to live up to his standards. Finally, after seeking solace in a solitary all-night Punch and Judy show that I put on with Bowser and Priscilla, I decided to quit my job and move in with my parents.

I dreaded telling him this, but when I did, all he said was, "Well, at least it's not the public dole," and returned to the task at hand, the smelting of three rusting vans from the next-door neighbor's yard.

My last contact with him was a congratulatory email he sent to me when *The Bowser & Priscilla Show* went into national syndication on PBS, where it replaced *Barney*. I knew we would not cross paths again, for the tracks of our lives were not parallel, but skew.

He returned every cent of my security deposit, with interest.

Unfinished Love Poem

Alexander Long

for James Wright

Like I've been saying
All along, I'm not sure
Where they've gone
Off to. Why can't I think
Of that place as full
Of lovers secretly kissing
In unmodified light?
This afternoon's rain settles
Along my jaw.
I hope my bus is late.
Three beers by noon,
And now I go to chop
The rows of onions
For my bosses who mark
Up the booze for us all.
We keep coming back.
This is the life I've got.
I make salads from hearts
Of iceberg picked by migrants
Who curse and bless
This country, state, and town;
Their corner with the motel
Whose windows acquire a sheen
Over them as they drink
Five-dollar Cuervo
And spit it into their hands
To slick back their hair,
Desiring the unattainable

Strippers who pass through
Once a month. Oh Sweet
Jesus, I keep imagining
The regulars and the lawyers drunk
Again, sliding off their chairs.
What I really like
About the clearest days
Isn't the light itself.
At the trolley stop in Sharon Hill,
Where I grew up and most can't
Leave, I'd stand there
With the two bums,
Big Bob and Chicken Man.
For being desolate, they dressed
Nice. They stank, though,
And sniffed glue every chance
They could. Otherwise,
They no longer seemed to desire a thing,
Not even the other's shadow
On the hottest afternoons, flirting
With oblivion, waving to it
As it floated by quiveringly
Over their ears,
White and light as milkweed.
Trying to think of them again,
In their polyester suits
And dress shirts
Buttoned all the way up
To their scruffed wattles,
Whose collars resembled a hit pigeon
I saw once by the curb—
Its wings lifting slightly
As another A. Duie Pyle rig
From Pittsburgh barreled through
Sharon Hill, where I grew up,
Without stopping until it hit
The limits of West Philly—
I can see they have
Completed that agenda the dead

Stars have laid out, and I don't know
Where they are now. So it is
This bus stop
We all end up at,
Telephone wires swaying
Between oceans, the sun
Hovering right there, between
Our fingers, with all its busted light.
I've heard it called a lot
Of things, not one of them
Accurate. The pines
And maples dripping with rain,
For example, have their Latin
Names that make them
Seem larger, which I can remember
Well enough most days,
Which I love.

Gift

Sharon Black

Here, I brought you an orange.

You prefer tangerines?
I like tangerines too
and might have made that choice
had I not thought of your hands
which are better suited for oranges.
I get a solid feeling about your hand
holding an orange.
Tangerine is prettier to say
and limes are like having short hair
and lemons remind me umbrellas
are for sun as well as rain
and I'm sorry I didn't think
of tangerines which are like wearing
clear bells around your ankles
I know that now
but oranges are cool too
because they make you feel
like going back to clay
even if it's parched and cracked
in a thousand places
the way your hand is creased
cradling one more deliriously
misguided gift from me.

Waiting for Test Results in the Kitchen

Laura Spagnoli

But the kitchen doesn't know
what you don't know.
It keeps its knives in a drawer.

No signs from the veined cabbage head
left out on the counter,
pale and dumb as the moon.

No telling which bell pepper cut apart
will bear a smaller self, stuck to the core,
hopeful, embryonic, near green.

No, no knowing in the dark
which egg
holds the furtive spot of blood.

Fortune

Ivy Goldstein

Boarding to Siyang is called. It's early morning, and the bus station is filled. I have to push through the crowd to reach the doorway where my bus is waiting. Everyone is carrying red plastic bags filled with food to give—fruit, peanuts, seeds. I am carrying my own plastic bag containing ten oranges and ten bananas. A middle-aged Chinese woman stressed the importance of bringing ten of each kind of fruit. I left ten pears at home, but the bag is still heavy. I hear a few passengers say *laowai*, foreigner, as I walk down the aisle to my seat.

Four hours later, we pull into the bus station at Siyang. This place is much smaller than Zhenjiang , where I have been living—more north and colder. Through the bus window I see my student smiling at me, and I wave. It's the Spring Festival Holiday, the celebration of the Chinese Lunar New Year, and he has invited me to visit him. He and his father have come to receive me. His father has a wide smile and a cowlick in the back of his hair. My student walks ahead purposefully when I mention I need to buy a return ticket at the station. We stand in line, and he takes out a pink 100-yuan bill.

"I can pay," I weakly insist.

"Ivy, I'll pay. Let me show you around."

That's my student, Changjiang. His name means " Long River " and refers to the Yangtze, the longest river in China. Changjiang will be seventeen next month. He's tall and thin. He has wispy, wavy hair that falls into his face and an easy laugh. When he looks at me, his eyebrows arch over his glasses, and he grins.

To go to their house, we ride in a "bread car," a small van. There are other passengers in the bread car, and we fly along the road together. The driver stops every so often and calls out for more passengers. More people get on with their bags of fruit.

The lane to their house is muddy—the van cannot go on that. It's made of dirt, and has brick houses on either side. As we walk, I see bales of hay, goats, some cows, chickens, and a donkey. The mud clings to my sneakers. Changjiang has my bookbag on his shoulders, and his father carries the fruit. When we arrive at his house, his mother and grandmother come to the doorway and together we go to the concrete courtyard. His grandmother is stooped over, wears a blue apron.

"She can't understand *putonghua* (standard Mandarin) so maybe you can't speak to her," Chanjiang says.

I can't tell if his grandmother can really see me. During my visit, she wanders in and out of rooms, putting a handful of candies next to us on the sofa, leaning over the table and tapping her foot, or standing behind her grandsons examining them,

"My grandmother often does things with no result," Changjiang says.

We come to a room with a wooden table, a TV set, a DVD player, and a sofa. Here we will spend most of our time. The ceiling is very high, and the walls have posters on them—famous Chinese TV and movie stars, blue and green tinted landscapes. There are two rooms off to either side, the room they all will sleep in, and the room I will sleep in, alone. It is cold outside, and the door to the courtyard remains open all day. We see our breath as we watch DVDs, putting our feet under a blanket as our toes slowly freeze.

We leave the room for meals. For dinner, we eat corn porridge, bread, and vegetables; for breakfast, dumplings and glutinous sweet dough balls in soup. We eat crabs, turtle, pork, and vegetables for lunch. After meals we take in a mouthful of warm water from a shared cup, swish it around our mouths and spit it into the dirt off the courtyard.

If I rest for a few seconds between bites of food, his mother points to a bowl with her chopstick. "Ivy, *chi, chi.*"

"You can eat as you like," Changjiang says.

The first night, his mother introduces me to my room. There are two plastic basins on the floor filled with warm water and two towels. "This one is for washing your *pigu* (butt) and this one, your feet." She leaves. I don't touch the *pigu* basin, but I halfheartedly rub the other towel over my feet. She comes back, knows I haven't washed properly. She kneels down, holds my feet, and washes them thoroughly, rubbing between my toes.

The bed is covered with a thick blanket. When I wake up, I am warm. My head is entirely covered by the blanket and my coat, and a second blanket covers my feet. I don't remember wrapping myself so warmly.

"Ivy?" It's Changjiang, outside the door.

"Yes?" I say.

"Wake up," he says.

It snows today. We pass the day watching TV or movies. Neighbors come by. The grandmother gives them handfuls of watermelon seeds. An old man in a Russian fur hat visits, sits on the narrow wooden bench by the doorway, and the grandmother sits next to him. The light falls on the creases in their faces. I want to take a picture of them, but I don't. A young girl also visits. She leans against Changjiang, crowding him on a narrow bench. She brings a long, new firecracker into the house. He pulls it from her and throws it into the yard. The snow is coming down quickly. I laugh in surprise.

"Why did you do that?" I hit him lightly, and he laughs too. We light firecrackers on New Year's Eve. We watch from the doorway as the father lights them in the yard and runs off. We watch them burn down and throw off light, banging the air, until one goes off improperly, and the sound is unbelievable. "*Tai jinjang*, too intense," Changjiang says.

The next night, he borrows a pad and pen from his father. We talk about words in Chinese and English, draw crude pictures to show each other our meaning. Soon the page is covered with random drawings and words at all angles. "Art," his brother says. His father tells a story, and Changjiang translates. "When I was young, the other children in my neighborhood wanted to steal some money. I just stood next to them and watched. I was afraid someone would say I was guilty too."

Changjiang looks at me and laughs. "Oh, that's it," he says.

"I thought there was more."

Later I eat lunch with an all-male party—three young cousins, their father, Changjiang, his father and brother. They all have shots of *baijiu*, clear rice wine. I alone have grape wine. Everyone toasts each other. I am toasted several times and drink the weak wine. Changjiang sits beside me, worriedly telling me I only have to drink a little, only have to just touch my lips to the glass. He has had several shots of *baijiu*. He is ripping small holes in the plastic table covering. After awhile he asks me if I'm full. I nod, and he tells me I can just have a seat on the sofa. The men stay at the table toasting each other, so I get a book to read. Later, he asks to see the book, holds it in his hands, and asks me what happens in the stories I read. He sits next to me on the couch and carefully reads each word aloud on the book jacket. Floating with the *baijiu*, he steadies himself by following the words with his finger. I get my camera and hold it up to the table scene. He takes it, frames his father in the camera screen, and waits for him to laugh.

The day before I leave, I make a fortune-telling game out of a square piece of paper. I must think of several "fortunes" to hide under the folds. One that I write is, "You will marry someone ten years older or younger than yourself." And I write nine more fortunes. When I am done, I tell Changjiang to pick a number. He chooses the marriage fortune. I wrote it as a silly joke, but when I read it out to him, we just look at each other. I am twenty-six years old. I put the paper down. Later, I see his grandmother crumple it in confusion and sweep it into the trash.

That night, Changjiang, his brother, and I watch *Total Recall*. The room is dark, and their parents have gone to bed. When the movie is over, I go outside to brush my teeth and to use the outhouse. I am amazed at the stars, which are plentiful and twinkling. Changjiang and his brother come outside to look at them with me. We stand next to each other.

"I've never seen stars so clearly," I say.

After I say that, Changjiang and I look at each other.

"Maybe you can take a picture," his brother says. I get my camera, hold the screen up to the sky, but all I see is black. We also look at the airplanes. They are coming from different directions, their lights flashing.

"You can wave to me when I leave for America. Maybe you even saw me when I came to China," I say. I wonder if that could happen.

The next day, I walk with the brothers on the road to the main street. Their father stays behind but shouts several times with reminders. Tell Ivy to send a message when she returns, things like that. We walk awhile without speaking.

"Maybe we should talk," Changjiang says.

I tell him that sometimes "Silence is golden," like in a movie theater. He tells me this is also a saying in Chinese. When we get to the road, he tells his brother to go back home, and the two of us board a mini-bus. When we have to move over to make room for another man, my arm lands on Changjiang's arm. For the rest of the ride, we don't move, and we hardly talk. I experience something that I have experienced before, but rarely—I can actually feel heat along the entire right side of my body—from him. I don't know if I'm imagining the heat.

"Are you OK?" he asks me.

The Siyang bus station has an extremely dirty bathroom. No one closes the doors to the toilets, and the toilets don't flush. I squat down, face a child opposite me. Both of our doors are open. When I exit the bathroom, an attendant comes over, tells me the bus to Zhenjiang is boarding early. My student comes on the bus to wait with me. People rush to fill in the seats before the early departure. Chanjiang and I wait together in silence.

2007

Atlantic City
Justin St. Germain

Andy watched the cars around them puff vapor as his grandfather's Cadillac slid through the Sunday church traffic on Cheltenham Ave. Pop flicked cigarette ash out the driver's window. "Lock your doors when you drive through Olney," he said. "You were born in Olney."

Andy held his breath to keep the smoke out of his lungs and closed his eyes. His temples throbbed; the backs of his eyes ached. He'd had seven shots of airplane gin the night before, on a flight that landed late in Philly thanks to driving sleet. Four hours of sleep had done nothing to ease the pain.

Pop swung the Caddy through a gap in the wrought-iron fencing. The car plowed through a puddle and passed a low stone building with green landscaping trucks parked outside. A bronze crucifix stood by the door.

"Holy Sepulchre. Remember that. Lots of graveyards in Philadelphia," Pop said, turning to Andy, eyebrows arching above his fishbowl glasses. The road branched into a network of smaller lanes marked with letters. "Lane D," Pop said. They approached a fork and Pop pointed to a tomb with brass doors gone green from age. "Turn left at Felix Hanlon. Remember that name—left at Felix Hanlon."

Andy knew he was only telling him all of this because Pop thought he was going to die soon. Andy had been doing the same thing since his mother died three months earlier, covering all of his bases, even though he was forty years younger than Pop. He'd even had the estate lawyer draw up his will. But Pop could have saved himself the trouble: Andy wouldn't remember the way to his mother's grave. He wasn't sure if he wanted to.

They passed a line of limestone mausoleums strung along a side hill. A thin man stood in the middle of a plot by the side of the road, hands stretching the pockets of his jacket. Pop pulled over behind a silver Buick and parked.

"There's Eddie," Pop said, and Andy realized that the man standing among the graves was his great-uncle.

They slid off the leather seats and closed the doors softly. The grass was slick underfoot. When they reached Eddie, he nodded; his great-uncle was the tallest person in the family, and he looked down on everybody.

"How you been, Andy?" Eddie shook Andy's hand.

"Still living," Andy said, shrugging. He was surprised that Eddie had called him by the right name; most of the family confused him with his older brother, Josh.

Eddie said hello to Pop and the brothers hugged awkwardly, as if they were trying to lift each other but couldn't find the proper hold.

"Your brother couldn't make it?" Eddie asked Andy, frowning.

"He had to work," Andy said. It was a lame excuse, but the one Josh had given. Andy knew his brother had stayed home in an attempt to move on; he was rejecting the family's protracted mourning. Andy had considered doing the same but felt obligated to see this through to the end: he wanted to watch his mother's ashes lowered into the earth. He'd toss the dirt over her himself, if it meant it would finally be over.

Andy's eyes drifted to the crest of the hill, where angels and crosses shared the gray skyline with apartment buildings and the parapets of Beaver College, the unfortunately named all-girls school a block over. At least the weather's right, he thought. The storm had passed in the night, and now a dirty fog lingered at the bottom of the hill, erasing the gravestones. The December cold had already begun to stiffen his fingers. Living in Arizona hadn't prepared him for this.

"He's late," Pop said, glancing at the tarnished watch on his wrist.

"The priest?" Andy asked.

Pop nodded. "He's going to do a ceremony." Pop spread his hands in front of him, as if to illustrate.

Eddie muttered something under his breath. He was probably still upset that the funeral hadn't happened in Philly, where the family had lived for four generations. It was her birthplace, Andy's birthplace, everybody's birthplace. But Andy knew she'd moved to Arizona for a reason, raised them there, died there. He didn't know for what reason, but it had taken a crematorium and a box to get her back.

Andy tried to read the names inscribed behind the filthy windows of the family mausoleum. Pop and Eddie wandered the gravestones that lay flat and black in the grass of the family plot, like windows into the underworld. Pop began to read the names aloud. It took Andy a moment to realize that it was for his benefit. Pop pointed to the grave that held his parents. "Cancer," he said. "Both of 'em." He stopped at another and introduced Andy to the great-great uncle he would never meet. "Japs got him," he said. "Sank his boat and let the sharks do the rest." At the next stone, Pop didn't say anything. Andy read the inscription:

BENNETT
John M., Jr.
February 15, 1938—

Miriam A.
May 13, 1938—December 29, 2000
Together in life, together at rest.

Pop had already had his name put on, right above his wife's. A few years earlier, Grandma Mary had started to forget things. Then Pop woke up at midnight to an empty bed and the whine of a vacuum. He found her in the living room, dressed in an evening gown and slippers, vacuuming the drapes. She'd died soon after of a brain disease the doctors couldn't identify. The last time Pop saw her, she didn't know who he was. Andy had heard the story from his mother before she died. He'd never talked to Pop about anything other than Philadelphia sports.

"What's your middle name?" Andy asked.

"Moylan."

Andy chuckled, despite himself. "Seriously?"

Pop's lips moved silently, then words came out. "This is where I'll be soon, Josh."

"Andy. I'm Andy." It sounded angrier than he meant it to, and his grandfather looked up with hurt in his eyes. Andy felt bad for saying it, but he was sick of making arrangements, sick of spending perfectly good and vital days of his life making order out of death: who inherited what, where to have the funeral, where to bury the ashes. It struck him that he still didn't know exactly where they were burying her—he hadn't yet seen her grave. He asked and Pop pointed to a plot in the back corner, next to a pathway for lawnmowers, where a canvas tarp stretched across a hole in the ground. Andy felt a surge of resentment toward those strange dead relatives who had taken all the good spots.

Pop's face flickered. "And then you can go above her," he said, shuffling his hands in a stacking motion. Andy looked at Pop in disbelief. They stack caskets, he thought, like cars at parking lots in Newark. Pop squatted and began to rub the letters of his own name.

Brakes creaked behind him and Andy turned to see a landscaping truck pull up next to the Caddy. A priest in a black parka got out and walked toward them. He introduced himself and apologized for his lateness.

"I'll go get her," Pop said, and walked to the car. As Pop reached into the trunk, the priest looked to the sky, as if afraid of rain. Pop walked over holding the urn, a small pewter-colored box with an inscription Andy knew by heart:

Deborah Ann Bennett
August 10, 1957—September 19, 2001
A loving daughter, a loving mother.

Andy had chosen the words himself, because his brother didn't want to, and neither of them trusted anybody else. He'd agonized over how best to describe his mother; he wanted to give speeches, loud long eulogies to crowds full of everyone who'd ever known her, and everyone who hadn't, to tell them all what she was—retired Army, a small-business owner, a single mother of two from a bad part of a bad city who got by on her smarts and her sweat instead of a welfare check. How remarkable she had been, how much better than all the useless people still breathing everywhere he went. He soon realized he couldn't sum that up, so he went with relativity: who she was to those who loved her. A daughter, a mother. His mother.

Pop set the urn in the dirt next to the tarp. The priest pulled a prayer card from his jacket pocket and read the prayer of committal. Andy followed along in his head: We commend to Almighty God our sister Deborah...Ashes to ashes, and all that.

The priest finished. Andy waited for him to move the tarp and put her into the grave. The priest stood there for a moment, expressed his regrets, and shook hands with Pop and Eddie. He reached for Andy's hand, and it extended mechanically, but Andy didn't let go.

"That's it?"

The priest nodded. "The prayers of committal have been read. Now she can be interred." He tugged against Andy's grip, and Andy relented. He looked to his grandfather and pointed at the tarp, then at the urn nestled in the grass.

"They take care of that later," Eddie said. He clenched Andy's shoulder. "It's OK, son. You don't want to see that, anyway."

●●●●●●●●●●●

Andy read the Lee's Hoagie House menu while his grandfather and Eddie ordered their usuals. Pop got a pizza steak, Eddie a cheesesteak. The man behind the counter stared at Andy from below a dirty Phillies hat. Andy ordered a turkey hoagie.

They stood by the pickup counter tapping their feet.

"You sure you ought to have a pizza steak, Pop?" He'd had a heart attack a decade ago, and he was six months removed from triple-bypass surgery. The whole family had been praying that his heart would hold up, that he could survive the death of his only child less than a year after the death of his wife, that they wouldn't have to have another funeral—for him.

Pop shrugged and said he only had one every blue moon. Andy saw Eddie glaring at him and dropped the subject. They slid into a green vinyl booth.

"What was she like?" Andy asked. "As a kid, I mean."

Pop's jowls fell, then a wan smile creased his cheeks. He cleared his throat.

"How you like that new Cadillac?" Eddie asked. He nodded toward the parking lot, where the Caddy squatted alone among the weeds poking through the cracked asphalt.

Pop's head turned from Andy to Eddie, then back again. "Good car," he said. "Rides real nice. Lots of power." He rubbed his nose where the glasses pinched his skin, then put his sandwich down and excused himself. As Pop disappeared into the bathroom, Eddie flicked onion bits from his lips and spoke directly to Andy. "Jesus, kid, don't you know what he's been through?"

"Yeah, I've got a pretty good idea."

Eddie wiped his mouth with the back of his hand. "Why don't you two do something to take his mind off it? Go see a game."

"You know how hard it is to get Eagles tickets, Eddie?" Andy glanced at the yellowed Yuengling signboard on the wall.

Eddie leaned across the table. "You ain't got to tell me. I been here all my life, remember. Sixty-eight years I been watching that sorry-ass team." That didn't keep him from telling Andy about the old Eagle greats—Van Buren, Bednarik, Jaworski—until Pop came back to the table. They made small talk while they finished their lunch. Andy left most of his hoagie sitting on the grease-spotted wrapper.

In the parking lot, Eddie snuck a few bills into Andy's goodbye handshake, shooting him a wink.

"You kids go have yourselves some fun," he said, slamming the door of his new Buick. Andy watched his brake lights plunge as he drove down the steep curb. They got into the Cadillac. Andy reached into the center console for a breath mint to kill the taste of onions.

"So what do you want to do?" Pop asked. He cranked the

key and the Caddy rumbled. *Go home*, Andy thought. *I'd like to go home.* But he couldn't say that any more than he could do it. He turned on the radio:

"Put your makeup on, fix your hair up pretty..."

He'd know Springsteen anywhere; he'd heard his voice so many times, crackling on Mom's record player, wailing through the house every time she broke up with one of her boyfriends, or one of her husbands. The harmonica came in, screaming, as if somebody were sobbing into the mouthpiece.

"Atlantic City," Andy said.

"Good song." Pop reached for the volume knob.

"We should go," Andy said, and the moment he heard his own words inside his head, he knew that it was right. He saw Pop's face settling and knew what he would say—too far, he hadn't been in years, it would all be different now.

"C'mon, Pop. It's what, an hour away? It'll be fun. You can show me around." They needed to do something besides sit and eat and mourn; it had been too long, three months that felt like his entire lifetime, one long learning curve of grief. They had to do something to remind themselves that they were still alive. Their luck had to change.

Pop took off his glasses and wiped them. His eyes were red around the edges.

"OK, pal," Pop said. "What the hell, right?"

•••••••••••

Andy watched Pop behind the wheel. One of his grandfather's hands held his cigarette up to the cracked window; the heel of the other rested on the steering wheel, when he wasn't gesturing. Pop was telling jokes.

"What do you call a white man in Camden?"

Andy winced.

"Officer!" Pop chuckled.

Andy forced a grin while he wondered how it was ever normal to talk like that. It was another reminder of the generation gap between them, the one his mother used to bridge. Now it was just them, two men who shared blood and nothing else, who hardly knew each other at all.

There's still time, he thought. They were young enough: Pop was sixty-five, but he could have passed for sixty easily, and besides, Andy was twenty-three and he felt fifty and sixty and seven hundred, ancient, like he was carved in rock. Together, he thought, they could burn up the blackjack banks. They could take Atlantic City; make a memory or two that didn't involve death or long-distance phone charges.

He was dreaming stacks of green when the car shuddered. Pop had let it drift onto the rumble strips on the side of the highway. He whipped the wheel, crossing the dotted line, nearly side-swiping a Volkswagen. Andy gripped his chest with one hand and shoved the other against the dash. He closed his eyes and considered saying a prayer.

"Don't worry," Pop said, slapping Andy's hand away from the dashboard with his own, which should have been steering the car. "Safest road in America, right here. They did a survey."

The road was the least of Andy's worries. He had spent most of the trip envisioning the Caddy blowing a tire, them veering across the median into oncoming traffic, their caskets lowering into the family plot, one on top of the other. Strips of rubber, lug nuts, Pop's surgically repaired arteries: their lives relied on so many things.

Pop pointed to the horizon, where angular casinos reared above the tree line. They passed a sign announcing the end of the expressway, rounded a corner, and Andy got his first glimpse of Atlantic City. It was not what he expected: no lights or marquees or bright casino entrances beckoning. Bars covered the windows and graffiti covered everything else. Gas stations and liquor stores fought for space with fast-food restaurants and check-cashing centers. A homeless old woman in a little girl's coat staggered down the sidewalk pushing a shopping cart half-full of clothes stained with dark blotches. They drove down the street in silence, like observers in a war, until they could see the ocean peeking out between the high-rises on the boardwalk.

•••••••••••

Their brief sense of dread dissipated in the winter breeze blowing in off the beach.

The table was hot. Pop flicked chips from the Technicolor puddle in front of his ashtray. Andy plucked his carefully from neat stacks.

"You gamble a lot back home?" Pop asked.

"Nope, not much," Andy said. The woman dealing shot him a look; for the last hour, he'd been splitting eights and aces, doubling every eleven. There was no reason to lie. "I go to Vegas a few times a year." Actually, there was a reason to lie—Andy wasn't going to tell him that he'd donated most of his mother's modest life insurance money to tip jars and chip racks.

"No kidding? We used to go, Mary and me."

The dealer flipped her hole card, a king, then dropped a nine next to the six already showing. Bust. Easy money.

"Always stayed at the Flamingo," Pop continued. "Ever been there? That's a classy joint."

"Sure is," Andy said. It once was, judging by the pictures in the lobby. When he had gone, the bedspreads smelled like pipe tobacco and the flamingos were molting.

Pop squirmed in his seat and stretched. "How about we make things interesting before we head to the boardwalk?" he said, sliding his whole stack into the circle: four blacks and a ten-stack of green. Andy had less; a glance told him about three-fifty. He'd bought in with the three hundred Eddie had given him, taken a dive right away, then climbed back up during the hot shoe they'd just finished.

The dealer tapped a long red fingernail against the felt in front of Andy. "Bet?" she asked, in a shrill foreign accent that irritated him.

He'd told himself he wouldn't gamble anymore. The money in his hand could delay the collection calls for a month, buy him another two weeks without an eviction notice. Now that he'd dropped out, the banks were sending letters about his student loans. He refused to ask Pop for money, because he didn't want him to think he was after an inheritance. That wasn't why he was there. He had come to settle things. He had come to start anew.

Andy slid his whole stack into the circle. They were still young.

The cards came quickly: an ace each. Andy's chest stretched tight across his ribs as the deal came around to fill them up: Pop caught a seven, Andy another ace. The dealer flipped a queen.

"Jeez," Pop said. "This ought to be good." He winked at Andy and tapped his finger. She dealt him a ten that made his soft eighteen hard. She turned to Andy.

"Twelve," she said, her accent butchering the word.

Andy considered for another moment. Always split aces. Always. He turned to Pop.

"How much cash you got?"

Pop pulled out his money clip and counted twenties. "Two forty," he said.

"Twelve," the dealer said again. *Twerve*, he thought, feeling a sneer start and scolding himself. It was a ten-dollar table on a Tuesday afternoon in December, and if they lost they wouldn't have anything left to tip her. They were being assholes, but he didn't give a shit. The world owed them that much. More.

He looked at her name tag. "Where's the fire, Fong?"

The woman scowled as he counted the money in his wallet: five twenties, a five, four crumpled ones. He checked his pockets: three quarters and three dimes. He had a nickel to spare.

"Split 'em," he said, taking Pop's offering and slapping it all down on the table. "You can keep the change." He winked at Fong and felt his blood rising for the first time in forever.

She flipped an eight and smirked; it widened into a smile when she turned another ace. Nineteen and twelve against a face card showing. Pop had eighteen. They were going to lose everything.

She pointed her fiery fingernail at the leftmost hand, the pair of aces. "Split again, Bugsy?"

Andy leaned against the back of his chair and exhaled. He saw that a small crowd of degenerates had gathered behind them. That kind of hand didn't happen every day. The pit boss appeared behind the dealer, arms folded. Andy doubted he'd give them a marker for three-fifty after the way he'd been acting. He had resigned himself to another loss when Pop spoke.

"Three-fifty now, I'll pay you five or a Rolex in thirty seconds," Pop said to the handful of onlookers. He slid his watch off his wrist and dangled it between his fingers. It had diamonds on the face and, Andy knew, an inscription on the back: "Thanks for the best twenty years of my life. Love, Mary."

"Pop, what are you—"

Pop extended a palm. His face was flushed. A tattooed man in a tank top took the watch and looked it over. The diamonds did their job; old as it was, the watch was worth a few large, easy.

"My kind of guy," said tank top. He dug a handful of chips from his jeans. The pit boss moved toward Pop.

"You got a problem?" Pop spat. The pit boss blinked to a stop, surveyed the empty casino floor, and shook his head before stepping back. Pop was old, but he wasn't one to back down. He swept the chips from tank top's hand into his own and then dropped them into Andy's cupped palms like an offering. Tank top put the watch on the table, and Andy saw Pop's eyes linger on it.

"You don't have to," Andy said.

Pop shot him a smile that showed he wasn't sure about it either. "All I've got is time, pal."

Fong's fingernails massaged the deck as Andy counted how much was at stake. In his head, Springsteen again: "I got debts no honest man can pay." He held his breath as the cards came down.

King of diamonds.

Suicide Jack.

He let it out. He was buying dinner, no matter what she had. Fong let the slot machines jingle for a long second before she showed her hand.

Deuce. Twelve, the dealer's ace, Andy thought.

Then a Queen fell, and the table erupted. A grandmother slapped Andy's hand. He looked over and saw tank top put his arm around Pop. They'd pay him back, keep the watch, and clear more than fifteen hundred in profit.

"Color us up," he said to Fong, but she was watching Pop with widened eyes. Andy turned to see his grandfather clutching at his chest. Sweat beaded above his glasses.

"Pop?" Andy said. He shot out of his stool, knocking it over. He slapped tank top's arm away from Pop's shoulders and replaced it with his own. He felt the group crushing in around him. The stale smoke clogged his nose and the slot machines rang in his ears. *Should I tell him I love him? Is this my last chance?*

"I'm...OK," Pop said, wiping his forehead. "Just...out of breath...is all."

Andy put his fingers against Pop's damp neck, trying to remember the CPR class he'd taken in high school. He felt a pulse pushing back against his skin and said a silent prayer of thanks, to God, to his mother, to whoever was watching over them.

"Let's get you out of here," he said, helping Pop out of his chair.

Two steps from the table, Pop wheezed: "The money." Andy turned and stuffed the stack of black and gold chips into his pockets. He cleared a path for them with a glare and they walked to the door, the soft red carpet sucking at their shoes.

•••••••••••

The waves crashed along the boardwalk and the wind cut through their clothes. Pop leaned back against the marble wall and blinked slowly.

"Scared you, didn't I?"

Andy giggled, even though he didn't find it funny. His head felt light and airy, and his skin prickled from the cold and the relief. He looked down the boardwalk, past the T-shirt shops and food booths, to the palatial Taj Mahal at the far end.

"You ever played a hand like that?" Pop asked.

"Nope. You?"

Pop shook his head. "Mary didn't like to gamble. She was real classy, you know, and even back then A.C. was going to hell in a bucket." They watched a homeless man walk by. "I used to bring your mom down here, when she was just a kid."

At the mention of his mother, Andy blinked, then smiled, as his mind reacted in its usual way: picturing her alive, pushing brown curls behind her ear, and then picturing the urn with her name engraved on it.

"We were both kids, really." Pop had his only child at nineteen; Andy knew that much. He imagined himself with a four-year-old child. What a disaster that would be. "She loved the water, that girl. Couldn't get her to come out until her fingers were all shriveled up—" Pop clenched his hands, "and her skin looked like a stop sign." He sighed. "She just wouldn't listen."

Andy wondered whether Pop had pulled the watch stunt so that he'd have a similar story to tell about them. *I used to take him down the shore to A.C. Kid had brass balls—split aces three times once, almost cost me my watch.* Or was it for Andy's sake, to give him something to remember about his grandfather? *Next thing I know Pop's waving his watch around. He bet a Rolly on me. That's the kind of faith he had.* A funeral anecdote.

"I'm glad we came down here, Pop."

"Me too, pal." Pop smiled. "Haven't been in years. Glad we got a chance to see it—"

Andy sensed Pop's "before" coming and interjected. "You could come down whenever, Pop. It's not far."

Pop shrugged his shoulders and looked around. "With who?"

Andy followed his grandfather's eyes to the waves eating away at the empty beach, the trash blowing down the boardwalk, the lights chasing each other around buildings. Overhead, flags popped in the wind like the knuckles of some giant, closing hand. He realized how terrible it would feel to be here alone, and he wanted to say that they could go together, he and Pop. He could come to visit more often, they could come back to A.C. for a weekend or two. If he could get Pop to fly out, maybe they could even hit Vegas for a weekend. But he didn't say it, because he thought it might sound too much like a promise, or too much like a dream.

"Hell of a place you picked to rest," Pop said. Andy looked behind him for the first time. He'd thrown open the doors of the casino and led Pop to the nearest place to sit, a low marble slab that he now saw was part of some monument. A huge bronze plaque of names stretched along a marble wall, and a statue of an officer stood in the middle of the plaza. The officer held his helmet at his side and stared down his arm at a fistful of dog tags, as if he didn't know what they were.

Pop pushed himself up with one arm, and they walked slowly over to the sign.

"New Jersey Korean War Memorial," Andy read.

"Wonderful spot for it," Pop said, looking from the casino entrance on one side to the pizza joint on the other.

"Eight hundred twenty-two dead or missing," Andy said. "And this is what they get."

•••••••••••

Andy had checked twice on the way back from A.C. to make sure his grandfather was breathing, but Pop stopped snoring and stirred as they climbed the rise of the Walt Whitman Bridge. The city unrolled before them, its lights cutting through the dusk. Past twinkling Center City sat the concrete face of the Vet, and behind it lurked the long, dark arms of the cranes brought in to build the two new stadiums that would make it obsolete. Between the Whitman and the Ben Franklin, the dying light curdled the water of the Delaware, and above the swaying masts at the landing, William Penn straddled the gold-lit steeple of City Hall.

"There used to be a law that said you couldn't build anything taller than the tip of his hat," Pop said, pointing at the city's founder, then at the bank buildings dwarfing him. "That was a long time ago."

It was dark outside by the time they parked outside Pop's condo. He had fallen asleep again, cheek pressed against the seat, his mouth trailing moisture onto the leather. Andy got out of the car, closed the door softly, and stretched. The lights of the city seemed far away now, hidden behind the buildings of Pop's complex, so he could only see the halo they cast into the sky. Between the homes, sprinklers threw sheets of water across the grass, and Andy stood watching his breath escape into the cold air, not wanting to wake Pop. They would go inside, and Andy would sleep in his mother's old room, where the strange metallic wallpaper kept him awake with its reflections. Pop would sleep in his recliner, next to the nightstand he'd moved out into the living room, because his bedroom reminded him of his dead wife, and the other bedroom reminded him of his dead daughter.

Andy would leave in the morning, go back to Arizona with the money that stuffed his pockets. It was enough to make rent, pay the bills for another month. He'd have to find a job, something to do with himself. Maybe he'd enroll in spring classes at the local community college.

And Pop would stay right here, Andy knew, no matter what he said or did or tried to plan to change it. He'd sleep in the same empty condo and drive the same old Caddy until he moved across Philadelphia to join his wife and daughter. It was just a matter of time, now; the grave had already been marked with his name.

Andy thought of the family plot, where they had been that morning. He wondered if his mother's ashes had been buried yet, whether the grass had begun to take root in the raw dirt above her. He wondered how long it would take to grow over, for the brown earth to turn green.

Northern Liberties

Toussaint St. Negritude

Thanks
to a gracious wind from
Chestnut Hill

333,000 brown residents
of North Philadelphia

were found buried today
in a drift of war-torn apologies.

While their opportunities
were left inoperable

the citizens of the ghetto
are eternally bemused

2008

The Robbery

Christina Delia

Todd steals things. He takes tips off wet diner tables, jerks the bills from underneath the water glass you purposefully placed over them.

You say, "Don't do that," but your voice is passive and no match for his muscles. He has worked jobs that scare you, jobs where he has shoved people out of nightclubs and menaced trees with axes. He is the only wayward art school lumberjack you have ever met, and it is your life's mission to concoct his pancake piles.

He went by "Toad" during his cover band years. Seventeen reinterpretations of the same Quiet Riot song later, here you are. Toad's band was The John Goodman Arachnophobia Experience. Toad likes movies where insects best humans.

"Molly," he says, "you relax." Your name is not Molly, but that is Todd's definition of a little baby girl name. Molly wants an ice cream cone, don't she? Go ahead, Molly, tell the big badass manager that our man stole an orange. You are convinced he refers to himself as "our man" to let you know there are other morons like you, who let him sleep in your bed after watching him go through your purse. You are convinced that he belongs mostly to himself, while you have the submissive misfortune of being his. What happened to your feminist theory textbooks? Todd sold them. What did he do with the money? Todd bought pills. Why did he? Don't question our man!

So you make do:

—You stop keeping a diary after Todd sells it on eBay.

—Now at restaurants you get up to go to the bathroom before he makes a scene.

—On the occasion you find another woman in your shower, you say, "Hey there."

—Your friends pity you and this makes you cry; that people think you are worthy of pity.

—You remember that you are alive, so you work with this fact.

You are making a plan to hit yourself out of the park, like a home run, but first you need money. He keeps taking yours, and you are afraid of him. Not just because he talks to himself in the kitchen when he thinks you're sleeping, but also because he talks to himself while hovering over your bed when he thinks you're sleeping.

He won't see a doctor, any kind of doctor. The only way you'll see a doctor is if you get pregnant with Todd Junior. Yes, you are on the pill, but what if? You keep your legs closed so tightly at night your muscles ache.

Our man is a bully. Our man is a punk. You have nowhere to go. There is a part of you that finds comfort in this: Living in the present means you have nowhere else to go. Once in a while your mind clears and you feel like a Buddhist, which is way cooler than feeling like a victim.

You are not fighting back, because you are a planner. Little outbursts will have him suspecting. You don't want to awaken his inner Toad. You pack bras and panties in small, yellow supermarket bags and toss them in the trunk of your car. Soon you will have the balls—no, the breasts—to pack the big-ticket items: sweaters, a pair of dress slacks.

Now he wants to get on your medical insurance. The two of you should get married. Molly, there's nothing I wouldn't steal for you, he says.

You thank him for his proposal, and take a deep breath. Somewhere beneath the curves of your female form, probably above the hips, is a star. It's kind of like a soul, but a little less passive. It's a Holy Spirit divine inner compass, and it's telling you to get the hell out into the universe, darling! Make something of this flesh gift, this life.

At the Mutter Museum of Medical Oddities

Eileen Moeller

It's a miracle we survive at all,
I say, as we walk the cases,
wincing at a colon as big as a stove pipe,
scowling at ribs deformed
by corsets, and spines collapsed
into little broken heaps, the horns
and warts and tumors
jutting out of waxen faces,
carbuncles and gouty toes,
a lady whose fat has turned her into soap.

But my brother, being a man, jokes on.
He sees a petrified penis and gasps,
I'll never look at beef jerky the same way again,
as I giggle and cringe.

Until a whole wall of bloodless
babies in jars breaks over us like a wave,
all stages of fetal development,
followed by the terrible web of maladies;
so many damaged dolls,
each one a lesson in fragility.

He points to the anencephalic ones,
saying they look like trolls,
but then a lonely floater
in its little sea of tears
sends him into silence,
for we could be at the grave
of the little ghost he's been
tethered to for seventeen years:
his first girl, all tangled in her cord,
born still and cold as snow.
I can't bring myself
to tell him about the tiny
pearl of a zygote my heart tows.

Like Nothing in the World
Jacob Russell

The world is filled with gods
They are like nothing else in the world
This is how you know they are gods

The gods did not make the world
The gods were made by the world
They are more helpless than they have ever been

I asked them if they were once
Like the gods of our storied past
But they did not answer

Their tongues were made of stone
And their teeth of wool
They neither sing nor speak

I found them one day searching
For change, but my pockets were empty
Everything now must remain as it was

Only the world changes
As stars withdraw to the beginning of time
As we found ourselves at the edge of the forest

Following the animals over the plains
Listening to their lies, their endless
Stories of gods who will not let them be

My Charlie Manson

Helen W. Mallon

Our wedding was in a graveyard in November darkness. I had recently turned eighteen, old enough to make hash of my life and do it legally, and my fiancée, Kemp, was for-ty-two. I wore light makeup and under a raincoat, my best dress of striped wool. My hair was long and straight, and my Mary-Jane style shoes were better suited to a little girl. I felt numb and disconnected, as if I were about to sign up after stumbling into a meeting of bomb-assembling anar-chists. I was also a little disappointed. It would have been festive to show off my dress, but the night was too chilly to take the raincoat off.

A brick wall surrounded the graveyard of Saint Peter's Episcopal Church in Philadelphia's Old City; it was the nearest thing we had to a park, given where Kemp and I were living in the city. I was worried that someone who belonged to the church would boot us off the property, even though Kemp said they'd told him we could do anything on the premises, as long as it was legal and took place *outside* the church.

The absence of light at the wedding was due to a mis-calculation. We'd scheduled the ceremony for five p.m. We didn't realize—but how could my physics-trained fiancé not have realized?—that light fails early once autumn cold begins to shrivel the sycamore leaves.

I don't remember what Kemp wore that night, but he was a man who considered his coiffure. He bleached his dark hair brassy blond on the optimistic—but faulty— premise that if his hair were similar in color to his scalp, he could pass himself off as not-balding. The stringy comb-over rarely stayed put, but he had an appealing, little-boy grin and nice, agate-colored eyes. He was endlessly authoritative when relating my own passion, visual art, to his interest in science. He encouraged me even as he dictated the kind of painting I did. You're an artist now, he said. Why wait till you're twenty-one to call yourself one? From him I learned terms like *sexual revolution* and *Renaissance man*. Years later, I found out from a former student of Kemp's that in the early days of our relationship, he pinned my panties to the wall of his apartment.

Nobody gave me away at the wedding. My father stayed away, but my mother showed up with an elderly friend for moral support. The aisle I walked down was the worn brick path on which Kemp and I met the Ethical Culture minister. Mr. Smith was not exactly a believer, not Episcopalian, nor Quaker, as my family was, but the price he'd quoted to do the ceremony must have been right because Kemp hired him.

As I stood in the darkness beside the tilted gravestones of long-dead Episcopalians, my mother's mute presence felt like the still point of tradition from which my adolescence had fled. Perhaps her inscrutable sense of duty drew her; perhaps she felt compelled to witness the unthinkable. Introductions were made, hands shaken. My mother didn't kiss me, and I looked away to the brick wall, thinking I had dragged her into something cheap. At the head of our tight circle, the minister held his book at an unnatural angle to catch the sallow illumination of a street lamp. He read from Genesis about a man leaving his parents and cleaving unto his wife. *But I'm the one who's leaving*, I thought.

The June before our wedding, I had graduated from Germantown Friends, a private school where Kemp had been a science teacher. I was a "lifer" there: K through 12. My great-grandmother, my grandfather, my father's first cousin, and my mother had all gone there. It was a world in which the staid traditions of Philadelphia Quakerism— Meeting membership by "birthright" or family succession and the quiet tending of old wealth—set the stage for their own eclipse, at least in part, by their liberal embrace of the social revolutions of the sixties and seventies. As a teenager, I was proud to be such a revolutionary, convinced that Kemp was proof of my emancipation. As my great-grandmother had, I attended mandatory weekly meeting for worship in a plain, high-ceilinged room with rows of wooden benches, where faintly rippled, tall glass windows revealed a pensive sky.

Quaker meeting for worship is simple. People steep themselves in relaxed silence, waiting until God's spirit moves someone to speak. The first time I encountered Kemp was when he stood up in meeting. I don't remember much of what he said—I believe it had to do with *Guernica*, Picasso's tortured painting of the Spanish Civil War—but his mouth revealed the subtle overflow of his heart. Kemp was a predator on the lookout, and I had a vulnerable and sensitive ear. A few days afterward, I described on lined notebook paper how impressed I was by his brief talk. At thirteen, I was reluctant to speak my own name out loud, and I avoided writing it except on school papers. With my face latticed behind untrimmed hair, I gave him my unsigned note at a chance encounter on the stairs of the science building. The next week, one of his students handed me his reply. All I remember is one line: *i don't even know your name.* His use of the lowercase "i" impressed me; it seemed poetic and humble; like e.e. cummings. I was in eighth grade. He got fired at the end of my ninth grade year for "inappropriate conduct," but I never found out whether the school knew our relationship was indeed a sexual one. From my point of view, little changed with his firing; I simply continued seeing him on the sly.

At the end of our wedding ceremony, the minister intoned the traditional warning: "If anyone...let him speak now, or forever hold his peace." Silence crackled like a pause in a military assault. I glanced at the blue silk scarf tucked into the neck of my mother's coat, wondering if she would yell or perhaps grab the vows from Mr. Smith and tear them up. My eyes slipped down to her no-longer-parallel feet.

No one stirred. No words were spoken. Because nothing appreciably changed, the minister's words felt like an incantation, the power of which would only be revealed over time: *I now pronounce you husband and wife...*

The night speeded up. My mother bid me goodbye, sort of, and staggered back to her respectably antiqued house on the arm of her friend. Kemp and I had arranged to meet a few friends in our city apartment. I proceeded to get drunk and fell asleep fully clothed in the bathtub. He woke me in the middle of the night. It was time to clean up.

At the time, I believed that my parents would count me as dead, but as if my heart were swathed in bandages, the conviction brought no feeling. My loyalty to my new husband could have fueled an insurgency. A few weeks after the wedding, I received a set of place mats from my parents. Other than this, we had very little contact.

I was married for years before my commitment disintegrated. Cut off from my family and my privileged life, and perhaps the only one in my graduating class not to go to college, I explored the realm of the spirit. Years of Quaker worship spent in listening silence had cultivated my instinct for the reality of the unseen. Lonely, I responded when televangelists told me that God, the spirit, was also a person whom I could know. I was used to doing outrageous things. Belief wasn't a huge stretch. The conservative church teaching fueled my zeal to serve my husband, to smile when he cuffed me, and to organize his drawer of unmatched socks, although he claimed I'd interfered with his "system." Whatever the personal cost, my life had an aura of divine sanction. My church friends didn't agree; they spoke of give and take, of mutual submission. If one of them criticized Kemp, I sharply defended an alcoholic man whose permission I had to seek to go out to dinner with my brother, now back in town after college. *You don't understand,* I argued. *You don't know what he really is.*

Consider the loyalty of the Manson Family. Or the seductive influence of those who believe it pleases God to strap a bomb to a mentally challenged man and send him into a marketplace when the whole town is shopping. When there's enough of an emotional payoff, fanaticism can trump rational morality. The reality is that even if someone does something really, really nasty, there may be a girl who won't stop loving him.

Kemp, in fact, had not been my first love. An English cousin of my mother's had visited us when I was six years old. I adored Tony. With his open lap and his gentle teasing, he charmed me. He enticed. He was handsome as a wolf. Early one Saturday morning, I crept up to our third-floor guest room to surprise him; I remember the sensation of flight on the stairs. Tony was happy when I appeared in the bathroom, where he stood in his boxers and undershirt, having just shaved. He closed the door. He imprinted on my body and in my brain things that I was compelled to forget. Afterward, he said: *Don't tell anyone you came up here today.* While my parents fussed over breakfast downstairs, I stood in the weird light of my bedroom. What should I do? Pray? No. God was about *Now I lay me down to sleep* and *Be present at our table, Lord...* He wasn't concerned with the fallout from events that couldn't even be named. Tell my parents that Tony had done something bad? But they would believe him and not me. In terror I saw that my mind would snap like a china plate should they turn from me in this way, and I resolved never to think about Tony again.

Adolescence churned up more than the usual burden of confusions. In seventh grade, I considered myself preternaturally grown up, advanced beyond other girls who worried about boy crushes and parties, yet I felt envious to the point of nausea when no one passed me notes in class. Kemp was an escape from middle-school drama. He also offered me a chance to revisit the moral and spiritual dilemmas instigated when Tony's eyes changed from inviting to hard and glittering. In his mesmeric influence, Kemp was not unlike Charles Manson, minus the highly developed people skills.

When we were in high school, my brother challenged my father about the relationship: "Why don't you put a stop to it?"

"Your mother and I don't want your sister's name in the papers," was his response. The damage Kemp inflicted wasn't spectacular enough to make the newspaper.

Fortunately, Kemp's precocious interest in sex with schoolgirls translated into beer-fueled impotence in mar-

riage. I wasn't really interested in Eros, anyway. I was
an alchemist who poured out devotion in an attempt to
transmute sleaze into gold. Kemp needed a housekeeper,
nursemaid, and receptacle for his rants. In our last few
years together, I learned to manage him. When he dissected
my flaws with his maddeningly persuasive condemnation,
instead of defending myself I developed the instincts of
survival in a cage. Nodding. Yes-ing. Pretending to swallow
his wisdom. After four quarts of beer, he'd fall asleep, sometimes with his eyes half-open, and I would escape for a walk
in the woods. Life was simultaneously boring and chaotic.
But thanks to my long-suffering and, ultimately, supportive
parents, I went to Tyler School of Art and obtained a degree.

Clarity came to me, over time, bit by bit. The major
revolution occurred after nine years of marriage. Kemp's
mother, a serious churchgoer, had gotten me to visit a
hand-clapping fundamentalist congregation. It was God
on your taste buds as against the cerebral quiet of Quaker
meeting. At my progressive school, I'd envied the Black
kids for the easy, familial solidarity they shared. Now I met
cheerfully zealous people who might not have recognized
the names of most of the poets I'd studied in my senior
English seminar at Germantown Friends, but they invited me to their houses, hugged expansively, and called me
"sister." And they meant it. One summer, my mother-in-law
invited me to a church conference, and Kemp urged me to
attend, since he transformed himself into an authority on
any topic that caught my interest. He expected me to come
home chastened for my sins, and he sent me off with certain
verses underlined in my Bible as preparation.

Maybe I was sick of having glasses of beer tossed into
bookshelves I had recently cleaned, or maybe my heart was
exhausted. I didn't expect anything from the conference
beyond company for my loneliness and the possibility of
becoming a better person. But that week, I began to tie the
Christian notion of God as father around the fragmented
pieces of my inner self. Throughout the last night there, I
sat hyper-alert in my quiet dorm room, praying and touch-
ing the parts of my body I didn't like. I repeated over and

over, in shock and delight, that God loved me—*my mouth that binged on junk food, **my** breasts, **my** pallid skin.* Something was re-ordering my spiritual DNA. On the long train ride home, I knew things were going to change.

Kemp's Mansonesque diatribes began to sound bombastic, even silly. He told me that what stood between me and God's love was the fact that I had just rolled my eyes, revealing that my nature was as stiff-necked as the Israelites wandering in the desert. I didn't argue or pretend to agree. I started sassing back.

I moved out after he described a dream he'd had, involving me and a knife. I went home to my parents. It was a relief to say, "You were right about him." Our kisses were unpracticed and stiff, but genuine. I lived with them for a while, waiting for my divorce to finalize and figuring out what to do with my life.

Today, those shadow years lie at the periphery of my thoughts. I am happy and productive. I am married again— this time, to a gentle and loving man. I never saw Kemp or Tony again, but a mental breakdown while pregnant with my first child catapulted me into a war. I had dismissed my past as over and done. I'd been to hell and back, but here, reflected in my husband's admiring face, were my years of Jubilee. But as I stared at the pattern on the Persian rug in my therapist's office session after session, my past proved to be tenacious as vermin. As a young mother, while my heart sometimes threatened to explode under the pressure of change, I never lost my gratitude at having been granted a second, ordinary life. There was a time when I believed I'd spend the rest of my life in a grubby apartment, the target of Kemp's theories that I was the genetic inferior of people who were outgoing and successful. Scary as each hour of my new life could be, I lived it in the light of day.

Today, my children know only that I was married before. That I was young and he was old. That I made a mistake. They know that I have returned to Quakerism from a more conservative place, but they are not aware that the thick walls of fundamentalism once offered refuge for my sanity. Someday, when they're ready, I'll tell them this story. But am I the one who hesitates, knowing that their vision of order in the world is colored, however subtly, by their view of me? Once they know, they will think no less of me. They'll also realize that I used to be pretty strange, the kind of kid that they would choose to avoid. My straightforward parental authority has tangled roots. For now, I'm simply Mom, who volunteers at the school store, someone who would never do anything seriously outrageous or unsafe. I wish I could remain simple forever.

I'll introduce my story casually, as if pain were not at its heart. "It was only love," I'll tell them. "Granted, that can be complicated."

2009

I-80
DJ Kinney

They woke together at a rest stop on the interstate, car windows dimmed by frozen breath and through the glass, anemic blue dawn swelling over Wyoming.

She struggled out of the sleeping bag, wrestled with the nest of blankets and pulled at the door. She poured herself out into the empty lot and shuffled a few paces from the car before she buckled over a strip of grass and vomited. It slapped the ground and steam rose from it. The man got out of the car and went to her and put his hands on her shoulders to steady her, to hold her. She heaved again, just water and foam.

"Get your hands off me."

"What can I do?"

"This isn't your problem." She wiped her mouth with the back of her hand. "Drive. We shouldn't have stopped."

They got back into the beaten silver Saturn and pushed the blankets to the back seat, which was piled with unpacked clothes, some still on hangers, some tangled at the floorboards.

"Jesus, Peter. Why don't you just hate me?"

He started the car, which struggled in the cold. The engine knocked and shuddered. He drove.

•••••••••••

She slapped his hand away from the radio and it stung, and when he pulled away it made him swerve over the line, into the red gravel shoulder, which probably made her hate him all the more.

"Christ. Learn how to drive."

"You hit me."

"I hit your hand."

"I was turning it off."

"I'm listening."

"There's nothing to listen to, Annie. It's just Jesus radio. There's nothing there."

She folded her arms and turned to the window and was sullen for a while.

"I thought they might say something about it."

They were silent for a long time more, listening to AM static rise and fall because Peter was afraid to touch the radio and upset her again, and Annie was too proud to admit that she had been wrong and there was really nothing on the radio about this horrible thing that had happened. Just hallelujah. Just praise the Lord.

And so it was the End of Days through the long Wyoming desert.

Eventually, when the voices faded, Annie turned off the radio and there was only wind and the hiss of the road.

"This is crazy," she said.

"Yep."

"Yep? What's that supposed to mean?"

"I was agreeing."

"*Yep.* Are you a fucking cowboy?"

He didn't answer. He shifted and drove with one hand.

She didn't look at him. "Which part?"

"What?"

"I said this was crazy and you agreed."

"Yep."

"Which part did you agree to?"

The road was empty and wide, and so he turned and stared at her. "All of it," he said.

"Keep your eyes on the road."

He turned back.

"And that isn't an answer. Tell me what you think is crazy."

"That there are no radio stations. That we haven't been through a town in sixty miles. There's a storm coming and we don't have anywhere to stay. Everything."

"What's *everything*?"

"Everything that's happened. Every goddamned thing, Annie. You and me. New York. All of it."

She nodded. That was enough.

Then it was back to the radio.

Annie hit scan and it rolled through the entire AM band without stopping. It started again and stopped on static. She switched to FM and hit a station. Christian. Like everything.

The voice was rattled. It said, *What will become of the children?*

There were coughs in the pause and shuffling papers.

In the final days when God's wrath is descended over the Earth and the horsemen have strode among us. What will become of the children?

Annie drew back her hand.

Some say that children are the innocent, but God almighty, the child will pay for the sins of their fathers and death will befall them as it did the children of Pharaoh, and locusts will consume their flesh and flies will fill their eyes.

"Jesus Christ, Annie. Turn it off."

"No."

Peter flicked his finger over the volume knob and the radio went dead. He looked at her and waited for her to scream or hit him again. But she was silent. And then tears came.

"I hate you," she said.

"That's probably true."

"This is such shitty timing."

"The worst."

"We can't have a baby now."

He took his hand from the wheel and shifted it toward her. He put it on her leg, covered by the bloated down coat, which he loathed, and had always loathed. She put her hand on top of his and they held each other this way while the long desolation passed outside, while miles of fences flickered by and the morning sun settled on the land like ash.

"I still love you," he said. "I don't know if that makes any difference, but I do."

"It does." She squeezed his hand. "I don't know why, but it does."

•••••••••••

Miles piled upon miles, and the exits were useless and barren.

"*No Services,*" he said as another sign slipped by.

"How can there be no services? How do people live here if there are no services?"

"I think they drive a long way for services."

"Stop saying 'services.'"

"Sorry."

"Fuck this place."

"We'll find something."

"Fuck you too."

They were quiet for a while.

"I'm hungry," she said.

"Me too."

"I mean it. I'm really hungry."

"When we get to an exit, we'll see if we can find some services."

"Go to hell." She folded her arms and leaned against the window. "Why didn't we bring any food with us?"

"Because we were in a hurry. And yesterday I didn't think we'd have trouble finding some."

•••••••••••

They did come to an exit, which wasn't a town, just a clutter of lots and gravel on either side of the highway, two gas stations, a junkyard, and a McDonald's.

It was a nameless settlement that had sprouted simply because one old local road rambled out of the country and crossed the interstate.

They came off the highway and crept to the top of the ramp, slick with ice and snowblown. The car slipped and then caught the pavement again.

The station at the end of the ramp had put out orange barricades and a slab of plywood that said *NO GAS.* They turned left and the tires slipped as they moved onto the overpass and skidded down the other side.

At the other station, a long line of pickup trucks had stacked up at the pumps.

"There's a McDonald's," she said.

"You never eat that shit."

"I need to eat. I don't care what it is."

The snow on the local road had gathered in eddies and he drove slowly over black ice where the tires had no grip. He turned into the parking lot and turned off the engine.

"I don't want to get caught in the storm," he said. "I think we can make it to Laramie before it hits. If we hurry."

She nodded. "Yeah. Alright."

They got out and the dry wind bit them. Snow blew around their ankles and packed in dusty drifts at the edge of the lot. They shuffled for the door.

Inside, it was yesterday in America. Yesterday, when nothing had happened at all.

Annie ordered breakfast, but the kid behind the counter, an Indian with long black hair and bad skin, told her that it was too late, so she muttered under her breath and walked away. Peter ordered for her.

The kid disappeared into the back and Peter waited. The place was bright. The place was warm. It was good to be warm after the bitter winter night at the side of the road.

Annie sat in a booth against the front window, staring at her open hands. She pulled off her dowdy knit hat and frazzled hair splayed out in wild directions. When Peter had met her, she had been so prim and ordered. Her hair precise, her clothes immaculate, her body angelic.

But this had changed and she had become tangled and wrecked, as they together had wheeled wildly off the rails, and whatever they'd been once, they were no longer.

At the end, they cheated on each other ferociously, for vengeance, to push the other away, to disgust the other and bring the thorny bramble of their undone love to a permanent, fiery end.

And it had worked, and they had ended, squarely and without remorse.

Then on Monday came into their lives news of the baby.

Then on Tuesday came the end of the world.

The kid came back to the counter. "Sorry it's taking so long. A lot of people didn't show up today."

"It's alright."

"We don't even got the guy that cleans the shitter."

"Damn."

"Just didn't come in." The kid looked around to see if he was being watched. He leaned in and almost whispered. "Hey. You heard anything?"

Peter shook his head. "No."

"They don't let us turn on the radio or nothing. So I ain't heard. But if you heard something—"

"I haven't. Sorry."

"OK. Yeah. I'll bring it out to you in a minute."

Peter left the counter and walked to the table by the window. He hung over Annie for a while. She looked up at him, regarded him, exhausted and confused, the same way she had looked at her hands. Perplexed by her appendages, baffled that he was still attached to her, and she to him.

He sat across from her. "I have a plan."

She stared.

"We eat. Then we find gas. We can wait in line over there. Then if we drive all day, we can make it to Omaha. If we drive hard, we could make it to Chicago by tomorrow night. We'll be there for Christmas. Everything will be OK when we get home."

"That isn't a plan, Peter. That's just what we were doing anyway."

"It makes me feel better to say it."

The kid came over with a tray of Big Macs in their greasy boxes.

"Sorry it took so long. Some of 'em might be a little fucked up because the guy who knows how to put them together on Tuesdays didn't show up today, so I just guessed from the pictures."

"It's OK," Annie said, which was unusually kind.

He lingered, then shuffled back to the counter.

There was honking. A lot of honking and Annie craned her neck to see over Peter's shoulder.

"What is it?" He turned.

At the gas station, two men were scuffling. One pushed the other and a clumsy swing landed them both in a pile of snow.

From the passenger side of one of the fueling pickups, a woman dropped down, drunk and morbidly obese, shouting incoherent obscenity. While she ranted, she pulled the nozzle from the tank and dragged the hose to the opposite side of the pump island, dousing the truck that was parked there.

A couple of burley men tried to stop her, but they were driven off by a spray of gasoline to the eyes. They howled and scuttered away. She grabbed at one of her breasts. She flipped her middle finger as the gas pooled around her.

Peter switched places at the table. He sat next to Annie so he could watch.

The rest of the pickups in the line started to scatter, banging into each other, honking, jamming up against the wall of the station, against the pumps and islands, steel slapping steel and glass snapping.

The woman chased a few trucks to the extent of the hose. She turned circles and wrapped her legs in it. She fell, struggling, rolling in the gas. She untangled herself and stood and held a lighter to the grill of the truck.

One of the men in the snow, all battered now and dripping with blood, stood up and yelled. He might have been trying to reason with her. She couldn't hear or didn't care. She sparked the lighter and lit the pickup on fire.

The flames flashed back up her arm and burned the gas that had soaked into her sweatshirt. People ran from the tangle of trucks as fire chased out over the slicks that had gathered.

The woman screamed and ran and flailed her arm, but the fire jumped to her hair and covered her body. She set fire to the ground as she ran.

The next pickup in line caught fire. The station was a roiling black cloud, a filthy billowing torch, all alight in the snowy morning.

The bloody man tried to stop the burning woman, but she was frantic and slapped at him, and some of the flame jumped across to his coat and his hair.

He tried to get away, but walls of fire rolled up from the pools on the ground. He ran through it but was consumed and collapsed into the snowbank. The fat woman fell behind him and burned.

Annie had taken a bite of the Big Mac. She put it back in the box and pushed it away.

"Why is this happening?

"Why's what happening?"

"You know what."

"They're fighting over gas."

"Not that. All of it."

"The usual reasons, I guess."

Annie took the Big Mac and bit it. She stuffed her mouth with it.

Peter felt the heat of the fire on his face through the glass.

He said, "If it would have happened a month ago, would we have broken up? Do you think we would have been so terrible to each other?"

She worked pieces of food around in her cheeks as she thought. "No. No, I don't think so."

"Why not?"

"We need different things now. Things are different."

"What things?"

"We have new priorities." She looked at him and wiped her mouth with a bunched paper napkin. "It changes everything."

The glass rattled and rumbled. A broad and sucking bulge of fire rose up over the gas station.

"So what do we do?"

"We do what we have to. We make it work."

"Wait," he said. "Wait, are we talking about the bomb or the baby?"

She shook her head. "We're talking about us."

••••••••••

They left the place behind. The fire department never came. As they slid by the gas station, Annie pressed her hands over her eyes. The burned bodies stuck in Peter's periphery like shadows, black and stiff against the snow, which melted around them in the heat of the soaring fire.

They crept out onto the ramp and back to the interstate.

"We can make it to Laramie," he said.

"Don't you think we should find gas?"

"Look at the gauge."

"It's on *E*."

"Exactly."

"Exactly what? That means it's empty."

"No, it means we probably have sixty miles left on this tank."

"Sixty miles? It's on empty, you asshole."

"We'll be fine, Annie."

••••••••••••

At the side of I-80, where the car had run out of gas, Annie paced along the muddy red gravel shoulder, clutching her hands and doubling over, and cursing in a way that kept her warm with hellfire.

Peter sat in the car and waited for her rage to pass.

"You stupid fuck!" She kicked the ground and a hail of gravel hit the car. She turned and walked off.

On the crests of the rocky brown hills around them, pumpjacks nodded in slow succession, draining oil from the earth, scattered across the washes and ridges.

He watched her walk away and thought, as terrible as she was, as bad as they had been to each other, she was the most important thing left in the world.

He opened the door and called after her. She stopped and turned back.

"What are we going to do, Peter? We don't have any gas."

"We'll wait for somebody. We'll wait for a car."

"There are no cars. There's a storm coming. Nobody's driving except us."

"We're not driving either, actually."

She bit down hard.

"It's warmer in here," he said. "Just get in the car."

••••••••••••

The storm did come, and it consumed them.

They sat together in the back seat on their clothes, bundled under sleeping bags and blankets. The car rocked and shuddered in the wind.

The last pale sun came through the deepening snow on the glass, blue and icy light.

"There'll be a plow through soon. Or maybe highway patrol. We'll be fine."

"It's getting dark."

"It's just the snow on the windows."

"No. It's late. The sun's going down and it'll get colder."

"We'll be alright. We can still make it to my mom and dad's tomorrow night. We'll have Christmas. It'll be normal. Everything will be OK when we get home."

"It isn't fucking normal."

"I'm glad you'll get to meet them."

"Were you ever going to introduce me?"

"Of course."

"When? We've been together for eight months."

"They live fourteen hundred miles away."

"You could have figured something out."

"What about you? I've only met your mother once, and she lives in Vegas."

"Once is enough for anyone."

"I liked her."

"That's because you were both drunk and disgusting."

Annie shifted and brought herself closer to him. "Do you think she's all right? Do you think she's safe?"

"Definitely. She's on vacation."

"So?"

"She's out of the country. I'm sure everything's fine in Europe."

She put her head on his shoulder, heavy and smelling of wool and sweat. The ridiculous ball on top of her hat tickled his cheek.

"What if they don't like me?"

"They'll like you."

"But what if they don't? Or what if I don't like them?"

"Annie, everybody is going to like everybody else. Everything is going to be fine."

"But that isn't true, is it." She slid her arm behind him and held him. "Everything isn't going to be fine."

"Things will be different, that's all. It might get harder for a while, but it doesn't mean it'll be bad. It doesn't have to be."

"Are you talking about the bomb again?"

"No. The baby. Weren't we talking about the baby?"

"I'm cold," she said. "Do you want to make love?"

"What?"

"Do you?"

"I didn't know that was still an option."

"Well, it is."

"Then yes. Yes, I do."

••••••••••••

They did make love, with their clothes mostly on and swaddled in blankets. The windows gathered fog, which froze and glowed in the dusk.

When they had finished, and all of the light had gone out of the sky and the snow that covered the glass had gone dark, they sat together and thought of home.

Sound came from behind them. A slow vibration in the ground became a shudder and a quake. The growl from the highway became a torrent of raging engines and rattling steel.

"Jesus, what is it?" She sat up and scratched at the ice on the rear window.

Headlights burned through the snow and filled the car. Peter wrestled with the blankets and pushed his shoulder against the door to break the seal of ice that had formed. Clumps of snow fell over his freezing hands.

Standing in the gravel with his back to the wind, he watched the tanks pass with armored trucks and Humvees heading south. The headlights on the highway snaked back along the road for miles.

Annie climbed out, still wrapped in her blanket. They watched the convoy pass, too loud to speak over the whistling and growling and screaming of machines.

Annie waved her arms. She moved closer to the road, but none of them slowed.

Eventually, when the end of the convoy came, and the road was silent, a few military semis brought up the rear.

A tanker passed, and another pulled to the shoulder and stopped behind them, flooding the place where they stood with light.

The engine rattled and knocked. The driver dropped down.

"Are you in need of assistance, ma'am?" The soldier jogged toward them with hands deep in his coat. "They called back and said you were trying to flag us down."

"We ran out of gas," she said. "What's happening?"

"Gas? Not a problem." He turned and shouted into the light. "Diaz. Grab a gas can."

The passenger door opened and slammed and there was a shuffling in the gravel.

"What's going on?" Peter said.

"Can't say."

"Do you know anything about New York?"

"Really can't say."

The other soldier hustled toward them lugging a brown plastic gas can. She was small and wore thick glasses.

Peter had to pry the frozen gas tank door with a key. He twisted off the cap and the soldier started to pour.

"Where are you two headed?" she asked.

"Home," Peter said.

"Where's home?"

"West of Chicago."

"How far west?"

"Suburbs."

She nodded. "Where you coming from?"

"Salt Lake."

"You picked a very bad time to take a very long road trip."

"We're going to see his family for Christmas," Annie said.

"Have you spoken to them?"

"We couldn't get through."

The soldier who had been driving scraped his boot in the dirt. "No one can," he said. "Are you married?"

"No," Peter said.

"You two should get married. Make it right in the eyes of the Lord."

Annie took Peter's hand.

"So," he said, "you planning to take I-80 all the way?"

"Yeah," Peter said.

"Well, maybe when you get to Des Moines, you should quit the interstate."

"Why?" Annie squeezed harder.

"I think you might find the old U.S...uh, the old U.S. highways a more scenic way to travel."

"We're kind of in a hurry."

"Then you better quit the interstate at Des Moines. You follow?" He stepped closer. "This thing ain't over, brother. Do yourself a favor and stay off the highway."

He turned and headed back to the truck.

The other one finished with the gas can and put the cap back on the tank.

"I don't know what kind of mileage you get, but that should get you to Cheyenne. You can find gas there."

"Why are you doing this?" Annie said.

"We're just here to serve, ma'am."

"That isn't true."

The soldier stood for a while, quiet and staring, the last of the snow falling between them.

"Sins," she said.

"What?"

"It was Jackson's idea. To make up for the sins we gotta go do now."

"Diaz! Let's roll."

"What sins?"

The soldier turned away and jogged back to the truck.

"What fucking sins?"

"Annie, shut up."

"Why?"

"I don't know. Just shut up."

The engine growled and knocked and the truck rattled back onto the road, heading south.

They stood alone in the dark at the roadside, smelling ice and sage, silent for a while. Too long.

"Start the car," Annie said. "I'm cold."

"I love you," he said.

"I'm cold," she said. "I love you, too."

They sang. They were beset by the madness that comes on long ribbons of American road. They sang through the snarled and snowblown streets of Cheyenne, they sang through the last of Wyoming and six more hours into Nebraska. They told stories about their lives all the way to Omaha.

They laughed and were giddy and then fell into silence in a 24-hour Walmart parking lot which bustled and hummed through the night as lines backed out of doors for generators and pallets of bottled water and Band-Aids and all of the other things that had suddenly become the stuff of life.

They slept in the white glare of mercury vapor lights and in the morning Annie was sick again before they set out at dawn.

Civilization began to coalesce along the road, exits with new frequency, populated by chain restaurants and big box stores.

The radio, which had possessed her the day before, was silent. They had decided, without saying so, that neither cared to know what new and terrible things had happened to the world in the night. All they needed to know of that came from emergency vehicles flickering past and clusters of military trucks at intervals on an otherwise vacant highway.

At the edge of Des Moines, she said, "You never asked me what I was going to do."

She fiddled with the vents and the heat controls.

"Do with what?"

"If I was going to keep it."

"I just assumed."

"How could you assume something like that?"

"I don't know. I just did."

"You were right. I just mean that I'm curious. That's all. Why did you think that?"

"It was the way you said it."

"How did I say it?"

"You didn't say, *I'm pregnant*. You said, *I'm having a baby*."

She shook her head. She flicked off the heat. "No, I didn't."
"Yes you did."
"No I didn't. I said *we're* having a baby."
And that was true. She had.

•••••••••••

They came to signs that warned of a roadblock. Not the usual orange construction fare, but olive and white military signs that were clearly not suggestions of caution but statements of very serious intent.

They left the interstate, off onto the snowy, vacant surface streets of the suburbs. The soldier in Wyoming had told them to quit the interstate and, from an overpass, they saw why.

A tangle of trucks and flickering lights scattered across cordons. Semis were being searched, minivans turned inside out. An entire living room had been assembled on the side of the road from a moving truck that was being taken apart. Lamps and sofas and an oversized television in proper arrangement in the snow.

•••••••••••

On old US Highway 30, things were clear. The wind had kept the snow off the road, blown into drifts and culverts.

They drove all day through old America, town after tiny town forgotten when the interstate had opened and sucked away what traffic had flowed through these old veins. And surrounded by wide, white fields were main streets lined by storefronts, now vacant, and other streets that crept off to the edges, shaded by broad old oaks that covered dignified, forgotten houses.

The sun fell behind them and winter dusk came early again, and then finally they came to the Mississippi and Illinois beyond.

They stopped so that Annie could piss.

There had been no town for miles, and there wouldn't be for miles more, and even when they found one, nothing would be open. So this place was as good as any.

She walked away from the road, crunching snow out into a field. Peter leaned against the car and looked down the road, out into the strange silver dark, which wasn't dark at all. The light of unencumbered stars and sliver of moon shone on the snow which had gathered against the broken stalks of harvested corn, and in the stillness he heard a river of traffic from the interstate two or three miles away—a brief stretch of reprieve, unhindered by barricades after Daven-port.

It was this way that he remembered home. Still and per-fect in winter, the smell of snow, if there was such a thing, and the rush of traffic somewhere out in the dark.

And then a light swelled in the sky.

The sky went blue like day. Annie was forty feet away, squatting in the field in sudden noonday. She fell backward and scrambled to her knees and then the light faded. It drew back across the sky, painting stars again as it receded to the east.

He heard Annie struggle in the snow, then saw her again, jogging toward the road.

"What the fuck? Peter, what was that?"

He listened.

"Peter?"

He listened and watched the sky, but there was nothing. She moved forward and fell into him. He held her, squeezed her in his arms. She was shaking.

He had stopped counting by thousands when the sound came, a low roar a minute late, which was the end of Chicago.

•••••••••••

They drove and said nothing.

They drove until the places they passed by and through became familiar to him, became places he had been before, roads he had driven once, roads he had crossed twice, and then places that he called home.

They stopped in front of his house, which was an aver-age sort of American house in an average American suburb, part of the sprawl pressing fingers out into the fields.

The lights were still on. That was good. Strands of Christmas lights lined the eaves and angles. A tree glim-mered in the window. The lights wouldn't stay on forever, but tonight at least, they were bright, and they were home.

A woman came to the glass and cupped her hands over her eyes to see outside.

"Is that your mother?"

"Yep."

"Fucking *yep*. Honest to God."

"Don't be nervous."

"I'm not nervous. I'm scared."

"Yeah. Me too."

They got out of the car and walked together toward the house. His mother disappeared and he could hear her yelling to his father somewhere inside.

To the east, the sky was burning red, and at its edges, orange light broke through strange clouds, all black and scattered out over the horizon.

A breeze had swelled toward them, but it would shift by morning. He was sure that it had to. He was sure of it.

"Everything's OK now," he said. "We're here."

"Yes," she said. "We're here."

"We shouldn't stay outside though."

"No. We shouldn't."

"Come in."

She took his hand. She squeezed it. They walked together out of the cold and into the house.

A.M.

Leonard Gontarek

I think Death will come
when my face is wrapped
in warm towels in a barber shop.
We will exchange witty, brilliant,

noir chit-chat and comebacks in the delicious,
ambiguous moments of postponement
before the inevitable and ineffable.
I will feel rich, at last,

elegantly dressed as a mobster.
One cool customer.
I will finally have shaved this damn beard.
Until then, birdsong slits

the fabric of morning and aromatic shadows
spill on the trees and gold grass.
The coffee, black, hot, but not too hot,
the way I like it.

Devon Drive

Pat O'Brien

I am trying to remember blackberries
on my tongue, and my mother's rolling pin
flattening out the oily dough for pies,
and didn't dad lay the slate porch we etched in chalk,
and didn't we nap on the hot slate
until our eyelids glowed orange,
and how many times did the woods drip secrets,
and how many steps were there to sock island
where silver minnows darted back
and forth like underwater flags rippling,
and wasn't it below the abandoned railroad tracks
where we dug in clay mines to shape ashtrays,
and what it was like to win that crab-apple fight
with the Rockwood gang. I know there was always
wonder, and when the sky streaked pink under
a pulling moon, weren't our mothers
always calling us home.

Water, Communion

Alexandra Gold

"My mother is a fish"
As I Lay Dying, William Faulkner

She'd anoint the dock with blood
And baptize the gills to save my
White mouth from swallowing
Insolent sea religion.

Blame the fisherman for biting
Silence and sanity and sin and
The worm-bait that begged her
Green algae kisses.

Marry the midwife that birthed
The last tide change and she'd
Steal the ebbing burden of
Quiet pressing waves.

My mother is a fish
And when the weight of scales
Scraped my eye like a hook,
Did you ever doubt she'd fight
To consecrate my water-grave?

Bunker

Jonathan Kemmerer-Scovner

Everything still worked that morning, one week into the new year. The automated elevator sang, "Seventh floor, good morning!" The keycard opened the office door. Halogen yet buzzed like a life-support system.

Beside the copy machine sat a dumpster, old and dented, scratched with graffiti. It would have looked at home in a refuse-swept alley running behind a row of cheap storefronts, an emblem of decay normally exorcised from any modern workspace. Someone must have carted it in earlier that morning. It was, as yet—I could not help but note—empty.

People were huddled in their offices, whispering. They glanced up with intense faces, returned to private conversation.

This is it, I thought. *It's happening today.*

The fax machine was warm, filled with copyright forms to be scanned, processed, filed, forgotten. My computer turned on. The password worked. The inbox filled up with panicked emails from production editors waiting for the next issue's line-up, authors demanding to know what had happened to their manuscripts, notes about upcoming meetings, projects which needed completing. But all I could think about was that dumpster.

How would it come? An email? A phone call? A trusted friend stopping by?

Beyond the walls of my cubicle, a voice said, "Grace, may I see you in my office, please?"

Grace was a stalwart of organized chaos, surrounded by stacks of journals, calendars, catalogues of office supplies. If the question began with, "How should I...?" or "Who do I ask about...?" The answer was always, "Ask Grace."

I heard Grace answer, "Sure," followed by the slow creak of her chair.

A moment later, an office door shut.

Everything that happens beyond my cubicle is faceless, without form. Every day, there are private conversations, conference calls, inner-machinations, corporate politics. I hear without listening. They don't know my name. They don't know I'm there. Usually, I drown it out. On this day, however, I find that I am hyper-aware.

"Diane, may I see you in my office, please?"

Diane, my God. She's the one who hired me. She'd been in the business nearly as long as I'd been alive. I caught a glimpse of her as she passed my cubicle, on the way to the back office. She looked afraid, but also professional. Professionally afraid.

The office door shut.

All morning, that was how it went. Each time they were led past my cubicle, dead-man-walking style.

The only one who stopped was Carl. He'd always been my favorite publisher. He had one kid and another on the way. He stood at my cubicle and announced, "Well, I got the email!" all giddy with fear.

He told me everything he knew. It's not just Philadelphia, he said, it's Baltimore. It's New York. He gave me names, and the list kept going.

That afternoon, I got a sandwich from the Wawa down Walnut Street, and the man who took my money was in his fifties, well groomed, well spoken. I could easily imagine him wearing a suit and tie, sitting in on board meetings. Perhaps a month ago, he did.

Outside the entrance, a woman sat on the steps—no way to get around her. The layers of jacket and sweatshirt, coat and sweater, made her twice as large. She demanded a dollar, real indignant.

And what will I do when it's me who has to beg? I wondered. There's a million end-of-the-world scenarios to choose from. Nuclear annihilation is the big one, of course, humanity forced into underground bunkers. I'd read all those books, watched all those movies. But maybe we're all just meant to slowly go mad, slowly starve, slowly horde until everything is depleted.

On the other hand, why not imagine more utopian scenarios, wherein we turn our parks into massive gardens, feeding our families with all the food we'll grow? We'll use those green slips of paper—what in an earlier era had been known as "money"—to wallpaper our eco-friendly cob homes. We'll live in socialist collectives, contributing equally and singing Hosannas to the God who in His tender mercy allowed those corporate towers of Babel to crumble, so that a new world would rise based on love!

Either that or cannibalism, hard to say.

"Seventh floor, good morning!"

The dumpster by the copy machine was half-full. Mounds of textbooks, folders, medical journals, pens, pencils, staplers, all thrown together in a bubbling cauldron, a button-down Oxford witch's brew.

People were no longer huddled, no longer whispering. They talked openly, stood around the proverbial water cooler. For two years, I'd passed some of them in the halls and never known their names, but a demonic presence had been lifted, we could all feel it.

"It's over, that's what I heard," said one.

"They're done."

"We're safe."

Later that afternoon, Judy and I went outside to smoke a cigarette. I hadn't smoked in six months. I called my wife and told her I was fine. It was over. For now, we were safe. The relief in her voice made me want to cry. Many phone calls had been made that day which had not brought relief.

My friend Saul once gave me some advice. "You should be fine, Jon, at your level," he said. "Just don't get promoted."

Blessed are we, the underachievers.

2010

East of the Sierra

Allison Alsup

The following story won the second annual Marguerite McGlinn Prize for Fiction.

The boy stays close. From the moment the steamship docks, his son's jacket brushes his own. Lin-Hui thinks they must make for an odd sight: the taller, wide-shouldered youth crouching in the armpit of a man almost old enough to be a grandfather. But Lin-Hui remembers he was no different the first time he came to *Dai Fao*, San Francisco. He nearly climbed on his uncle's back at the first sight of so many blue-eyed barbarians, their guns, their red goat beards. And now, even though he has seen ten thousand Americans, he thinks it better to keep the boy near. Anything can happen on Gold Mountain. It is not so certain as its name. Lin-Hui has paid for insurance. Should he or his son meet with death on this trip, they will not be left to lie in this ghostland. Their bodies will be shipped home; their spirits tended to.

They travel by ferry from San Francisco to Oakland where they board a train, passing Stockton, Sacramento, and then climb into the Sierra: Auburn, Donner Lake, Truckee, over tracks Lin-Hui helped to stitch across the soil. They cross into Nevada whose mountains, their fellow *tong yun* now say, contain hidden clefts of silver.

They will have to rename it now, one of the men jokes. Silver Mountain.

A second-class dream, Lin-Hui thinks, and still it is enough to lure men across an ocean.

Like Lin-Hui, the men are from Sunning County. They are staked outside of Reno, close to where Lin-Hui and his son are headed. As a precaution, Lin-Hui tells them he and his son will stop by their claim once they have finished. If the men do not see Lin-Hui or Chi within ten days, they are to come looking.

Perhaps you have forgotten what the desert is like, one of the men says.

Lin-Hui looks out the window. But it is late and the window shows nothing.

Much can happen before ten days.

I have not forgotten, Lin-Hui replies. He is glad his son is sleeping.

At Reno, they get out. Lin-Hui buys Chi his first leather boots. They rent a small wagon, a single horse. They load bedrolls, rice, longan beans, dried fish, pots, and two shovels onto the bed. Lin-Hui also brings tea, a tin of liver pills. He does not want to exhaust the horse. There is not money enough to buy it if it dies. Lin-Hui tells Chi they must walk alongside the wagon.

They pin up their braids and wear wide straw hats to block the sun. They are careful not to stray far from the tracks. The land is as dead as Lin-Hui has remembered, like something cooked too long. Immediately his feet begin to flatten against the baked earth.

Where are the trees? Chi asks.

Lin-Hui has tried to warn his son. But such talk is pointless. How can one prepare for something one has never known?

His son is not used to his new leather boots. The father cannot have his son limping with blisters; Chi must walk. Lin-Hui regrets not having purchased boots in Hong Kong and breaking them in during the weeks on the steamship. A foolish oversight. At least he has had the sense to bring binding cloth. Tonight they must wrap his son's feet.

As a younger man, Lin-Hui traveled to Gold Mountain twice: once for gold, which he found, and once for the railroads, for which he laid track. Six years after his second return, his uncle came to him. The villagers wanted Lin-Hui to return a third time, he explained to his nephew, to fulfill a *jup seen yu*, a final task. His uncle held up his fingers. Four men still waited to return home. Lin-Hui understood. He was to comb the deserts for the bodies of those taken by the railroads. He was to return east of the Sierra.

Lin-Hui listened out of obligation to the uncle who had herded him safely through the first trip. But Lin-Hui said he would not return. In the following days, his relatives and neighbors plagued him.

It is not right that these fellow spirits lay in untended graves, they reminded Lin-Hui. Our ancestors will not know peace until they are home, until they are properly buried in the family plots and provided for with incense, oranges, eggs, and money.

Still, Lin-Hui refused.

These men are clan, they insisted. To neglect them is a shame on the entire village.

Lin-Hui knew all this. He was done with *gum san*. Find a younger man, he told them. Find two. Younger men, he repeated.

But you already have one, they pointed out. Seventeen and true to his name. Chi is a boy of strong intentions, nearly a man. We have saved, they revealed, pooled our money for two passages from Hong Kong.

Others have gone to Gold Mountain, he said. Ask Sun Wen. Ask Wing.

No. Sun Wen has no sons. Wing has lost all his money to dice. Sun Wen and Wing are not lucky men. But you, Lin-Hui, have a house and a little land, a healthy son and an obedient wife who has not frittered, as others did, money on silk and pearls. You are lucky. *Ji.*

Lin-Hui knew they were flattering him so he would agree. And he supposed he was lucky. At least compared to them. Many returned from Gold Mountain with nothing but holes in their pockets. Some did not return at all. There were men with other wives across the water. Others sent money home only to have it wasted by foolish women. Fortunately, his own wife showed more sense. She had borne him a son and only one daughter—the girl already married and settled. If he was lucky, Lin-Hui thought, it was because his parents chose well.

At first, their task seems hopeless. The light is too bright. It is too hot, the eighth breath of the year, the time of ripening grain. But there is no grain here; it is too dry for fields. The sand, the stone, the scrub blur into one.

Lin-Hui catches his son dipping his bowl into a stream.

The water runs slow, the father explains. It must all be boiled. Cold tea for day, hot for night. The Americans and Irish miners never understood this. They drank dirty water and whiskey and wondered why they were always painting the dust with their shit. He must watch his son closely. Chi may look like a man but he is not. He has not gone hungry or had to sleep on the ground. He has not had to carry all he owned on his back or been threatened with a knife. He has not seen a man fall to his death. Lin-Hui has tried to keep his son from such things. Now, however, he wonders if some part of him has brought Chi here as a test.

They camp, search the surrounding area, and move on. Lin-Hui's sense of distance has changed. They must move further from Reno than he remembers.

After the third visit from the villagers, Lin-Hui's mind began the journey back east of the Sierra. He did not want to return, but the darkness over his bed opened like a door and he found himself back on the high plains, whipped by dust. He found himself back on a land that cost too much to blast and scrape for track, a place to be traveled over and not one to stay, a place where white men feared their wagons might break a wheel, their horses an ankle, where the snow might fall early. From this worn, faded, stubborn soil leaves did not grow so much green as gray. Here the wind could twist the trunk of a tree into the knots of an old man's knuckle.

Here in the bleached sweep between the Sierra and the Washoe, winter fell hard and fast in December 1866. Men disappeared under drifts that crashed like waves. Here he made promises to the broken and dying; he swore to men like his friend Shen that he would not leave his fellow *tong yun* to spend eternity in the fallow soil of the eastern Sierra or even worse, in the rusty stretches of Nevada's sands. He would help them with their *ronggui*, their glorious return home to Pearl River, to Sunning County, so that their children and grandchildren could see them into the spirit world with chickens, lychees, and all the money the men never made working themselves to death on Gold Mountain.

The door closed and Lin-Hui stared into the darkness. He could not refuse an obligation of his own making. He would settle his debts, right his wrong to Shen. Reaching out a hand, he found the soft hump of his wife's hip.

I am going back to Gold Mountain, he said. I am taking Chi.

She rolled from his hand onto her back. Chi wants this?

Her words surprised him. They suggested he should have asked his son's permission.

It is an honor, he reminded her.

Yes, she said. In the moonlight, he saw her hands go to her face.

Lin-Hui thought again. Chi must see *gum san* for himself, he said. All the young men talk about it. Better that Chi go now and be done with it. You know he has already asked me about such a trip, he lied.

Neither spoke for some time.

See the fortune teller, she finally said. Begin the trip on an auspicious day.

Did his wife think he had lost his head? Of course, Lin-Hui said. Then: I am sorry to leave again.

The first time he left, he was gone over two years, the second almost as long. He knew the song the washerwomen sang down at the river, the one about marrying Gold Mountain men, about dusty sheets and spider webs on the bed. He did not like to think of his own wife calling out the words.

He said his wife's name, pulled the hands from her eyes.

It will not be as long this time, he reassured. There is a new steamship, an iron giant. The passage is now four weeks, half of what it was. We will be gone only a season, three months. In the meantime, first uncle will help with the fields.

Have you forgotten what it was like there? she asked.

No.

And I have not forgotten how to wait.

Gradually, their eyes adjust and they begin to see the small ridges and humps, the exceptions to an otherwise endless span. On the third day, they spot a telltale pile of rocks rising up from the scrub, a wooden stake placed to catch the eye. They dig. Lin-Hui watches his son.

Do not force the pace, the father says. Be slow but persistent.

The remains are wrapped in a tent fly. Lin-Hui tells his son to reach down and find the bottle. Chi hits the glass against his pants to shake off the dust and hands the bottle to his father. Lin-Hui breaks the wax seal and extracts a strip of cotton that he guesses was once part of a shirt. But the father cannot read as well as his schooled son, and so he hands the cotton back. Chi must decipher the painted characters that sum up this life. They are few: a name, a date, a place of birth.

It is hard to read, his son says.

It was written in grief. Concentrate.

His son shakes his head. No. This man is from Kaiping.

They recap the bottle, shovel the dirt back over the body. Lin-Hui has let himself forget. All he can be sure of is that no one was buried out of sight of the tracks. There was no time to travel further, to find a proper spot. They move ten, fifteen miles from Reno. They find one body. The remains are loaded onto the wagon and brought back to camp. They find other things, too: a rusted mallet, a jackrabbit's skull, a tin cup, a chipped miniature of Tien Hou, the patron goddess of wanderers. Lin-Hui slips the cracked figure into his pocket.

To hear the coyotes at night in the deserts east of the Sierra is to think this world is endless suffering. The boy has never heard such cries except in dreams. Lin-Hui remembers the wailing from before. His dreams are not of wild dogs but of Shen, white-faced and flying among the Washoe's bony ridges.

Night makes a quick stranger of the day's heat and they build a fire. When Chi tells his father he wishes for a thicker jacket, his father nods and explains that the men who worked the track were like them, Pearl Delta men, many from their own county. Some did not even own socks. They had never known the cold of a five-layer morning. It was the way they came to call that cold.

It is not lucky to be buried in five layers, his schooled son reminds him. The character for five sounds too much like the character for causing evil.

Lin-Hui nods. It is why we called it so.

To ease his son's fears, to ease his own, the father tells his son about the emperor's robe. It is all things, he explains: the sea, the heavens and of course, the brilliant yellow earth. From the emperor's left shoulder shines a red sun and a rooster, from his right, a silver moon and a hare. His chest bears the three constellations, his nape, the rock of strength. He explains the five qualities and colors, the twelve symbols of the emperor's twelve powers. He describes the waves along the hem, the mountains rising above, the clouds along the chest, and the most important, the emperor's symbol: the five-clawed dragon that brings rain each spring.

Lin-Hui has never seen the robe of course, never been within one thousand miles of the Dragon Throne, but he has learned about it from his own father, repeated its patterns until they became as familiar as his own cotton jacket. It comforts him to think of the universe contained in silk.

When the emperor dies, time stops. The emperor becomes a dragon again and a new emperor must rise from the depths. Time is renamed and begins anew. But the robe remains the same. The robe does not change. To not wear the robe is to invite the end of the world.

His son sleeps. Lin-Hui watches the stars. In them, he sees the pale hands of the emperor. The father tells himself that his fears are pointless; all is as it should be. A perfect grip holds him, even here, even in the fallow desert east of the Sierra.

They must wait out the hottest part of the day under the shade of the tent. To dig when the sun is overhead is to risk headache, cramps. Lin-Hui curses himself for trusting a scholar's tea leaves before his own experience. He should have set his own date, waited until autumn.

When the sun begins to sink, they head out. It is easy to miss the rocks; most of the markers have eroded and blown away. They spread to cover more ground but keep each other within sight. Lin-Hui cannot now fathom how he worked this ground for track, how they blasted through granite to get here. Even memory exhausts him. The day the lines from the east met the lines of the west, the newspapers wrote of conquest and progress. But the photographs of the two trains showed no Chinese, only American men in tight wool suits, their fingers clasped around clean mallets.

Chi calls out. He has found rocks. They dig.

On the sixth day, they find Shen's grave. They move the rocks and Chi digs. His shovel lifts the bottle into the air. The vial is closer to the surface than they would have expected. Indeed the cloth inside bears Shen's name. They continue to dig. Lin-Hui prepares himself for the worst; he cannot remember if a tent fly was spared to cover the body. The hole grows deeper. Finally, they catch a glimpse of canvas. Chi bends down to brush away the dirt but Lin-Hui stops his son, bends down himself. He scoops the dirt to the side, expecting to touch bone through the fabric. But there is nothing. The canvas is empty. Shen's body is gone.

Chi gasps.

Stop that, Lin-Hui demands. His son is crying. The father refuses to let the boy see his own fear. Coyotes, wolves, he says and waves a hand towards the hills.

Chi shakes his head. It was covered in dirt. Dogs do not cover empty graves.

Lin-Hui could tell his son that when Shen died, he could not find the strength to shovel the frozen ground and bury his closest friend. He could tell his son Shen's body lay in the snow for seven days until fearing animals, others took on the task. But Lin-Hui does not tell his son any of this. He does not want his son to think that the world rewards such behavior. The desert snatches weak men. Even more, Lin-Hui does not want his son to see him as such a man. Lin-Hui is tired and raw and cannot control his anger.

He hits the ground with his shovel again and again. This is nothing! You have been spared the worst stories. You will never know what it was to suffer here.

His son continues to cry, mumbling about ghosts, curses. Lin-Hui raises his hand and slaps his son hard across the jaw.

There is no more crying. They speak of the task at hand: of shovels, of cloth strips, of boiling water for rice and tea. At night, when Lin-Hui tests his son to see what he has learned of the emperor's robe, his son rolls his back to the fire and pretends to sleep.

After eight days, Lin-Hui calls off the search. They have recovered three of the four men. The skeletons are all burned to remove any remaining flesh, then dried on flat rocks. They place the bones in white muslin sacks brought from home, soft coffins sewn and embroidered by a wife or mother who, thousands of miles away, sits waiting for her man to return.

It is a two-day walk back to Reno. The miners offer dinner. As they board the train for San Francisco, Lin-Hui knows he is abandoning Shen forever. Shen has been lost to the desert, a sand ghost. Lin-Hui wonders if curses are strong enough to cross an ocean.

In *Dai Fao*, San Francisco, they pamper themselves like merchant men. They sit on polished bamboo stools and eat shark fin soup on the top floor of a restaurant. They do not talk about the desert. Lin-Hui sends word ahead about Shen and the other three and then vows that no part of him—foot, mind, or tongue—will ever return east of the Sierra. With one week to fill before the steamship departs, they check into a boarding house and tour the streets. Lin-Hui marvels at the buildings and stops in Chy Lung's Bazaar for gifts. They eat salted plums, spit the seeds as they meander. So many new places, shops, sidewalks. Little China has grown, he tells his son. A city now, eight blocks!

But the father also sees what has not changed: the tide of men, the endless bobbing waves of black jackets, hats, and braids. He sees the old men, young enough when the gold was found, who now sit on stoops and peddle old cups and spoons. Lin-Hui has always believed that what the universe intends for *tong yun* is clear: fields, a wife and sons, a daughter to help clean and cook. This bachelor society, with fifteen males for every female, is not natural. And children, what few exist, are spoiled by lonely men who pay to be Sunday uncles. No, there can be no family here. At most, *Dai Fao* is a place for work, not one to stay.

As Lin-Hui turns to share these thoughts with his son, he realizes he is looking at the back of his Chi's jacket. The boy now walks two steps ahead as if he already knows his way around Fifteen Cent Street. Lin-Hui watches his son's braid snap from side to side. They have just been to the barber's shop and now his son's braid hangs thick and polished as an ink brush. The father decides the desert has, in fact, yielded treasure. It has revealed the man hidden in the depths of his boy.

On Sunday, they sip tea and eat sweet bean cakes in a darkened theater on Jackson Street. They watch four plays sung by painted men who tell of heroes and gods, of ancient battles and sacrifice. Like everyone in the audience, Lin-Hui and his son know how the stories will end. But they watch anyway and are no less moved. Between the acts, Lin-Hui talks with old friends, men he worked with when they were able to crouch in the dirt for hours. One man sets and swings himself forward on a crutch. He points to the empty space below his ankle: dynamite.

Your father is a clever man, they tell Chi. Sifting the dust from the floor of cabins abandoned by American miners. Content to gather small treasures when others looked for the mother lode. They tap their foreheads to show their admiration. Lin-Hui shakes his hands and pretends to quiet them. He was a little lucky, that is all. In truth, he is pleased his son hears their words.

They will be going back to Sunning County, they all say, land of oranges and lychees. To not come back to the delta is like wearing silk in the dark. If no one can see the money, what does it all matter?

Some press letters into Lin-Hui's hand to pass on. Others give him coins and make him promise to stop by their lands.

Soon, very soon we will see you there, they repeat.

Lin-Hui nods. Yes. Very soon.

But he knows he will not see them in Sunning. His friends are now *gum san ghi*, Gold Mountain men. They are Chinese yes, but this place has made them something else—not American—they can never be that, but between. They drink whiskey and coffee. They have traded slippers for boots, round caps for felt bowlers. Some have even cut their hair. From the back, perhaps, they could be mistaken for American. Lin-Hui wonders if, in fact, this is what his friends desire. They have stayed too long. Sunning County is no longer home, no longer even a place. It is like the emperor's robe, an idea to think about, a comfort in this ghostland.

The next morning Chi announces he will not be boarding the ship.

Lin-Hui laughs. The gold is long gone, the railroad done. Many men, even American men, are out of work. They blame Chinese and rough them up. No, the time for Gold Mountain is over.

Chi repeats that he will stay.

Have you so quickly forgotten why we have come? Lin-Hui asks. The white muslin sacks waiting to return home? And what of the others who never will, spirits like Shen? They are trapped here forever.

I will not end up like them.

Don't you see why the city grows? Lin-Hui pleads. The

men do not return. When it is time for their leaves to fall, they will not find their roots.

Old sayings are for old men.

Lin-Hui raises his hand to slap his son for a second time but the boy does not turn away. He juts his chin, offering his cheek. I am not a coward. Opening his pocketknife, Chi holds the blade to the back of his neck.

Lin-Hui cries out. He reaches for the knife, but he is too late. The blade slices through the braid. His son's hair falls, sounding with a knock against the floorboards.

I too, am clever and dutiful, the boy tells his father. I will make my own *ronggui*. I will return to Pearl River to buy more land, to build new rooms for your house! In the meantime, I will send money just as you did.

Lin-Hui does not hear any of this. He sits on his bunk. It is done. To return now will mean a fine or prison, misfortune on the village. His son must remain on Gold Mountain long enough to grow his braid back. His son's remaining hair falls forward in a jagged hem along his jaw. It cannot remain like this, crazed, unkempt. They must return to the barber to have it shaped American-style like the other *gum san ghi*.

The next morning, the boy's passage is sold. The boy tries to give the money to his father but Lin-Hui tells him to keep it. He tells his son to sell his hair. It is all he can offer now. The son helps his father carry a trunk with gifts and the three muslin sacks onto the steamer and waves goodbye. As Lin-Hui settles into the hold with the other Chinese, he realizes he now has twenty-six days to practice what he will tell his wife.

Lin-Hui sits on a bench in the shade of a longan tree. He looks over fields bought long ago with *gum san* money. Today marks the start of *bai lu*, white dew, the fifteenth joint of the year, the pause before autumn's amber breath. He is an old man now, more than sixty. He has lived longer than a man should, longer than Sun Wen who died three years ago from water in the chest, ten years longer than first uncle. This morning, over rice and dried fish, Lin-Hui's wife said they must go to the tailor to commission burial robes. It is the third time she has said this.

Death is an eternal winter, she reminded him. One must dress warmly for it.

He can hear the women singing down at the river, chanting the same songs as their mothers. Dusty sheets. Spider webs on the bed. He closes his eyes to hear the words but is quickly interrupted by a man's voice. It has been years since Lin-Hui has allowed himself to hope. He received a few letters: one posted from a silver mine, a fishing camp, then artichoke fields, then nothing.

Lin-Hui opens his eyes. It is only Wing—Wing who was too unlucky to be sent to Gold Mountain, so unlucky that he is now grandfather to five boys, so unlucky that his eldest son has recently presented him with a burial suit embroidered with silk cranes. Lin-Hui's friend stops to sit. Of late, Wing likes to talk of the southern rebels and their growing numbers. He draws lines in the dirt with his cane. Sometimes, Lin-Hui thinks, Wing talks as if he himself were riding in the rebels' flanks. Lin-Hui does not think Wing sees these battles for what they are. After all these years, his friend is still a gambler. Wing sees this world as a game to be won or lost, then played again. But Lin-Hui understands the stakes—the end of the emperor's robe, the unraveling of the universe.

Wing raises a finger in the air. Even some of the soldiers now side with the rebels, he pronounces. Soon, no more Manchu.

Lin-Hui sees his wife toss scraps to the chickens. He has seen enough change.

Wing laughs. Ai-yah! For thousands of years, China has been sleeping. Now it will wake up! A new century. A new China. Such news is wasted on you, Lin-Hui.

Lin-Hui watches Wing make his way down to the river to bother the washerwomen. He watches a leaf fall and sail with the wind. Tomorrow, Lin-Hui decides, he will go to the tailor. He knows winter, its many layers.

He has not kept his promise never to return east of the Sierra. In his mind, he has gone back many, many times.

He cannot say when the door will open—as he listens to his wife turn at night, as he watches her with the chickens, as the women gather at the river. In his mind, he makes it right. He holds his calloused hand back from his son's cheek. He explains that Sunning men were not meant for this place. He touches his son's shoulder and tells him that older, stronger men wept there. He tells him it is wrong to bring a boy into the desert to make amends for his father.

He sits and waits. At the river, the women are singing again. Perhaps, they have grown tired of Wing's war talk and sent him away. Such battles are not their stories. What happens now will be decided by young men. Lin-Hui listens to the voices for a moment, then hums to their song.

A Supermarket in Pennsylvania

Kathryn Elisa Ionata

I saw my old psychiatrist at Trader Joe's,
sampling organic hand lotion.
We last faced off

50 milligrams ago, when he talked
about stress, and I watched the clock's hands
march, an army of gears ticking

like the rattle of pills. This 2-pill-day,
I gather dried fruit, herbs,
everything organic. My old shrink,

smaller and greyer, bags peppers
and free-range chicken
with his dark-haired wife.

Tense despite the lavender plant I hold,
my gaze flings to my love, the engineer,
weighing cranberries

versus apricots. He has seen me
through deflated 1-pill-days.
My old shrink has brown bags

happier than dopamine, and I want
to block his exit, show him my fruit bars
and engineer, whose perfect serotonin

levels mock health insurance. I am 8 years,
200 milligrams better. I buy only organic and
my lavender plant doesn't talk back.

I see my shrink slip away, like an expired prescription—

We pay for the plant and dried cranberries,
which, I have told the engineer, taste best.

The White Deer

Paul Lisicky

I can't exactly say why I went to church on Saturday
for the five o'clock mass, but that's just what I did. I don't
know why that feels like I'm confessing to some dirty im-
pulse—maybe it's just that I'm still drawn to the liturgy—
the music, the patterns of it—in spite of my exasperation
with the Church. I hadn't gone to church by myself since my
teens, and as I walked into the sanctuary, I thought, OK,
I'm home. When I'm with someone else—for Christmas Midnight Mass, or a funeral—I usually feel some tug of loss, a
loss I can't quite explain. But not this time. Maybe it helps
that the church is a progressive church—many gay and
lesbian parishioners, people of all ages and nationalities.
Think of it as a Unitarian Church—but with communion.

I'm usually not so big on homilies. I usually think of
that as the time when the celebrant makes meaningless
noises in order to fill up some space; time to look at the
songbook, but this was different. He was talking about hos-
pitality—what does it mean to welcome the people we love?
I was thinking on that, my arms outstretched on the back
of the pew, when a line of his jumped out at me: "The closer
we get to someone, the more we must stand humbly before
his freedom." Every molecule in me was turned to him. He
said it once more, as if he wanted it to sink in. "The closer
we get to someone, the more we must stand humbly before
his freedom." What on earth could such a thing mean?

Later that night a friend told me about a white dog
showing up at another friend's house. The other friend
looked at the dog's tags—the address was three miles away,
all the way on the other side of town. There were fireworks

in town, extravagant fireworks, and it was likely the dog had run across woods, marshes, highways to get to the friend's house. The friend looked out the door and saw what she thought was a white deer. But it wasn't any white deer. It was a dog, a white fluffy dog, who walked right into her living room and dining room, muddy paws and all. The dog looked around a bit, submitted to the friend's petting, then slumped, turned on his side and fell asleep.

The friend called the numbers on the dog's tags. No one answered at the numbers. The friend left a message, and when she didn't hear back after a while, she started to get suspicious. Maybe the dog was hers, the mystery beast coming up the street in the dark, out of the briars, the woods.

The next day the phone rang. A terse, gruff boy on the line, and the story comes darker, clearer. The dog's human, his protector, his *mother*, drowned in the pool the night before. Did the dog see it happen? Did the dog jump in the water after her, try to rescue her? Was it a suicide, a heart attack, a slip off the side while she was heading back into the house with armful of dry clothes? The friend didn't feel she had the right to such questions, but she did ask the boy—the woman's daughter's boyfriend—if he'd be willing to let the dog stay with her for a while. "He seems so comfortable here," she said. And the boy agreed to that, if reluctantly. And who could blame the friend if she started to make plans, if she thought about driving to the store for dog food. Life with the white dog, the white deer—and wasn't she already relieved that she had a reason to keep herself from going so many places? A root in her midst. Finally, after so much running around.

I suppose I don't need to say that the family wanted the dog back the next day. I suppose I don't need to say that the friend was inconsolable, as the dog jumped in the back of the family's car, so grateful to be back with his familiars. Of course his mother wouldn't be there at the house when he jumped out of the car, but he didn't know that yet. And all the losses of the friend rose up before her like ghosts turning to flesh, needing to be dealt with.

Night Diving

Sean Finucane Toner

No wheels, no license, no ability to drive—I'm a little hesitant, a little ashamed. I pause for a two-beat before I dial Ursula to arrange our weekend together. She's a teacher and single mother in Pottstown; I'm a late-thirtyish man living at my granny's Drexel Hill Tudor-style house. During this pause, I'm sitting at my adapted computer, my finger poised over my phone's Velcro-marked "five" button. I feel like I'm the sighted adolescent again, standing at a mall payphone, arranging a pick up.

The adult me pushes through, and dials. But I don't get Ursula. It's her daughter.

"Hi, is your mom home?"

"Stop making that funny voice," Ursula's daughter says, right away without a "howdy-do."

"Is your mom home?" I repeat in my higher-pitched "everything is OK, kid" voice.

"Stop that," the girl shouts. "Daddy, stop talking like that!" Then slam. Dial tone.

My chair creaks under me as my heart becomes all inaudible bass beat. I fidget with the phone cord then work at disentanglement. I fill the silence with a movie image. Today it's *Big*, and Tom Hanks is hoofing "Heart and Soul" on the oversized walking piano. How many takes were there? Did he break a sweat?

••••••••••••

It's the weekend and Ursula gathers me from the Reading bus station. We drop off my bags at her place, then take a walk through her neighborhood. As we stroll, my ears tell me what my eyes would. Traffic is infrequent, sound is sponged up by lawns and bushes, the stationary eloquence of a robin several stories above me hints at tree heights.

We head uphill, past the pools, and to the pond, circle it at leisure with my hand resting on her right shoulder for guidance. I hold my white cane upright, dandy-style in my free palm. Ursula pulls me aside when we meet an oncoming couple who haven't done the white cane and black glasses math.

"We're coming to a footbridge," she says. "No rails."

I scrutinize her tone for weariness or resignation. I still can't figure if I'm man or encumbrance to her. Her divorce is not final and I fear I am a cliché in tennis shoes—the Transitional Man.

A brush of her long hair against my arm tells me she's turned her head away. I Photoshop her locks Day-glo apricot to contrast her picket-fence spirit. Only, I'm thinking about the steady quiet of her neighborhood, its pond, its pools, the nearby market. I could easily tap-tap-tap along the pickets as well.

There's the faintest of paddling noises from the water. I'm sure there are duck feet, upended, as a Mallard goes under for a morsel.

"Still going swimming tomorrow?" Ursula asks.

While she's in the kitchen drawing up a shopping list, I'm out of the way, in the bedroom, attending to medical concerns. Diabetic, I test my blood sugar, the meter counting down aloud and voicing a number I'm satisfied with. It's time for my afternoon meds, so I take the four anti-rejection transplant pills, the pair of blood pressure, the anti-nausea pill.

Ursula calls out, "Can you think of anything besides soda and chicken you want?"

"Strawberry Pop Tarts. The glazed kind, please." They are my current form of emergency sugar. But still, I blush.

Before she leaves, Ursula refreshes my memory about the stairway threshold and projecting TV shelf. She grabs her keys, says, "I have to stop at my husband's with my daughter's schoolbag." The door closes behind her. It's not long before the stillness conjures the creepy twin girls from *The Shining*.

•••••••••••

We wait for the senior citizen hour at the lap pool because the main pool is a mined bay of bobbing children in nosecoat and water wings ready to sink my ship.

"Marco!"

"Polo!"

Ursula gives me a quick description of the layout, and then I'm swimming, first time in the dark. Splash splash, then a little bit of a crawl, and then I'm going freestyle. I bump into walls and tangle myself in lane dividers. But this isn't good enough.

Hand out, I trace my way to the ladder. Once I'm up, Ursula walks me around to the deep end and sets up her towel. I perch on the coping, work up nerve, then jump. I try to go coast-to-coast underwater, and put my hand up to meet wall. I fall short the first dozen tries. This game still isn't good enough, though. I encounter my first flotation worm and get ideas.

The Styrofoam worms are a little shorter than my white cane, but when I'm up and poolside I find I can hold them ski-pole style and make it to the diving board.

Once up, I edge cautiously past the handrails. Tap with the left pool toy. Tap with the right, then another tap ahead to discern my placement on the board. I don't want to pitch forward unprepared.

I find the end and ready myself. Ursula, poolside, and a senior couple treading in the water, wait in sparkly daylight. This is not nighttime, shades drawn, lights out. My body is exposed, on display with my shrunken eyes, my transplant scars, my insulin injection bruises. I am a Google map of doctor visits and hospitalizations, hinting at many more unpaved miles ahead. Is Ursula up for that trip?

I am eager to dive. But my mind conjures a dry excavation in front of me. Then, the crypt full of snakes from *Raiders of the Lost Ark*. Next, a chamber filled with a thousand armed Chinese terra cotta soldiers.

"Are you watching?" I ask.

"Go ahead," Ursula says, and the words hang in the air. I picture her floating as well, Chagall-like, five feet over cement pool deck. "Just go."

Finally, I toss the worms into the pool. I trust there will be water, soft and buoyant, to catch me as I leap.

Little Magpie

Randall Brown

I find Maggie squatting on the kitchen floor beside the door to the garage. My eyes always go to her belly first, as if she has swallowed a globe. There've been two miscarriages, both early. Never have we gotten so far. Then I notice she's picking something off the floor, putting it in her mouth. Get closer. They surround her. Hundreds of them. Ants. Maggie is eating ants.

A lifetime of sitcoms has prepared me for cravings—pickles, hamburgers. Running out in the middle of the night for a pint of Haagen Daz Vanilla Swiss Almond. Strawberry Frosted Pop Tarts. But insects?

Maggie looks up. She removes the finger from her mouth. "Must be the baby," she says. Her hand follows the curve of her belly. "She wants bugs."

"Really? They sell crickets at pet stores. I could get some."

"Crickets?" She purses her lips, gazes up to the ceiling. Then nods. "OK."

The girl at Pet World brings them to me in a clear plastic bag, twist-tied at the top. She holds them up, dozens of them, hopping against the plastic. "You'll have one happy lizard," she says.

"Yeah. That's all one can really hope for in life, isn't it? A happy lizard."

She nods, a sign that we share some deep understanding. She tells me she threw in an extra dozen, then winks.

In high school Maggie wrote a piece about the opening of fishing season and the senseless slaughter of the earthworm. In graphic detail, she captured the wriggling on the hook, the oozing entrails, the practice of cutting them in half to double the bait. Together we collected money, went to bait shops, released nightcrawlers, earthworms, grubs back to the wild of gardens.

At home, in the garage, I hold up the bag. A cricket stares back; all eyes, bugs are. Crunchy. Gooey in the middle. Like pretzel snacks with cheese in the center.

I picture the bugs skittering down her throat, at the bottom, a baby open-mouthed—a miracle baby. Dozens of times, the brown bleeding began, and we were told she was lost, only to see her on the ultrasound, hear the beat-beat of her heart. How useless and helpless I feel during these races to the hospital, as if there's nothing I can do for them.

I carry the bag of crickets upstairs, find Maggie lying among the dozen flower pillows, her face the center, the cushions as petals. I swish the bag back and forth, imagine her sitting up, tossing cricket after cricket into her mouth, as if chomping on popcorn.

But instead the crickets bring tears. "What?" I say. "Beetles? You want beetles?"

The crickets pop in my ear.

"I'm bleeding again," she says. "Heavier this time."

A blur—the car ride, Maggie holding the bag of crickets, tapping against the plastic, then opening it, taking one out. "She's still hungry."

The breakneck drive, the crickets, the hospital waiting for our arrival—it's all part of the blur, something to hide the truth from both of us, that nothing matters except the desires of Fate for our baby to live. But that's nothing to tell Maggie.

"It has to be a good sign," I tell her.

"It does, doesn't it?" Maggie answers, then opens her mouth and feeds our baby's desire.

To the Garden

B.G. Firmani

*The following story is the winner of the third annual
Marguerite McGlinn Prize for Fiction.*

It seems like during a certain period of time no one in
Delaware ever smiled.

They look out at me from terrible photographs, grim,
frightened, their faces fucked by poverty. Most of them
look like they expect to be punished. Father Peter Donaghy
and his charges at St. Joseph's on the Brandywine, built
for the Irish workers at the famously exploding Dupont
powder mill nearby, stand up against the wall as if facing
a firing squad. The children have been told to cross their
arms against their skinny chests, probably in an attempt
to appear uniform and tidy; instead they look like sulky
criminals. It's 1890 and Father Peter, their protector, is
unshaven and defiant in a Cockney-looking bowler hat. His
pleasureless face still rings with childhood famine.

Halfway into the twentieth century, however, St. Joseph's would become known as the fancy Catholic church
in the area. Among the many other parishes in that mute,
Catholic city, there was a second congregation called St.
Joseph's, on French Street, "in town" as they used to say to
mean the City of Wilmington, a parish that had been found-
ed in the Jim Crow days of segregation to serve the Negro
community.

In the fifties my mother was working for the Dupont
company as a technical illustrator and being courted by
a rich young man, a chemist, very Catholic just as she
was. Each Friday he would say to her: Well, I'll see you

in church. She would smile and say yes. Each Sunday she would look for him, but never see him there. Then each Monday they would pass each other in the halls of Dupont and one of them would say, Well, I suppose you didn't go to mass—? And the other would say, How funny, because I was there. Mutual suspicion grew until my mother began avoiding the man in the hallway. She was a moral young woman, almost insufferably prim actually, and could not abide liars. Only later did she realize that the young man had been going to the fancy St. Joseph's, while she had been going to the humble St. Joseph's in town all this time. It was too late by then, however, because she had already married my failure of a father, and so I grew up poor.

It seems strange to be haunted by such a mundane place.

I was a clueless young person, at once distracted and self-regarding, and—when I made the mistake of bringing myself back to earth to face a lousy reality—furious. I kept my head in permanent escape mode. My father always championed education, always told us how far a good education could take you, but here he was with his numerous degrees from highly selective universities, the angriest man alive, raising his sullen, insulted children inside a crappy little house in a neighborhood of hard-luck white people.

I remember one family in particular who lived almost directly across the street, their house a bad mirror to our own. The parents were in a biker club called the Pagans, and their youngest kid, Jody, would do things like eat mud and walk around the neighborhood in his underpants. He had a deep leathery tan like a homeless person, even at the age of nine, and terrible scarring all over his tiny belly as if someone had squeezed him with barbeque tongs.

Up the street was the Mooney family. My sister and I were kind of friends with the youngest Mooney, Mickey, a large, unbright boy, and his sister Peg, but the oldest kid, Jacko, was a "bad element." Their mom was a beautician, their dad a fireman for the City of Wilmington. When the dad was killed in the line of duty, burnt to death in a house fire on the East Side, even though the man was an abusive

S.O.B. much like our own father, Peg just went off. She would stand by her window for hours and try to hit you on the head with one of Mickey's Hot Wheels if you attempted to get past the house. Jacko was heavy into drugs, and his life ended when he was babysitting for a friend downstate near Smyrna. The friend and his girl had been drinking, and when they came back to their trailer Jacko was asleep on the couch. The friend took out his gun, put it to Jacko's head, jokingly cocked the trigger, and said, "Wake up, Jackie boy." Then he shot him in the head, an accident.

My mother carried her church around with her and I have no doubt she always believed she would one day escape this neighborhood, if only through death and her eternal reward in the garden of heaven. Her striving husband, our father, always had a foolish new scheme for getting us out, but each of these schemes crumbled in his hands. I had no doubt I would escape the whole sick life of Delaware, but I made no plans. Inertia pressed down on me from that chemical sky. All three of us kids went to Catholic school, all three of us hated it, but I was the youngest and probably the most fanciful and so instead of dealing in practical reality and applying to college or something like that, I sat and I waited. I fully expected some change to just happen to me. So in 1986, eighteen years old and graduated from the all-girls' Catholic high school that I hated, I found myself working as a file clerk at A.I. du Pont Institute, a children's hospital.

It used to be called the Hospital for Crippled Children, way back before my time. I had found the job through a placement agency and, since in my mind a job was a job and they all stank, I didn't think too much about what working at a pediatric hospital would entail—I'd only be biding my time there until life came to claim me, anyway. So I was completely unprepared for the parade of sick children I saw coming through the hospital's doors day after day. There were little girls with bruised-looking eyes, kerchiefs on their bald heads, their bodies wrecked with chemo. Boys with extensive braces all up their legs, crutching themselves down the long cement walkway, their frames spasmodic with exertion. The children with cystic fibrosis, permanently exhausted, shuffling slowly, fighting for breath. They were like flocks of tiny sparrows. You could only look away.

All of them shared a kind of ancient resignation, the same thousand-yard stare.

The records department had about a dozen employees as I remember it, big men in suits behind closed doors and women out "on the floor" in workstations. The women were nice to me, perhaps out of pity because I was so young and clueless. I saw them as figures in a benign but boring film, or as a kind of vaudeville backdrop being reeled behind me as I pantomimed walking in place. My head was where I lived, where my mythic self soared. The highlight of my workday was lunch, when I would walk out of the building, a utilitarian, Pentagon-like place, then down the grass-flanked walkway and across the parking lot to my car. I would drive to Route 202, Concord Pike, which was where all the fast-food places were, and take out some edible trash from places like Arby's or Taco Bell. Then, instead of staying and eating, I would drive around as I ate, mentally exploding all the buildings I passed. I would blow up the Concord Mall, the ugly Methodist church, little brick-building accountancies, the Arby's whose warm bacon-cheese-burger I was grinding to bits in my hot little mouth. I had a special hatred for something called the Rollins building, an oddly tall tower protected by an oversized, moat-like green. It was like a giant dick on an otherwise flat landscape.

Of course I always had to go back to work after lunch. One of the nice older ladies would always ask me what I had for lunch, and I'd lie just because I could. The lies were meaningless—Oh, Mickey D's, I'd say, when I'd actually had Wendy's. Lying was something to do. One day when I did this, I heard a sharp intake of breath from the other file clerk, a woman named Keesha who was, after me, the second youngest person there, about twenty-four; she was the A–M file clerk, I was the N–Z. Keesha and I were civil but didn't really have anything to say to each other. I always got the feeling around Black people that I didn't hold any interest for them, that their society was closed, and that I wouldn't know how to talk with them anyhow.

Later, when it was just us, Keesha said to me, "I seen you at Wendy's."

I was so shocked to have been found out in my meaningless lie that I immediately lied again.

"You did not," I said haughtily.

We looked at each other. I noticed Keesha now, as if I hadn't really looked at her before. She had seemed like a dry young church lady to me when I'd first shaken her hand, but now I saw she had a canny look about her. She kept her hair severely pulled flat in a charmless plastic clip, but her face was shapely and unusual, with a smattering of freckles across high cheekbones and wide-set, watching eyes. And there was amusement in those eyes, a boundless amusement.

"OK, the fuck, I was at Wendy's," I finally said.

"What is that mouth?" she said.

I closed the file drawer I was working on and wheeled my cart away. Behind me I could hear her making a sound like *tch*!

I began to be curious about Keesha.

She dressed about fifty years older than she was, in dowdy acrylic cardigans, "sensible" polyester slacks, and an eternal pair of crepe-soled puckered shoes in a terrible light ocher color. On her sweaters was a procession of novelty brooches, of the kind you would see heaped in cheap little gift boxes in big bargain bins at the front of discount stores like the Almart's on Kirkwood Highway. I pictured Keesha there, at Almart's, tenderly looking through the many cheap gift boxes of one-dollar jewelry until she found the brooch that spoke to her. This scenario that I had invented for Keesha in my head depressed me beyond belief, but the horrendous, sad-hilarious brooches—the rhinestone-studded Jack-in-the-Box, the pseudo-marcasite daisy, the cat with "emerald" eyes—also somehow made me like her. Most of the young Black women I saw around dressed very stylishly, very flash, with shingled hair and sleek red leather and enormous shrimp earrings in eighteen-karat gold, and so Keesha's old-lady ways marked her for me as a serious, unfrivolous person. An emissary from another era, if not another planet, truth be told. She looked like no one I'd ever seen.

I'm not sure exactly how it was we started talking one day. It wasn't long after the Wendy's episode, I do remember, and we'd drawn our carts up next to each other, on either side of the M-N divide. In my mind, she just opened her mouth and began. She had a kind of offhand, buzzy delivery and would always start very softly with a series of throwaway words; it was as if she had every expectation of being ignored and so wanted to give the other person an easy out if that person didn't choose to pick up the dialog.

"So I was reading, the other day, in a library book about the Second World War Two," she said, "about the Fas-kists, and how they come to power, and everyone like them at first because the country was a plain mess, and how the main guy, Mussoli, was a strong, powerful leader and they had one central person they could look up to now, and so everyone want to be a Fas-kist too."

I was holding a file in my hand, its edge marked with a bright red N sticker, staring at the letter and trying to figure out how I was supposed to respond. All sorts of things flashed through my mind. Was she bringing this up because I had an Italian last name? Was she making fun of me?

"It makes a soft sound, 'Fascist,'" I said.

"Fascist," she said loudly.

Was she calling me a Fascist?

"Yeah, I don't much like them," I said.

She asked me why not.

I said something about not liking people who insisted you only see their way. Hating intolerant, brutal people. Hating tyrants.

"Uh-huh," she said, edging her cart back up the alphabet, away from me.

I zoomed after her with my own cart, well out of my letter group, and found myself asking her if she'd seen a photograph, a famous photograph of Mussolini—and I was careful to pronounce the name slowly, to articulate all the syllables—had she ever seen that photograph of Mussolini, of his corpse actually, when they strung up him and his lover, strung them up upside-down from a beam in front of a gas station? Their arms were flying out in front of them, as if they were diving from a high ledge. They had tied up his lover's skirt, because otherwise it would flop down over her face and be even more indecent. They'd strung him up there in that place because he had ordered the killing of a group of partisans, I said, resistance fighters, anti-Fascists—the Fascists had killed them and dumped their bodies in that same place, and so hanging him there was a reprisal.

"A reprisal," Keesha repeated.

"Yeah, like what goes around comes around," I said.

We were staring deeply at each other. People in the records department generally talked about television, Weight Watchers, drug store purchases. Here I was telling a Black woman about a lynching.

"I'd best get back," I said, wheeling down the alphabet.

I'm not exactly sure how we started eating lunch together.

I had a crap car, a late 1970s lemon, which my father had bought at an auto auction for two hundred dollars cash. It was tan, seriously uncool, and had a muffler that would come undone and scrape the ground if I hit a pothole, of which there were many in the City of Wilmington as I remember it. Once you got out of the city, however, the roads changed. Once you got north to the area through which the Brandywine Creek wended its way—once you got to the part of New Castle County actually called "chateau country," which was studded with Dupont estates—everything stank of Champagne and caviar. In my mind greater Wilmington was like a cartoon from the Great Depression: here were we poor people, crammed into shitty little houses and itty-bitty apartments in and around the City of Wilmington, dressed in our rags and our beat-up bonnets and our boots with our toes sticking out of them—while sprawling to the north and west were the rich in their fat French houses, turned out in silk top-hats and evening clothes. They stood in the drawing rooms of their mansions lighting cigars with hundred-dollar bills, their enormous bellies and Margaret Dumont bosoms filled with surety over the natural order of things. The houses of chateau country were usually hidden by walls or trees, but they would show themselves to you, along routes like Kennett Pike or Montchanin Road, in cunning, winking ways. The slate top of a stucco wall would lower just slightly to give a view of the mansard-roofed manor house, a stone wall would interrupt itself with a wrought-iron fence to frame an up-sloping greensward: these were the gracious bones thrown to the commoners. The message being, Look, but don't touch. As I child I looked and looked and I ate my heart out over it. As a furious teenager, I only wanted to burn it all down.

Keesha didn't have a car and the one time she saw me at Wendy's her mother had taken her there for a birthday treat, it turned out. Otherwise Keesha was thrifty and always packed her lunch. Her mother, I learned, worked nearby, as a stocker at a chain drugstore on Concord Pike, and would drop her off each morning at the hospital; on the day her mother was off, Keesha would take the bus and then hoof it down the long skinny road that led to Alfred I. Keesha called her mother by her first name, Carla.

"Why don't you call your mom 'Mom?'" I asked her one day as we ate our lunch together, Keesha with her home-brought stuff and me with a bag of vaguely food-like shit from McDonald's.

"Because my mom one nasty piece of work," Keesha said, "and she don't much like me."

"Isn't she religious?" I found myself asking.

"She about as religious as a bull dyke can get."

"Your mother's *gay?*" I gasped. I had never encountered such a thing before.

"If you call it that," she said, "but she not frilly at all."

The usual routine we'd fallen into had us talking about history, sparked by the *World at War* series still endlessly running on Channel 12, WHYY in Philadelphia in those days, as well as the succession of books Keesha took out from the main library in town. It was basically extra-personal, talking about history, talking about books. I felt awkward getting into family stuff because—how can I put this—I had an idea she didn't want to share personal Black stuff with me. Because that might reveal too much, or call out our differences. So when we got to Keesha's gay mother, though I was plenty curious (where was her father? I wondered) I looked for something else to turn the subject to.

"That sandwich looks good," I said. "What is it?"

"This here's hummus," she said, showing it to me, "which I make myself with those canned chickpeas, and a lot of spices in it, like this stuff the people of Lebanon and those folks eat, which is a nice kind of brick color. I put it on Roman Meal, with the bean sprouts."

"That's all the stuff my mother likes," I said. It didn't need saying that I disdained all the stuff my mother liked— the wheat germ and miso and herbal teas that smelled like potting soil. As a kid I had once seen my mother comb the beach at Indian River Inlet for the perfect piece of seaweed, rinse it with her eternal jug of spring water, and crunch it right there in her mouth for all to see. I could have lost my shit, I was so embarrassed.

"That stuff you eating there, that mystery meat? That stuff'll kill you," Keesha told me.

"Whatever," I said. I remember thinking, God, she is one bossy Black woman—why is she telling me what to do?

At the end of that day, driving home, I passed Keesha waiting for the bus. Standing very straight, library book held up in front of her face, large and unlikely vinyl purse hanging from the crook of her arm like a tea-social old lady.

I was embarrassed about my shit car. Keep going, I said to myself. I looked in the rearview mirror, Keesha's figure spooling away from me. But then something made me pull over.

I backed up in the bus lane and pushed open the passenger door.

"Want a ride?" I called out.

She had looked away, expecting some creep no doubt, but then she leaned forward and saw me.

"Oh! It's you," she said.

And then: she smiled. Which was a previously unseen event.

She was uncommonly beautiful, I realized.

"Get in—I'll drive you home," I said, taken by a sudden kind of happiness.

"I'm good," she said.

"What?" I said. "The bus takes fucking forever."

"Hey, mouth!" she said.

But she got in. I told her she had to lift the door as she closed it, since it was a little out of whack. She did this flawlessly, then put on her seatbelt and looked around the car.

"Nice ride," she said.

"Huh?" I said. "What? Which way is nice?"

"You got a nice car," she said.

"This piece of shit?" I said.

"You got a car."

"Such as it is," I said.

"How much you pay?"

"My dad bought it for me," I said.

"That's a nice dad," she said.

This—the richest joke ever—made me snort.

"*So* not the case," I said.

And then there was a pause.

And I thought, she is thinking: You got a dad.

"Stay on 202 here," she said.

I hadn't even thought to ask, Where do you live? She lived where Black people lived, my mind had figured. Going "home" to where I lived, to the luckless white people area, I would first turn from Concord Pike onto a route called the Augustine Cutoff, and have a moment of driving through Alapocas, an area of beautiful old stone houses, and then past the John Wanamaker's, with its landscaped parking lot tiered like a wedding cake. From there the cutoff became a truss bridge passing over Brandywine Creek, which flowed down from chateau country, bringing its largesse into the City of Wilmington. And that place, down below the bridge, in the parkland beside the Brandywine, held a kind of magic for me, strange to say. It was beautiful there, and it was a beauty you could touch. It was a public park, but special. I would drive over the Augustine Bridge and picture what was below, that nineteenth-century park so perfectly made, with its winding paths that revealed, then hid, then revealed vistas so surprising and dreamlike. I think of the place we called Josephine Gardens, where there was an allée of cherry trees, blooming like pink heaven in early spring, that led to a fountain that seemed to me so wistful, a fountain with a statue of a woman with her head bowed, as if in mourning.

We stayed on 202 instead, and Concord Pike became Concord Avenue and then we were rolling through the City of Wilmington. We were rolling far over on the East Side, a place I never ventured. We chatted about this and that but my eyes roved all over the landscape. We kept going further out, further east, further over than where I'd imagined Keesha living. The road bent to the left, its name changed again, we made a turn onto another street and I felt my head contracting in a way that felt like ignorance, or fear.

Then we caught a red light and Keesha told me she'd get out right there.

"We're here?" I asked. I ducked to look out the window, seeing a block of row houses with second-floor bays. Some vinyl-shingled, some the old brick, some with enclosed porches with improvised windows. Much like the neighborhood where I lived. But Black.

"Yeah, it's fine," she said. She already had her hand on the door handle, her purse clutched to her chest.

"Which one is it?" I said.

"I just gotta get a little something, and then it's close from here." She seemed to be gesturing to a small grocery on the opposite corner.

"I can wait," I said, "I'm fine to drive you to your door."

"Thanks, girl," she said, already out of the car. She had remembered about the door, and she lifted and closed it with a click, then pressed it firmly to make sure it stayed closed. She leaned down at the window and looked at me, a sort of privacy in her eyes. Then she turned and crossed the street.

There were no other cars on the avenue, so I swooped the car around. The store had a big window, but I didn't see

Keesha there. How could she already be gone? But then as I drove away, I thought I saw her walking straight down the way, further out, further east. So far to keep walking! In my mind I held a speculative map of that place, Wilmington, with its neighborhoods and "hundreds" and boundaries and very rich and very poor, and Keesha was walking toward the neighborhood most unknown by me, a place to be glimpsed only from the train—a scanty, wretched, starveling collection of dead-end streets. Can't even call it a neighborhood. Later I would look at a map and see that the only street that continued past that way was East 12th, which led to Gander Hill Prison.

But she wasn't going to the prison, I knew. Nothing that complicated. She just wanted to keep me away from the sight of her shitty little house. I knew, I smelled this in her, because—you can drop me here—I did it all the time.

•••••••••••

Butt up against the children's hospital was a former Dupont estate, Nemours.

Not sure if it was because of this or because of the hospital, but the grounds around Alfred I. were enclosed by a stone wall, high and fearsome, that actually had shards of ancient broken glass embedded into the top of it. It looked like something out of Dickens. Driving along the course of that wall—which ran the length of Powder Mill Road, as I remember it—I would wonder: Is it to keep people out, or to keep them in?

I shared this thought with Keesha one afternoon as we sat eating our lunch by the big plate-glass window, watching a scene unfold on the lawn outside.

"I did read that writer, Charles Dickenson, and I do know what you mean," she said. "All those poor little waste kids in Victorian England."

"My favorite book by Charles Dickens is probably *Great Expectations*," I said. I would always do this thing, repeat a word the right way to her rather than outright correct her. Keesha had by now told me she'd never finished high school.

"I like the book with the dust heaps," she said, "where they always digging through the dust heaps."

"Wow, *Our Mutual Friend*? You read *Our Mutual Friend*?" I was fascinated. "Even I haven't read *Our Mutual Friend*."

Keesha had finished her sandwich and was carefully folding up the aluminum foil she'd wrapped it in, to save for the next day's sandwich. She did this every lunch and reused the foil until it was so creased and holey it almost looked like metallic lace.

She seemed to be weighing something in her head.

"You know," she said, "you a little hoity sometimes."

Let it be said that the scene we were looking at outside was a busload of Amish come down from Lancaster County. You would see this, and though you saw it numerous times, it would always do something to your heart. One child was sick, one among their numbers, and the whole clan would come down in support of that child. You would see fifty, sixty people. They couldn't take the buggies that far and probably they were too small, so they came by bus, driven by a Mennonite or just some regular-looking guy in a baseball cap. The child would be brought into Alfred I. and all the rest of the clan, for some reason, just stayed outside. They brought picnic baskets and blankets and spread out on the grassy expanses outside our window. Sometimes they seemed to just be praying out there. They seemed so peaceable and unlikely, the women in their long pinafores, thick black stockings, and gauzy, heart-shaped plain caps, the men in their broad-brimmed straw hats and black trousers and suspenders. Their shirts and dresses would be of a kind of cornflower blue or an odd sort of mauve, as if made by strong vegetable dyes. They were like apparitions there on the grass outside our utilitarian pentagon, collective hallucinations. And we were free to stare at them, because we looked at them through one-way glass, but if they tried to look in, all they would see was a distorted mirror of themselves.

"You a little hoity sometimes" rang in my ears.

I was chewing a cheese-covered chicken sandwich thing and it was turning to elastic in my mouth. My first reaction was, Did I ask you to be my friend? Did I? I chewed and chewed my disgusting expanding chicken gum and I realized tears were starting to come into my eyes. I was chewing and looking away from Keesha and out the window at the Amish, who suddenly seemed to me like a bunch of art-directed simpletons, extras from a freak movie. So many people for one child, what is the stupidity of this, why so many people for just one child? Why are you showing off for us like this? Then Keesha leaned forward and blocked my view.

"You like a soft little mouse," she said to me, not unkindly.

I stared at her, my mouth chewing, tears rolling out of my eyes.

"I'm so sorry I made you upset," she said.

"You didn't," I choked out.

"Yes I did, and I'm sorry. You talk a good game but now I see."

"What do you see?" I asked her, my voice finally breaking.

She sat back. She was wearing a pin on her sweater shaped like a parallelogram, and she raised her hand and touched it. She turned away.

"You're like me," she said. "You sad, like me."

••••••••••

Autumn came and I realized I was expecting school to start again. When it didn't I was somehow offended.

When was life coming to fetch me? I knew it was only a matter of time, but I was sick of the boring job, sick of being stuck in the house with my parents, sick of the shit life of Wilmington. My route to work took me by a municipal sign that marked the spot where the city began, the kind of thing made of pretend redwood with rustic lettering and inevitably flanked by hearty, ugly mums. The sign read: Wilmington, A Place To Be Somebody. Someone even angrier than I was had shot it full of BB pellets.

I hated that I was nineteen years old but that my parents insisted that I still eat with them at the table for dinner. It had always been the family custom, I always hated it, and it always left us kids open for any sort of abuse, mental or physical, that my father felt like dishing out. He would light into my brother or crack my sister across the face or pick up a plate and bring it down on the lip of the table, smashing it to pieces and sending melamine shards into the lentil stew we were all trying to choke down. It was because my Asperger's brother had got a B in calculus or my sister had said something "smart" or my defeated mother had made the same crap-tasting dinner again for the fourteenth time in a row, because how could you really feed a family of five on twenty-two thousand dollars a year? My brilliant father, our provider, Master of Education, Doctor of Laws, master of nothing.

He was always so angry, so quick to blame and yell and strike. But as the days grew shorter something different seemed to be happening. My sister had lost her job and come "home" that November, until she got back on her feet. This was a bad idea and there were the usual screaming matches and bullshit—and then she was quickly gone again. I still see her in my mind, standing on the sidewalk in front of the house, giving my dad the finger. It was freezing cold and she was so hot and angry it was like I could see steam coming off her in furious waves.

What had changed was that our father didn't have the strength to hit us anymore.

My strategy had always been to steer clear of him, to creep around and avoid detection. My sister had been the screamer, the provoker. But now it seemed like all he could do was let her scream, and yell and bluster back. When he raised his fist, she was too strong for him now.

After my sister was out of the house again, a strange new atmosphere settled over it. My brother was long gone and maybe my father sensed that I was all he and my mother had left. I saw him trying to summon up a new, mild tone for me. He tried to be "understanding." I only wanted him to fuck off, but I developed a way of dealing with him, answering when spoken to but mostly treating him like a flickering shadow on the wall. Dinners were no longer violent or dramatic; instead, my father leaned toward me as if supplicating and asked me endless questions. How was work? What was new with the hospital? Had I read a certain article in

the *News Journal*? I gave him short, clipped answers. My
mother, a defeated woman who had stood by while her children were beaten by her husband on an almost daily basis
for twenty years, had long ago gone into eternal-rewards
retreat and mostly just listened. If I were in a good mood,
which was a rarity, I would offer a bit more, perhaps a joke.
To such things they would respond with an almost pathetic
amount of laughter.

One evening, after dinner, I heard a knock on the door
to my basement room.

The bedrooms upstairs were empty now, but I preferred
to stay in the basement. Years before my father had tried to
make it into a rec room, but he had given up after covering
about half of it in imitation wood paneling. The idea was
that we'd be moving out of that house anyway, moving out
of that house soon, to our rightful place in a development
in north Wilmington, maybe to Alapocas with its beautiful
stone houses. That was the idea. The basement was a horrible place, damp and musty, cold in the winter and hot in the
summer, but it was mine. It was my lair and in it were my
books and my records and the things I loved. After I turned
eighteen my parents weren't allowed in it—that was part of
the deal—and had even installed a Radio Shack intercom as
a means to summon me to dinner. So when I heard a knock
on the old metal door, I jumped.

"What do you want?" I yelled.

"Honey?" It was my father.

I got up and ripped open the door.

"What do you *want*?" I yelled in his face.

He flinched. He reeled back. My tough-assed father
cringed before his youngest child. He stood blinking at me,
and I think of the look in his blue eyes, those oddly inappropriate, sensitive-looking blue eyes of his. He looked like a
little old dog.

"May I come in?" he actually said.

I pushed the door open, turned, and sat at my desk.

The only other chair in the room was a small, cushioned
one with a seat that slanted back, and he sat in it. It made
him lower than me, which I liked. He wanted to talk about
something but looked at my stereo. I made an exasperated

sigh and turned it off.

"OK," I said.

He looked around the room, studying my things: my posters, my books, the small, artful items I had bought at thrift shops. All the evidence of my dream life.

"Pretty nice set-up you've got here," he said.

"Right," I said. I didn't want him eyeing my things, I didn't want him near me at all. He tried to sit up in the slanting chair but was unsuccessful. I was bored and annoyed and only wanted him to leave.

"You know I want you to be happy, don't you?" my father said.

"What?" I said.

"I just want you to be happy in your life," he said.

"What are you asking?" I said.

"I love you," he said.

I shot up from my desk and was standing in the middle of the room.

"What do you need to know?" I shouted at him.

"Nothing, honey, I just want you to—"

"Want me to *what*?" I said. I leaned over him, in his face, and I spewed out: "What, dad? What, dad? What, dad? What, dad? What, dad?"

"What the fuck is wrong with you?" he finally said.

He stood up and came at me. A flash of the old fear leapt up. I stumbled back. He stopped. He corrected himself. He was supposed to be kind now.

"Honey—" he said.

"We're done," I said.

He stood, supplicating. He looked miserable and shrunken to me. He had never been that big, but he had strong arms, big fists. But now he looked so stooped and so small. I realized that he shrank as we grew. We grew and we grew and he shrank.

"I love my kids," he said in high-pitched, womanish, strangulated voice. "You know I love my kids."

I walked around him and went to the metal door and opened it. I waited outside until he had gone.

You pathetic little man, I thought.

If I had seen better, if I had eyes that could see, I would have realized that my father really was shrinking. His body was riddled with cancer—stage four, several kinds. All this would kill him by spring. What is funny with this was that I didn't cry at all.

When I went back to work everyone was so nice to me. All the older ladies and Keesha took me out to the Bennigan's on Concord Pike for lunch. I remember eating puffy breadsticks. I ate and ate, as much as I could stuff down. It was somehow surprising to me to see that during my weeks off folks had missed me. Keesha especially was full of new things to tell me, and it was a great comfort to me to fall back into our routine. We went back to eating our lunches at the large glass window that overlooked the hospital grounds, which were becoming green again with spring.

So this is the way people live, was a thought that came to me. Sometimes when we were sitting there eating I'd become aware of silence and realize that Keesha had asked me something and I hadn't been listening at all. I had floated away. I was floating away, looking at life even more abstractly than before, when I thought I would be rescued. There could be no expectations. Click! My mind had been recalibrated. I was a new mild person. I was beyond disappointment. I think Keesha was trying to summon me back, but the most real thing for me was a new kind of blinking dream that I kept in my head. In this new dream I was in my castle, untouchable, alone, beguiled by a piece of cut glass I held in my hand.

The food that I had craved and eaten for so long now became disgusting to me. Meat began to smell of death. I tried eating the things that Keesha liked. They didn't taste exactly good, but they were not disgusting. I tried all kinds of things and then I was packing my lunch and eating the same thing every day, smoked gouda on wholewheat pita bread with Roma tomatoes and Dijon mustard. That was a kind of craving I had. I would wake up in the middle of the night and crave this sandwich. I was thinking of my mother, alone two floors up, and wondering could she sleep? When I was home from work she would follow me around the house, talking at me, but I ignored her. I started staying out, did not eat dinner with her anymore. She was a flawed religious character anyway. Foolish family. I went to sleep dreaming of deeper sleep. Every morning when I woke up I was disappointed.

One of the nice older women pulled me aside and told me I had to clean up a bit, I was beginning to look slovenly. I knew Keesha had been trying to talk me back from this place where I was but her voice was like a thin echo, not applicable to where I was.

It was a day in April when Keesha and I were sitting at the window eating our lunch. I am not sure how we saw it at the same time, but both of us became riveted on a bird, flying in toward the hospital from way off. We both locked eyes on the bird and it was really nuts because we both knew the bird was sailing right toward the plate-glass window. We leapt up from our seats and we ran around either side of the table and we were both at the window jumping up and down and waving our arms and yelling. "Bird, bird! Look out, bird, stop it, look out!" We were frantic and yelling but the bird couldn't see us at all—was it looking at itself, sailing in to meet itself, seeing itself as a lover who would greet it? We were yelling. The bird sailed into the mirror glass and banged so hard it was like the glass buckled. The bird bounced right off and fell to the grass, dead.

I was aware of a terrible noise and I realized it was myself, screaming. I couldn't stop the noise coming off me. Keesha was bundling me in her arms and pressing my face into her sweater. The noise quit. There was some kind of thing and then the older ladies had got her something and she had my bag and my spring coat and we were in the parking lot. She was going to drive me home.

Keesha closed the passenger door on me with a soft click.

I put my hands on my face and my eyes were crying.

She got in and started the car.

"I don't want to go home," I said.

We had rolled smoothly out of the parking lot.

"Where you want to go to?" she said.

We passed beneath the trees and I looked out the window and thought how clear life was up here, in these rich private places.

"I want to go to the garden," I said to her.

She asked me what garden was that? As if there could be more than one garden. I told her I'd show her. How to get to the garden. She should bear right and go down the hill. There was a turn and it seemed like you were going the wrong way but then you were actually on the right path and it was only a question of finding a place to park. She would park. It would be spring of 1969, it is April, Easter Sunday, and my father has taken us to the garden to see the cherry trees in blossom. It is a fine clear day. We stand close together as if delighting in one another's company, and we are beautifully dressed, my mother in a hat with a veil and a burgundy suit, my brother in a tiny blazer with a crest on its pocket and a miniature bow tie, my sister in a velvet coat, white stockings, white Mary Janes, and bows in her hair. My father wears his best suit, a sharkskin suit about fifteen years out of date, but impeccable. And he is cradling the baby, who has been dressed in pale pink—bonnet, coat, stockings. He holds the baby so tenderly, cradling her in his arms. I reach my arms out oddly, as if I am expecting to fly. Behind us, the cherry trees are in blossom. Who has taken this picture? Someone else has taken this picture, to give to my father or mother so that years later they could look on it and wonder: were we actually happy then? Were we once actually happy?

"I don't know this place," Keesha said when we stopped the car.

"It's not that far," I said.

We got out and walked down the hill. Below us would be the park, which led to the garden with its fountain and cherry trees. As we got closer I couldn't wait and I grabbed Keesha's hand and ran her down to the garden. I ran her toward it but before we got there I saw the fountain from afar, the cloaked woman atop the fountain, and I realized we were too late. The trees had already bloomed and shed their blossoms. We had missed it.

And now we walked slowly, toward the fountain, toward the garden.

"It's beautiful here," Keesha said.

She didn't know how it should look, I thought, so to her it looks just fine.

"It was supposed to be in bloom," I told her, feeling anguish filling my mouth. "The cherry trees are supposed to be in bloom, but we missed it."

She looked at the trees above us.

"No," she said. "We didn't miss it—we just too early." She pointed up. There were buds in the trees. She looked back down to me and smiled her beautiful smile, bestowed so gracefully and so rarely.

What kind of dream life goes on with you? I wondered. What dream of self got her through her days? I felt my legs giving out under me and then I was kneeling in the muddy grass, banging my fists on the ground. Keesha was over me, her hands under my arms, trying to pull me up. I was like a stone to the earth, banging my fists on the ground. And then she just let go and she crouched in front of me, her face up against mine, watching me way up close. She crouched in front of me and it was like I was counting her freckles as I banged and banged my fists to the ground and when my arms started to fatigue she banged the earth and said, "More!" She banged the earth again and said, "More!" And I banged my fists on the ground and she said, "More, more, more, stupid ground, screw you, stupid ground, that's the stuff, that's it."

And then I remember her pulling me to my feet and buttoning up my coat for me like I was her child. She took an old tissue from her pocket, spat softly on it, and cleaned my hands with it. And I felt like she must really love me, she must really love me after all, to share her spit like this with no embarrassment. I collapsed into her with gratitude.

"You got to get it together," she told me, pushing me off in a moment. "I can't be your facilitator. I can't be your savior."

And with this she led me back up the hill.

•••••••••••

After this I would go home. I would go home and see my mother sitting alone at the dining room table, her small defeated hands cradling a cup of tea. I was raised to respect my husband, to believe my husband is always right, she would say to me. We would speak in a way we had not been able to before. I would make myself forgive her in some way. I would pity her but not enough to stay with her in that place.

I would forgive her enough to finally leave. No vindication, no day of triumph. Just finally putting that corrupted dream life behind me, and walking out the door.

Advice from an Opossum

Noel Sloboda

Ignore your brothers and sisters
until you secure your place
in the pouch. Then grow up quickly.
Once you step out on your own,
devour everything in your path,
from acorns to carrion. Revel
in delicacies to be discovered
in garbage cans. Sleep all day.
Develop the wiry muscles

in your pink, prehensile tail:
seeing the world upside down
is sometimes inspiring. Scavenge
country roads, but beware
white lights cascading across
the blacktop. If they approach,
bare all fifty of your teeth.
If that fails to stop them, perform
an Elvis: bask in the glow
as you bloat and stiffen; secrete
a horrible smell; hold
perfectly still; and dream
of swallowing the moon.

Are You Ready for the Country?

Tim Zatzariny, Jr.

I watched my old man's face, hoping he wouldn't notice my chubby fingers creeping toward the volume knob.

From the driver's seat came a grunt that sounded like "No." He hadn't even taken his eyes off the road.

I backed off, realizing I wouldn't win—this time, or maybe ever.

It was a game we played every time I rode shotgun in his old Ford Ranger—light green body with a forest green cap over the bed.

He listened to what he called his "hillbilly music"—cassettes by Loretta Lynn, George Jones, Tammy Wynette and other honky-tonk heroes, and I did my best to seize control of the stereo.

The picture is a little hazy—maybe it was all that secondhand smoke—but most of the details are still as clear and crisp as Loretta's sweet voice.

I fought it for years, but now I realize my father handed down to me a love of country music.

A forced inheritance at first, but now it's one I'm keeping in the family.

My father had bought the truck from an old high-school friend who owned a used car lot in our hometown of Vineland, NJ, a city that's equal parts green farm fields and shadowy urban areas, halfway between Philadelphia and Atlantic City.

The Ford's engine always seemed to be coughing, spitting or just plain dying. Frequent, wallet-busting trips to the mechanic left my father, a hard-nosed police detective, cursing the buddy who'd given him such a great "as is" deal.

The most dependable parts of this green lemon seemed to be the cassette player and the tinny speakers—there was never a time when my father, also named Tim, wasn't listening to music in the truck.

To this day, my old man is a hillbilly at heart, even though South Jersey is flat as a prairie and the only real time he ever spent in the South was during basic training at an Air Force base in Texas.

I blamed Elvis for my father's musical tastes.

My father swore he could listen to Presley's music all day, and he often did. My parents bickered constantly, but there was one thing they could agree on: The King.

Whenever Elvis's music was on the stereo, there was détente in our house.

He could soothe people, even from beyond the grave.

Elvis's own hillbilly bent led my father to seek out the mainstream country music that was popular in the late 1970s, a few years before the genre gussied itself up, "Urban Cowboy" style.

I was nine or ten years old, a chunky kid with straight blond hair hanging in my eyes, and a love of rock 'n roll inherited from my mother.

My father's music seemed hokey to me, as old-fashioned and corny as the *Hee-Haw* episodes that seemed to be on whenever we visited my mother's parents.

If I'd had veto power, the soundtrack for all those hours I rode in his truck would have been The Who, The Rolling Stones and Jimi Hendrix.

My younger brother, my cousin, and I used to throw the Stones' "Some Girls" LP on the stereo in my parents' wood-paneled basement and play furious air guitar. We fought over which one of us was Keith Richards. No one wanted to be Mick. We were weird kids. And it was no coincidence that we'd always skip the one country song on the album, "Far Away Eyes."

"My truck, my music." Sounds like ad copy, but this was my old man's standard reply when I complained.

And then he'd turn up Charley Pride's hit, "Just Between You and Me" like it was the first time he'd ever heard it.

Trying to extract even a small victory, I'd reach for the

knob on the air conditioner. The grumbling rose from the driver's seat: "The air wastes gas. Roll down your window."

Fine, but you don't get much of a cross-breeze going 25 miles an hour.

As I sweated through my Fonzie T-shirt, I swore that when I was old enough, country music would be banned from any vehicle or domicile I was in.

It was bad enough I had to endure these hicks singing about broken hearts and busted dreams, but what made things even worse were the cheap Garcia-Vega cigars my father puffed on in the truck.

A quarter apiece, the stogies smelled like they cost even less. I couldn't decide which was more foul—the sounds or the smoke.

Eventually, my father quit smoking, and I took up country music.

Some of those songs had insinuated themselves in my head, no matter how hard I'd tried to hate them. I knew every word to "I Will Always Love You" long before Whitney Houston had a monster hit with the song in 1992. My father played Dolly Parton's original—and superior—version all the time. And to this day, "He'll Have to Go" grabs me the second Jim Reeves croons that sad-but-hopeful opening line: *Put your sweet lips a little closer to the phone...*

When I was a senior in high school—taller and leaner now, but with my bangs still flopping in my eyes—my parents bought me my first stereo, at Macy's. The speakers were so bulky they barely fit in the trunk of our '76 Grand Prix—a slightly more reliable vehicle than the Ford Ranger.

I set up the equipment in my bedroom, underneath a poster of U2 in which Bono had a mullet as grand as his band's sound.

Finally, my own stereo, to play whatever records I wanted, whenever I wanted (more about the "whenever" part in a minute). I thought about having a sign made to hang alongside Bono's mullet: NO COUNTRY ALLOWED.

Back then, the main supplier for my music fix was a grocery store. I worked after school as a bagger at the local ShopRite, which had a small display aisle of LPs, located,

God knows why, near the meat counter. The LPs were left-overs; I never figured out if the pork loin was, too.

I'd spend a good chunk of my meager paycheck on albums by The Stones, Dire Straits, The Cars and AC/DC. Then I'd lie on the floor in my room and spin those records through the night, until the banging started. My father was on the other side of the wall, a critic expressing himself with his fist.

It was a game of attrition: I'd lower the volume a few notches; he'd stop pounding on the wall. I'd crank the volume back up when I thought he'd given up. But, then the banging started again. Eventually I invested in a set of headphones that cost me a week's paycheck. A small price to pay to save the plaster on our walls.

On to college, and my tastes shifted again.

R.E.M. and the Replacements might have been winking a little when they did it, but even they embraced country music, which seemed as incongruous for college-rock bands in the mid-'80s as wearing a plaid tie with a checkered suit (although that's how the Replacements normally dressed).

Were these bands—whose every move I followed well before the Internet made it possible to find out at any given moment what color socks they were wearing—saying it was OK to like country even if you loved punk rock? Maybe honky-tonk had seeped into their heads the same way it had wormed itself into mine, from hearing those old records played over and over again.

I started to think I should give country a chance, maybe sit down and have a drink or two with it, listen to what it had to say.

It took a little while longer for that meeting to happen, and it finally took place thanks to Steve Earle.

In 1995, Earle, recently released from jail on drug charges but now sober and on the comeback trail, was playing the Philadelphia Folk Festival. A local paper ran a feature in advance of his appearance. I had no idea who this tough-looking guy with the long hair and beard was, but the article mentioned that in the mid '80s, he'd played shows with the Replacements.

That was all I needed to know. I hustled to my favorite music store and bought a copy of Earle's new, acoustic album, "Train A' Comin'." I figured I'd just ignore the "country" parts.

Earle's attitude, which was just as punk as anything I listened to, grabbed me immediately. A true music fan, he wasn't afraid to let other genres seep into his own music. On "Train A' Comin'" there's a song by the Beatles *and* reggae, and they seemed to get along together pretty well.

What did this album teach me? Not to be a musical segregationist, because a good song is good song, whether it's a country weeper or a sparkling, three-minute pop tune.

So maybe this country stuff wasn't rotgut after all. Around this time, Johnny Cash had a career resurgence with a series of albums that introduced—or in my case, reintroduced—his music to a lot of people who didn't know him from Johnny Paycheck.

Hearing Cash's music with different, older ears led me back to his earlier albums, like "At Folsom Prison."

Like Earle's music, Cash's deep, ominous baritone straddled the divide I'd created in my mind between punk and country.

Was it possible my old man had much better taste in music than I'd ever thought?

After digging a little deeper, I decided Merle Haggard and Waylon Jennings were really rock 'n rollers in black cowboy hats.

This revelation was the end—or maybe it was the beginning—of a circuitous route, one started by my father. In that damned green truck, with the sour-smelling cigars.

"Daddy, play that 'workin' man' song again."

I almost had to ask my seven-year-old to repeat himself. On a road trip, we had been listening to Merle Haggard. When the song "Workin' Man Blues" finished, Ryan, his blond hair hanging in his eyes like mine used to, demanded an encore.

I'm not sure what made the song stick in his brain. It's catchy for sure, and throughout the song, there's repeated sound of a triangle, meant to replicate the clang of a laborer's hammer.

It's easy to connect with a song about blue-collar life when you're an adult, but what does a kid know about drinking beer in taverns to wash away the memory of another hard shift at the factory?

Whatever it was, the song spoke to him in the same way Elvis's music spoke to my father, and Steve Earle's music spoke to me.

In the case of my father and me, Elvis's and Earle's songs spoke *for* us, with a confidence we couldn't always muster on our own. After listening to Earle sing, *I wanna know what's over that rainbow...*for the thousandth time, I had to find out if there really was a world outside the place I grew up.

I'm still trying to figure that out. And now I have Waylon, Merle, Steve, and a bunch of their rowdy friends along for the ride.

Inheritance

Maria Ceferatti

When I look at my nine-year-old son, I see my husband's face. His square jaw, his chiseled cheekbones, his light brown hair, his delicate, perfectly proportioned nose. When my son turns to the side, however, I see myself. He has my ears. I have big ears. My father has big ears. Our ears don't stick out from the sides of our heads, they are not mal-formed, but they are big.

I wonder if this physical trait is shared among us be-cause we are all musicians: my father, a music teacher for thirty years, plays the saxophone, clarinet, and flute; I teach the violin and piano; and my son has been dutifully taking piano lessons for four years now. It makes sense that for musicians, large ears would be an asset.

I think back to the first time I saw his oversized ears. Nine years ago I wasn't concerned about piano lessons, I was just praying he'd survive. That's because he was born prematurely, weighing only one pound, three ounces. I was just over five months pregnant when I was put on strict bed rest at Lankenau Hospital because of pre-term labor. After three weeks, the contractions couldn't be stopped and my son came into the world sixteen weeks before he was due. I'd never seen a human being so small. It amazed me that his whole tiny body was already formed, from the wisps of hair on his head to his fragile little fingers and toes. Oh, and those precious ears.

Because he had arrived so early, my husband and I did not have a name ready for him. After four days the neo-natologists were getting impatient. "We need a name for this baby," they told us. "The nurses can't keep calling him

'Baby Boy Number Seven' when they talk to him through the incubator."

My husband and I scrambled. I'd been reading the Bible for solace and comfort during my weeks on bed rest, so we consulted the greatest story ever told to come up with a name.

"What about 'Simon'?" my husband said, popping his head up from the Book of Acts. "There are a lot of 'Simons' in the Bible."

"It's a good name," I said. "Simon was the man who helped Jesus carry the cross. Let's go with that."

We proudly reported our son's name to the head neonatologist.

"Simon says!" he answered, teasing us with a smile. I hadn't thought of that, but then again, in the game, Simon Says, Simon is always the boss. I wasn't concerned about the potential teasing. I was glad to have a name to call my little guy who was so delicate yet strong.

"You're gonna be OK, Simon," I whispered into the portholes on the sides of the incubator. "You're doing a great job, little guy, just keep growing." Even then, when he was one pound, those ears must have been listening.

Soon after naming him, we researched the name Simon: "He Heard," from Hebrew. I wondered how this meaning would pertain to my son in his future. I found out a few months later. The doctors and nurses had warned us about the rollercoaster ride that was the life of a micro preemie; the medical staff was encouraging (and bordering on saintly), but they did not give us any false hope. My husband and I sighed with relief when Simon seemed to dodge each potential illness that the hospital staff anticipated: no brain bleeds, no chronic infections, and no life-threatening heart issues. We celebrated each milestone that Simon achieved: breathing without the ventilator, graduating from a feeding tube to a baby bottle, and the most visible accomplishment—gaining weight. After two and a half months, Simon was no longer dependent on oxygen to breathe and he had grown to five pounds. Then, one evening as we left the house for our nighttime NICU visit, the nurse on duty called us to say that the pediatric ophthalmologist would meet us there when we arrived. The eye doctor explained that, earlier that day, Simon's eyes had been routinely checked for a condition called Retinopathy of Prematurity. The results were not good. Simon's retinas had completely detached. He would be blind.

My husband and I felt the sharp dip of the roller coaster that we thought we had eluded. We insisted on a second opinion, and on this occasion my parents were present for the results. The doctor came to the same conclusion—that our little fighter would never see. My mother asked if she could donate her eyes to Simon. The doctor solemnly shook his head. Again, we scrambled. We scoured the Internet for information and we eventually found an extremely gifted retina surgeon in Detroit, Michigan. We were told that people came from all over the world to see this doctor. Once Simon came out of the NICU, we flew to Detroit every two weeks for surgeries and subsequent check-ups. After three surgeries, Simon was able to see light. This may not seem like much of an accomplishment, but in the blind world, being able to see light means a lot: it means that you can distinguish daytime from nighttime; that your circadian rhythm of sleeping and waking is not disturbed; and that light can be used to orient the space around you, whether it's the light from windows in a room or fluorescent ceiling lights to guide you down a hallway.

Simon is now a healthy, chatty nine-year-old with a sharp wit and long pianist's fingers. He reads Braille and walks with a cane. He attends Saint Lucy Day School for Children with Visual Impairments in Juniata Park where he is mainstreamed with sighted students. And he's still got those big ears. Those ears that my father gave to me and that I gave to Simon. Those ears that help him to distinguish the voices of his favorite radio sportscasters on 610 AM WIP. Those ears that detect the smallest sound when I think I'm silently gesturing to my husband. Those ears that fill my heart with joy when Simon tells me that he doesn't need to see my face because he can hear me smile. I know that those big ears will serve him well throughout his life. He sees with those ears and I'm proud to share them with him.

The Rest of the World

Adam Schwartz

The following story is the winner of the fourth annual Marguerite McGlinn Prize for Fiction.

High rises, like towers made out of sidewalk. The minute they started talking about blowing us up, we forgot everything we didn't like about Freedom House Projects. No one fussed anymore about the spent lights, or sometimey hot water, or the elevator-jamming hustlers. Pretty soon, graffiti cried through stairwells and across doors: Save Freedom House.

•••••••••••

I had a job at a seafood restaurant called Barnacle Bob's. He'd hired me as a dishwasher. Straight away, though, he put me on his boat, working the crab pots. Out there, with the wind popsicling my bones and the boat tossing my stomach, I wanted to tell him to kick rocks. 'Cept then I would've been right back in the house with Excuse. So five, six days a week I hit that first empty #11 and rode the flickering lights down to the harbor where the streets were made of stone. Barnacle Bob was this old crusty dude with a fat face and a yellow beard and a really dirty hat that he called lucky even when it wasn't and he would be there waiting in the dark by the water.

Huddled down, chopping across that bay, gulls at our side, some days you couldn't help from praying those pots come up light. But Barnacle Bob had taken a chance on me, so I worked to keep his chains snubbed, the slack out of those cleats, his gaffs holstered, his ice iced, and everything else he wanted.

One day, after work, I got off the elevator and I could see, way down at the other end, the little girl who lived across the hall, sitting on the floor, locked out, again. She was nine with a mom probably wronger than mine. Jay-Z was rocking in my headphones and the long smooth hallway smelled like old mop and fried onions. I slipped off the headphones and stepped lightly, listening. I pictured the floor see-sawing, then dropping away. In my stomach I could feel how it'd be: all of us on seven kind of lifted together like wishes off a dandelion: Old Leopold practicing trumpet in ran-down Adidas and alligator pajamas, still pretending like he ain't heard the news, that little boy Lopez tapping a soccer ball off his heel like it's on a leash, Ms. B carrying around an old Campbell's soup can calling, "someone want this grease?," the old heads playing spades at their table, and the strange part was that no one was unhappy, considering.

When I got closer, I saw that the girl was eating cornstarch from a box. White powdered her chin. My key was turning the lock when I thought I'd better ask her inside to wait. Inside was half upside down. Odds and ends that hadn't been there that morning were at my feet: a couple dug-up plants from somebody's garden, too many fistfuls of still-good relish packets, and a stroller—one of those ones they got for running the baby—sleeping, a tall orange cone in it. I stepped around the mess and went in my room to change into dry clothes.

My mother—the one I call Excuse—will inch the socks off your sleeping feet and I knew at once something of mine was missing, but I felt I was better off not knowing what she took until I needed it since it was gone now and wouldn't be coming back, whatever it was. I put on button-fly Levi's, Converse, and a red hoody. Back in the living room, Maeya stood at the window.

"Where's your mom?" I asked.

"Out." Maeya shrugged, unfazed.

She watched me as I gathered up my crabber's gloves and yellow waders and CD player and locked them in my trunk. "You don't go to school?" she asked.

"They put me out."

"You must be bad," she said, looking me over.

"The principal got robbed."

Her mouth went slack. "Stop playing."

"Psyche," I said. "They got me for eating pop tarts in the bathroom."

"That's it?"

"I'm tired of school anyway. They always on you to write something. Even after you do your answers. They'll even take your scratch paper."

I walked to the window to see what she was looking at. Outside there were workmen everywhere. Some dudes in hardhats were wrapping columns in something. There was a trailer marked D E M O L I T I ON. Further off, other men in masked space helmets held blowtorches over manhole covers. I have no idea why. Even Animal Control was out there unloading cage traps from a van.

"Dag," I heard myself whisper, "they getting ready."

"They're sure in a hurry for something," she said.

"If they gonna get rid of us, they better do it before it gets hot."

"What's the difference?"

"It'll be whatever then, Crayola. People stay upset for nothing when it's hot."

"They're upset now."

"Upset crazy. Not upset bawling."

From seven, the concrete square below looked split by green spider legs of grass, all hairy and tall. We could see people clutching plastic bags or humping boxes. Every so often, people would stop and huddle, shaking their heads, hugging—might've even been crying—before stepping through that grass. They did not seem to be in a hurry, but kept on, going away. Some of these people I'd known my whole life and watching them gave me a funny feeling, like I was looking at something I might miss later.

"It must not have been as bad as everyone said," Maeya said.

"Or we got used to it."

She pressed her forehead against the window, looking

down. "I've been waiting for them to say it's all been a big mistake, they didn't mean it and everyone can come back now."

"They're not gonna say that," I said.

"I know," she said. "But they should."

"You think so, huh?"

"I mean, don't they feel bad putting people out?" She turned back to me.

I stepped away, rubbing the cold out of an elbow acting like it thought it was still outside. "You don't ask the hamster spinning the wheel when he's had enough."

She squinted at me, lost. She had a round face and little porcelain saucers for eyes. They were the kind of gentle eyes a little girl is supposed to have.

I stretched out on the couch. I hadn't realized how tired I was. That Rent-A-Center left-behind was just right. I reached under the couch and grabbed two comic books, one Fantastic Four, one Hulk. I felt good, happy even. People had a lot to say about me and my comic books. Excuse said I was too old for them, but I'd never seen her read anything. Other people said comics ain't real, but what I need real for? I had plenty of that right outside my door. Basically, people'll tell you anything, if you let them. I closed my eyes. The heel and pitch of the boat were still under me.

Even now, with a whole bunch of cyclone fencing around the nothing where our home used to be, people still feel sad the way Maeya felt sad then, tattooing FHP Forever on their arms or necks. That was funny to me—inking up your body with a place that doesn't even exist anymore. I guess they thought it'll make 'em feel a little less empty for the people that used to be there. My Nana called it nostalgia, like worrying about the Colts all these years later.

All of us—me, Excuse, Maeya—picked up and dragged ourselves to my Nana's on the west side, which is where all this mess started. By then Maeya had been staying with us during those last weeks before they blasted our building to the ground. Nana said she'd get custody of Maeya when someone started asking, but no one ever did.

•••••••••••

Nana was sixty-three, worked for Social Security, and drank a prune-gin cocktail before taking out her teeth each night. At night the teeth slept grinning, ready to talk, in the water glass on Nana's bathroom sink. I'd stayed with Nana before—once when I missed a lot of kindergarten and the school sent the police and declared Excuse unfit. Duh. Once when I was eight and Excuse had me steal razors from Safeway and they caught me. Once a couple years ago after this Mexican maid at the Quality Inn let me hold that room with a Jacuzzi for nothing until I got found out. Bunch of other reasons I can't remember right now. Nana was Excuse's mother, but they weren't nothing alike. Nana's is where you went when you wanted someone to ask what you wanna be when you grow up. She was never one of those pinch-your-cheek grandmas, but she looked after me and took pride in her house, hanging the windows with beige lace, feather-dusting the good china, which never came out the cabinet anyway, vacuuming when there was nothing to vacuum. She could cook too. Pans of lasagna, baked macaroni and cheese, big gravied roasts she served on egg noodles. And you didn't have to play sick to get any of it.

About Excuse, Nana'd say she uses the toilet on us just like spelling her name. I think Nana wanted to be free of her daughter and I was the thing that stopped her. Nana never said this. It's what I thought was all.

No one believed Excuse's promises about getting herself together once we were on the west side 'cause she never had herself together over east. That first week, though, we were counting our own shadows 'cause Excuse had trouble running her little outside scams and she'd steal the soap bar out the shower to try to sell it.

It might've been the second or third night after we got to Nana's. We sat around, trying to act normal. Maeya was messing with a rainbow hula-hoop Nana had brought home. Nana sat in her recliner, working the crossword. Excuse was smoking at the window and I could see Nana clocking her over the top of the opened newspaper. There was a sour-sounding piano in the living room that Nana claimed Excuse could play once, but I'd never believed it.

I stepped over to the piano. "Play me a song, Ma."

Excuse acted like she hadn't heard me.

"You can't play, can you?"

She blew smoke out the window.

"Nana, she can't play," I said.

"She loved that piano. She was the only one that could play," Nana said. "Scott Joplin, Fats Waller, even some Bartok."

I pressed down a handful of keys. It jangled like an old toy. "You got jokes, Nana."

"I wish I did," Nana said, working the crossword.

I opened the bench lid and looked at the thin books of sheet music, the old scribbled notes on some pages. "I don't care what Nana says. I don't think you can play," I said.

"And you can stop, Franklin, OK? I got enough to forget without you bringing shit up, but there you go asking about a piano." She twisted her cigarette into the brick sill outside and left it there.

I closed the seat lid again.

"It was a long time ago," Excuse said, getting up. "I played then. I don't now. What you wanna kick a can? I can't change nothing what happened. You ain't Chopin yourself."

She walked into the hall and was out there with her hands on her lower back for a minute trying to get herself together when she called me over, away from Nana and Maeya. We stared at each other, neither of us speaking. Then she said, "I'ma need something."

I kept quiet.

She said softly, "You know it's different over here. I don't know these people like that."

"What you expect—a marching band?" I said. "They out there, jamming."

"I'm in the hole with that little crew already. I need help. I'm going sick."

"I ain't got no money," I lied.

She searched my face, playing back the words in her ear. Then she said, "Can you ask your man Alvin to front you something?"

I let my gaze rest on Excuse's face. It wasn't a pretty face anymore: a bony jaw, a droopy lower lip, two scheming dusty eyes. She could be charming or ugly, depending. This was charming.

"Can you do that for me, Franklin?" she said.

"I ain't seen him."

"I'm quite sure he's on his little strip or whatever."

I cut a quick glance over at Nana. She was still eased back in her recliner, snapping her newspaper, making little humming sounds. "Then ask him yourself," I said.

"He don't know me from Ronald Reagan." This was a favorite phrase of hers, even when it wasn't true.

I'd known Alvin from all those times at Nana's. We'd clicked since the fourth grade. Six months might pass without seeing him, then next time, there he was, a bouncy little guy with a smile so full of golds it stayed lit in there. We battled about anything—who could burp loudest, who had the nicest crossover, who choked on that first Newport and who didn't, who could sweet talk a seven out the dice, who went harder, east side or west. I kept a box cutter up in the cupboard above the fridge and now I reached up and slipped it in my pocket. When my coat went on, Nana plucked off her glasses, fed up. At the door I told Excuse, "Stay here."

Nana's was an old street, sunken in its middle like the power lines above, dip-strung, party-ribboned end to end, one block after the next. I walked up to the carryout with the sign that said Mel's but everyone called Up Top. Two boys, almost yellow under the streetlights, were posted up outside the store. I didn't recognize them and I had to think if I really wanted to ask these corner boys anything. I stepped in front of one. "You seen Alvin?"

The boy was blowing into his hands. A Bin Laden coat swallowed him. On his head, a blue bandana. His eyes were empty. "You gonna make his money right?"

"I don't know nothing about that," I said.

He sized me up, sucked his teeth. "Yeah, you look like short money."

I took him for one of those clowns that'll come at you sideways just to impress his friends. In my pocket I felt for the switch on the box cutter. I started to say, "Tell him—"

"You can't read?" He undid his bandana and wrapped it again, knotting it off in the back. "Yo' illiterate," the boy laughed, doubling over.

I didn't move. Then I saw the white letters behind and above him eating into the red brick: RIP Alvin. Inside me something skipped and dropped away. I backed up slowly, then turned and started up the empty street. A necklace of unlit doorways, boxy and empty, stretched up the block. Then I thought of his sister. I had not seen her for a long time, but remembered Alvin saying she'd gone to Philly to go to college for hair and I knew she must be tore up, where ever she was. Later, I'd find out some of what had happened—he'd messed up somebody's money, wouldn't get low when most would've—but none of it mattered. Alvin had always wanted to be hard. Now he was gone and it didn't get any harder than that.

Back at the house, Excuse was sitting outside on the steps, arms clasped over her knees, rocking. When she saw me, she popped up. "What you got?"

"Nothing," I brushed past, opened the door and stepped into the house.

"Nothing?" She was on my hip. "What you mean?"

"Alvin ain't there."

"What about them others down there—you tell 'em you cool wit him?"

I stared at her wordlessly. "Alvin. Ain't. There," I whispered, biting off each word.

"Oh shit," she said, catching something final and done in my voice.

"Yeah," I said. "Tish ho."

"He wasn't no older than you," she said.

I put my coat on a hanger in the closet. Behind me I heard Excuse say to no one in particular, "It's rough out here."

I paused in the hollow of that closet, soft coats against my face. When I turned around, she was squared up with me and that lemme-hold-a-dollar hunger was back in her eyes.

"Let me have that little radio of yours," she said. "I'll pay you for it after."

"You can't have my CD player," I said, trying to brush her off.

"Then I'll just take Maeya down the store."

I laughed. "Yeah, OK."

"I'll have her back in five minutes."

"Or five days."

"You just being stingy now."

I turned and hooked her elbow. "Ain't I always?"

She wrenched free, started clawing her neck, screeching "Am I gonna be alright? Am I gonna be alright? Am I gonna be alright?" Spit, like sparks, flew from her lips. I saw Maeya coloring with markers, spying the whole thing. I saw Nana, still resting in her recliner, set down the newspaper. Then I did the thing I swore I wouldn't: I gave Excuse twenty dollars from my check I cashed the day before. The whole time I was thinking Barnacle Bob might as well be paying me in salt-water shivers for all this. I just wanted her out of the house. She snatched the money and was gone.

I stepped outside and watched her cut across the street and disappear around the corner. A sharp wind shaved the block of row houses. There'd be times she wouldn't come back for days. I used to worry she might be gone for good, but I learned that Excuse always made it home. Might forget her own birthday but she knew how to find home.

I closed the door. The house felt suddenly quiet. I let myself tip back, shoulders resting against the wall. Nana had been sitting on her purse. Now she stood, dug in her wallet, pulled out a twenty, walked it over and squeezed it into my hand. I accepted it silently.

I could tell you how awful it was having a mother who's a fiend, but I've accepted it. I could tell you it's just one side of her, but it's not. I could tell you that she wouldn't do anything for five dollars, but she would. I could tell you that when I was little and I needed her like I don't now, she loved me enough to stop, but she hadn't. I could tell you that I never saw this happening to Alvin, but I guess I had. I could tell you that when Excuse started running the streets over here, doing her little shiesty dirt, that the dude she hooked up with wasn't all bad, but Amon was.

Excuse introduced me to Amon this way. I was folding a bundle of clean laundry Nana had left on the couch. They came in together. Over her shoulder, Excuse said, "This a friend of mine," and breezed past, clattering down the hall, into the bathroom where she shut the door. Excuse wore a lot of noisy hoop bracelets, which she thought made her look legit.

I turned to face him. He was big and missing one eye. This surprised me, but I concentrated on keeping my gaze level, pretending he had two good eyes and one wasn't all milky with little smeary folds and creases that looked like they might be hissing.

I said, "Who are you?"

"The one and only, Amon." It sounded like an apology.

"Why is it the one and only?"

"Why is what?"

"Why is it the one and only?" I asked again.

He stepped into the kitchen, real smooth, like it was his house and always had been and he was helping himself to whatever. He came right out, holding a can of peaches that had been in the cupboard, and talking again. "How you gonna ask me a question like that?" he said.

I shrugged and continued separating clothes. I saw then that Nana had bought Maeya a lot of new clothes: Hollister Jeans, a yellow American Eagle sweatshirt, socks with moons on them.

"Well, how many people you ever been around named Amon?" he asked.

"No one, I guess."

"Now, if you knew that you'd never known anyone named Amon then why'd you ask the question?" He had a goofy way of talking, like his mouth was a gurgling drain, glub glub glub.

"Just something I said, I guess."

He stepped a few steps closer and a sweet smell of talc came with him. "You went and fucked up the origin, is what you did."

I felt my back stiffen. I said, "I just never heard a name like that before."

"It was my people's inspiration. My people are from Togo."

You never knew who Excuse might bring in. In general, she was the type of person that could get you hurt—put you in the middle of something you got nothing to do with. But this jackass beat all. He was wild looking. Everything on Amon was too big. His hands were too big, his belly was too big, and his red, flappy-eared, peanut head was too big. He had to cock his face to get any seeing out of his one good eye.

"You know about Togo?"

"No."

"Then speak up, boy. Don't sit there like you Mr. National Geographic or some shit."

My feet shifted a little.

He made a couple clucking sounds. "Think you slick. Your mom must notta raised you right."

"What's she got to do with it?"

"That ain't some soup du jour. That's your mother."

"And I raised myself," I said.

"Togo's in Africa," he went on, cutting me off. "It was German. A colony of it. That's what they called it anyway. A colony. Make it sound more proper for when they take yo' shit. Comes to the same thing anyway. When your tea leaves and spices ain't yours no more 'cause the laws they made said so, don't nobody care what you call it." Now he began to raise his voice. "Yes, indeed. You looking at a hybrid. Dues paid. For keeps. Sweetened by the taker and the tooken."

I was quiet, but in my head I was thinking, wasn't they German in that movie they showed at school, the one where the dude saved the Jews? And this jackass didn't look nothing like them. But I kept folding and didn't say squat.

I heard the top pop on that little can of peaches and looked up. He sipped the syrup first, keeping the rim close to his lips, and lasering that one eye into me. "I expect you one of those ain't no use explaining nothing to, ain't you?" he said, smacking those peaches.

We watched each other, waiting. When I did not answer, he flicked his face at me, and spoke through his teeth, "Thought not." Then he turned and pounded down the hall, "Diane!"

•••••••••••

A few days later, I came home from work and when I glanced out the window I saw Maeya standing in the alley. I clanged down the back metal steps. She was holding a shoebox. She stood beside some old tires and a torn mattress with popping springs. "What're you doing?" I asked.

"Looking for a butterfly," Maeya said.

I breathed in. Spoiled milk soured the air. Junk was everywhere.

"It was from school. I had it in here." She offered me the shoebox. Dime-sized holes had been cut on top. "Amon threw the whole thing out," she said, pointing up to the window.

"Why'd he do that?"

"Said we don't need no bugs in the house," she said.

I stood there, mad.

"It was red and black," she said.

I followed her as she picked her way deeper into the alley, stepping over a fan and plastic milk crate, looking behind a box spring. Then she stopped, turned around, straining to see between the spaces in all that junk. Her hands flapped out from her side and fell back.

"C'mon now," I said, "let's go in the house."

We started towards the mouth of the alley. "My teacher told us they don't taste good to birds," she said, hopefully.

Inside, Maeya sat down on the living room couch and I put on Oprah. I checked the rooms for Amon; he was gone. I dropped onto a cushion beside Maeya. Oprah was talking to dieters. These people had been on some crazy diets. They'd show a before picture of some humongous man and then some skinny dude would walk out and everyone would clap.

"Do you think my mother hates me?" Maeya asked.

"No," I said. "She loves you."

"She hasn't come looking for me, in case you hadn't noticed."

"She knows you're safe."

"She knows where I am?"

"Yes."

"Did she ask you to take me?"

"When you were staying with us all those nights and she didn't say nothing—that was like her asking."

Maeya seemed to think hard about this. "That's when my mom knew I was across the hall. Now we're over west."

"You don't like Nana's cooking?"

"No, I do."

"Doesn't Nana keep your hair done?"

"Yes, she does."

"You'd rather be with your mom somewhere?"

"Not when she's dropping me at different people's houses all the time. Her little while never is."

I didn't say anything. On the television Oprah was cheesing for some man that had lost a hundred and thirty seven pounds. "He did good," Maeya said.

"Listen," I said, "did you know that your mom and mine are just alike?"

She squinted at me. "Sort of."

"Oh, yeah. They have a lot in common."

"Like what?"

"Well, for one thing, they're both un-moms."

"What's an un-mom?" she asked.

"It's a mom that can't be a mom right now but might be a mom again later."

"Oh," she said.

We were silent.

"You have a un-mom?" she asked.

"Biggest in town."

"For how long?"

"Pretty much always, might as well say."

"Aren't you mad?"

"Used to be."

"Used to be?"

"I decided I can live with a mom that ain't a mom."

"Well, I'm mad," Maeya said.

"You gotta right."

She was quiet.

"It lasts long?" she asked.

I didn't have the heart to say long enough to make waiting for a normal life pointless, which is what I was thinking, so I just said, "Sometimes."

She was biting her lower lip. Oprah was talking about miracle berries and bloating.

"You know I used to fight for my mother?" The memory seemed sad and funny now and I felt a grunting snort come up. "Other kids would get to talking about her, calling her monkey fiend, or Junkie Diane, or whatever and I'd take up for her. I'd be out there, seven years old, scrapping in the street 'cause someone said she smelled like dukey, which she probably did."

Maeya was quiet.

"I was never too young for anything. That's just how she carried it," I said. "I wish somebody woulda pulled me up back then and told me: this woman's not changing for nothing."

"Who would've known that?"

"No one, I guess." I brushed some dirt off my tennis shoes and felt a sigh go out of me. "It's just something you tell yourself in your head."

We were quiet for a time.

Then Maeya asked, "How'd my mother look when you told her I was gonna come stay with you and Nana?"

"What d'you mean?"

"You know, did she have her regular game face on and everything?"

"Oh, that," I said. "No, not at all. She got real sad."

"Is that all?"

"You could tell, it just hurt her real bad. But she was glad too 'cause she knows Nana keeps a good home."

Maeya was quiet. The truth is I admired the little girl. At her age, I was already half-sprung. This child hardly frowned. Might be scared of Freddy Kruger, but she was ready for whatever the world put on her.

I looked at her. "You alright?"

She nodded.

I held out my fist. "FHP."

I waited.

Then she balled her little fist, extended it and we tapped knuckles. "FHP," she said.

•••••••••••

Everything looked different from the water. In the harbor the boats were shiny with linseed or resin, bobbing in their slips, and the light on the water was creased and flinty and the skyscrapers behind were struck glassy with sunlight and the city looked like a postcard a tourist might buy, and not at all like a place where anything could happen. Then as the boat moved further out, drawing a tail of foamy wake, the harbor spread out and the picture held your whole view and it could seem like a place you might leave one day, if you knew how, or someone showed you.

Barnacle Bob called himself an old salt and I guess that's how he talked too. When we got to the crab pots, he'd shift down to the little trolling motor and come out of his little pilothouse and start plucking my nerves with his sing-songy directions, Swing to now. Drop the brailer. Hook that float. Now heave. He would say the same thing three, five, seven times. His voice would be low and steady, like something he learned in church, and after a while it would seem like his little sayings were keeping time with the water.

There were heavy seeping chains and small anchors and big crab pots. These I hoisted up, hand over hand. Every time I dropped a pot or pulled up another coil of chains, Barnacle Bob was right there with Swing to now. And it was kind of funny, but his talk did sort of help you bring the weight up and over the edge and on to the deck.

And Barnacle Bob knew that bay like I knew the streets. He'd look at the moon and tell you about the tide, listen to the water against the hull and tell you about the wind, tell you what trap was coming from which side way before you got your first glimpse of blue marker buoy, tell you where the grasses grew underwater from how the water sat, smell the wind and guess just where the northerlies would've dried out the marshes. He probably could've done it all stone blind. He didn't fool with charts or sounding devices or tide tables. He knew the shoals and where the channels played out because he'd always known them. And if anyone ever cut his traps, Barnacle Bob was ready for blood.

Sometimes the pots were more or less empty, or had only a few eels, which we'd use for bait, and Barnacle Bob would get heated and start talking down the winter dredgers or the algae that had no business growing in the water or the government trying to keep him on the beach. But he didn't stay mad. It was like Barnacle Bob hadn't made up his mind about everything yet, which probably explained why he'd hired me to begin with, 'cause I know I looked like a roughneck bopping through his door that first time.

If the pots were empty, we'd drive out Route 1 to buy Barnacle's Catch from the freezers at Sysco. Along the way, he'd be playing Hank Garland or Chet Atkins in his truck and it was as if those empty pots out on the water had been someone else's. With his moon face and yellow beard and the sling shots going half up his back, Barnacle Bob was like something out of one of my comic books, except he never really wanted to get even with anybody.

One day we were far out and when I snagged the last float for the last pot and pulled it in, it was empty like the others before it. It had been another bad day, the fourth in a row. I reset the bait box with fresh chicken necks, raised it to the edge, and listened for Barnacle Bob's swing to now as I set the pot in the water and paid out the line. Then Barnacle Bob did something unusual. He cut the engine and let the boat drift. He was quiet and didn't seem in the mood for talking. I sat down on the rusty water breaker and zipped up my fleece hoody. Using my clenched teeth, I tightened my gloves and then crossed my arms against the cold. The bay was empty in every direction. There was little current. I felt that something might be wrong, like Barnacle Bob was hurting somehow and it made me feel bad forever wishing his pots be light.

Barnacle Bob stood looking out beyond the stern. In the open water, drifting, time felt slowed.

"The sky looks funny, sitting on the water like that," I said.

He did not answer for a time. "I suppose it does."

"What's out there?" I asked.

"A few shore towns gone so broke they're more mud hens than people," he said, still without turning around.

"What if you keep going?"

"You'll be in the Atlantic."

"And then, after that?"

"The rest of the world."

The weather was turning. The sky was paper-mâchéd in gray, a thousand shades of gray. It would be dead winter soon and the crabs would dig in and go in their holes and Barnacle Bob would pack it in 'til spring because he didn't believe in dredging. For a time, we drifted, listening to the bay slapping softly against the quarters. Then I said, "It's a long ways from here?"

He had turned back to me. "What's that?"

"The rest of the world."

•••••••••••

Amon came to the back door, pounding. Excuse started for it, but I headed her off. "Don't bring him in here again," I said.

"What you getting ready for tea and crumpets?"

Nana had been watching Jeopardy, but now she was up, steady crossing the room towards us. I felt like Nana was aging before our eyes. She looked a hundred and three.

"I don't like him," I said.

"Sit your tail down," Excuse said. "He ain't no harm to nobody."

"No more than you," Nana said. "And that's enough for anybody."

"Whatever," Excuse hissed.

He pounded the door again. Nana moved forward and slid back the dead bolt and pulled the knob. Stone-faced, Amon filled the doorway, one arm on the jamb.

"You'll have to take your good times outside, sir," Nana said. "There are children in this house." The door clicked shut again.

On the way out, Excuse wheeled on me. "That's the problem with you: you always think you better than somebody."

•••••••••••

Sometimes I sang Maeya to sleep with "I Believe I Can Fly" or "I'm Not Your Average Girl on the Video." I can sing a little bit, but only Maeya would know it. This night I didn't feel like singing so I was searching for a good radio station. I'd gotten tired of 92 Q playing the same songs.

She said, "You're like my father, Franklin."

"I'm not your father, Maeya."

"I think so."

"Sixteen's not old enough to be a father."

"Yes, it is."

"Not yours."

"Then why do you hold my hand when we get on the bus?"

"So you don't fall and bust your ass and everyone laugh at you."

"Isn't that like a father?"

"No."

"I think it is."

"Look, Maeya, your father's in Jessup. You know that."

"So?"

"So quit geeking."

"But I don't even talk to him."

"That's still your father," I said.

"Not to me."

"And he probably gave you those good smarts," I said, "least you could do is act like you use 'em."

We were quiet while I fiddled with the radio dial. Bits of songs flew by.

"Amon says he knew my father."

"That fool'll say anything. He never knew your father."

"He said you act like you're grown when you're not."

I thought about how kids my age always think they're grown and want to tell anyone who'll listen. But I didn't think I was grown. Instead, I thought about getting older and what my life would be like then. But I didn't say any of this to Maeya. I said, "He could be two hundred, but that don't make him grown."

"He said he's gonna teach me to kiss, since I'm gonna be a woman soon."

I cut the radio off. "What?"

"'Someone's gotta show you how a woman be'," she put her hands on her hips and puffed out her chest, imitating the glub-glub-glub of Amon's voice. "A woman's gotta know how to enjoy herself."

I got up and walked a tight circle, my shirtfront in my teeth, cursing. Then I threw open a window and spat. I asked Maeya a bunch of other questions, but she didn't say much more and I just got madder anyway.

Afterwards she said, "You shouldn't cuss."

"Even that bastard knows better than talking like that to you."

"I don't pay Amon no mind."

I said, "You stay by me or Nana. Me or Nana. OK?"

She was quiet.

I took her hands in mine. "Did you hear me?"

"Yes," she said.

"You promise now?"

She nodded.

My bed had been in the very small room Nana always called a sewing room. Now I dragged my little mattress down the hall and into Maeya's bedroom. I plumped the pillows and arranged the bedding on the floor where I slept for a time after this. She watched me, her face still with worry. I hadn't meant to scare her.

"Look," I said, "Amon ain't right. Even when he does something nice—like gives you a whole box of Krispy Kremes, all your own—he's really just plotting on something else."

She said, "His eye—that ugly one—it looks funny."

"Somebody told him no."

••••••••••

The next day Amon came in from the back. I was in the kitchen, making a bologna and Miracle Whip sandwich.

"You can't be in here no more."

"Say who?"

"This not your house."

He looked at me, surprised. "What you tipsy?"

"Wouldn't matter if I was," I said.

"Your Mama's already gave it her blessings," he said, like that settled it.

"That ain't even how she talks," I said. "She ain't

church." I placed my sandwich back on the plate and set it on the counter. "So you can bounce."

"Oh, you big time now," he said. "You decided."

"Maeya doesn't need you anywhere near her. None of us do."

Suspicion twisted his face. "You must be planning on keeping her to yourself." He opened the refrigerator door, closed it and swung back to me, getting louder. "'Cause you sure enough not running, what, an orphanage in here?"

"I'll take that key." My voice had gone tight.

When he moved closer, you could feel his size in the floor. "Nine ain't what it used to be. Girls grow up fast nowadays." And then he laughed, throat like a train tunnel.

"You make me sick," I said.

"OK," I heard him say, swallowing a giggle. "Do you."

I never felt him hit me. First, I was standing; then laid out. Darkness pooled around me and the smell of bologna became electric, crackling and sputtering behind my eyes. I lay there, trying for breath. I heard him changing TV stations. Then I remembered the weight of his shoulder rolling towards me before the fist shot out. High in the chest is where he'd hit me.

When I got to my elbows, he came over and put a heel on my throat, flattening me. "I seen so much I gave one of these sum bitches back." And he pointed to the empty socket in his face. "You lucky I left you something to chew your food wit."

I got to my feet and started for the bathroom. I was up and walking, but I was shaky. At the sink I steadied myself before the mirror. My wind felt small; it made a little rattle. Slowly, I cranked my head, right, then left, until my breathing got easier. I had not expected a warning and there had been none. I opened the medicine chest; the reflection of my eyes swung past. There was a box of Band-Aids and some mouthwash. I didn't need Band-Aids or mouthwash.

I headed down to the corner where Alvin used to be. I thought of asking one of them that took his place to kill Amon, but didn't. Then I went looking for Maeya.

•••••••••••

The next day I didn't go to work. Barnacle Bob would have to do it without me. I did hope the crabs were running for him, but I wanted to be in the house when Maeya came in from school, which I was.

The sun was gone from the sky. It was getting to be time for dinner. I'd gotten paid the day before, so I had some money. Maeya was eating cornstarch from the box, a habit I hadn't been able to break her from. She looked bored, flicking jacks around her lap on the carpet.

"You keep eating that, you gonna turn into a ghost," I said. "Watch."

"I wanna bake a cake," she said.

I was getting mad. "Fix your face. You look a mess."

"What's wrong with you?" she asked.

"It's not food."

"You're acting funny." She sounded insulted. "And bossy."

"Yeah, well, maybe I got things on my mind."

She closed up the box and brushed off her mouth and cheeks. "Anybody can bake a cake," she said. "Just follow the recipe."

We were quiet.

"We don't have no eggs, anyway," I said. "I'm quite sure that recipe says eggs. I know that much."

"Chinese people deliver," she said.

"If you think I'm calling that Chinese man and asking him for two eggs."

"Why not?" she said. "I don't mind calling."

I forced out a long breath, pinching the bridge of my nose. Maeya could argue if four quarters made a dollar when she wanted to. "You a nuisance," I sighed, giving in. "Let's go get what we need."

We walked down to the corner store and bought all the ingredients in the recipe. By the time we got back and got started, Nana was home. Later, after Meaya's yellow sheet cake had cooled and she was icing the top and Nana dozed in her chair and the whole house smelled cake-sweet, I let myself fall into that butterscotched air where you could tell yourself nothing bad was going to happen.

I asked some dudes around the way about Amon. He'd done a lot of cruddy things. Stolen his uncle's methadone so he could sell him real dope. Called the fire department once faking concussion for an Advil. Ran in the Arabber's pockets and, when all he got was a peach pit and someone laughed, Amon killed the dude's sable-back horse right there; after that, was like a fruit drought hit the whole neighborhood. Always ready to mix in. Always wants a Newport but never has one for anybody else. Some of the old heads called him Mustah Bin, 'cause after Amon bled some poor bastard, it's always, Oh well, must've been meant to happen.

If I called the police on Amon, they'd come in here and take Maeya away, put her in some crazy foster home or group home or in DSS. Might even try to put me somewhere.

I thought of tricking Amon into coming out on the boat—telling him we can rob Barnacle Bob—then knocking Amon's big ass in the water. I doubted he could swim and no one would miss him. But I didn't think Barnacle Bob would appreciate me using his boat like that.

I wished so hard that something would happen to Amon, but nothing did. Life was like that. Amon could rob and steal and scheme and get over and nothing hardly happened to him. But Alvin tries to sell a few pills for back-to-school clothes, and he gets got.

•••••••••••

A day later I went down the back steps to where Amon always came in. I slipped into the alley, beside the steps.

I turned a metal trashcan upside down, pulled it into a sliver of darkness, away from the streetlight and sat. Patience filled me. I'd wait 'til next spring if it took that. I felt the grapple in my hand. It was iron, heavy, and had three small hooks. I did worry that I didn't have it in me to crack his skull, or that I wouldn't hit him hard enough and then he'd just burn me up with the revolver he kept in his dip. So many dudes say, "I don't care if I get shot. Live by, die by. Real knows real." But when they're on that sidewalk leaking out of themselves, they care. Crying for their Mama-God-ambulance, they care.

Hours passed and the sun went down and I set myself against these worries. There was an old head of cabbage under the steps and the rats ate from it, taking their time. And I got to wondering about the things I always wonder about: the stars of course and what's so great about this country that everyone wants to come here for anyway, and Nana's teeth in that water glass at night and what Alvin saw when that cap went in his nose—maybe it just feels like clicking off the TV, that sucking sound and everything shrink-popping black. And the rats came out deep, scurrying here and there and I could hear a TV from someone's house. It was a re-run of Martin.

Then I heard him, walking that shuffling walk, mumbling, re-living a bad turn he owed somebody. My ears pricked up. My breath dropped away. I bent my knees and clenched back the grapple with my moisty grip. I could feel blood thumping my head. He got so close I smelled that sweet powdery talc he wore and I saw his face emerging from a curtain of cigarette smoke, and at the last moment he turned that one good eye toward me and I swear I heard Barnacle Bob in my head.

"Swing to! Swing to! Swing to now!"

On Seeing Old Footage of Norman Snead Playing for the Philadelphia Eagles[1]

Brian Heston

Dad, he truly was a bum, a defenses'
dream, a knock-kneed, cockeyed excuse
for a quarterback. Just as you said,
when we sat and talked—you just back
from a ten-hour shift at Jeffrey and Manz,
me before running streets with "punks
up to no good." Snead, the thorn
of your twenties, mocking your faith
in the American Dream. Fleet
as cinder block in the pocket, crushed
every time he floated a duck, always
managing to get back to his feet,
jersey bloodied, ready to begin again.
"If the poor bastard had ever played
for someone who cared, he'd probably be
in the hall of fame," you said.
So how'd you do it? Five squawking kids,
another on the way, the 70s economy
an oozing wound. Days spent
in summer heat, lumbering up and down
Chestnut and Walnut in gaudy,
almost out of style suits, begging for work
from "big mahoffs" sitting behind
shiny nameplates. Week after week:
light and gas unpaid, meals of cornflakes

and fried baloney, winter stalking
in the air. I remember none of it,
the baby you held your ears against,
screaming you awake whenever
you managed to sleep. Then there was Snead
every Sunday with his failure,
leaving you to sit alone nights
in the kitchen when the house
finally quieted, unshaven face buried
in your hands, wondering when life
would grow tired of kicking your ass.

[1]A version of this poem was published in the Spring 2012 edition of *Philadelphia Stories* under the title "Clip of Norm Snead Playing for the Philadelphia Eagles."

Sep Tepy (The First Time)[1]
Caitie Barrett

If we assume two things—one, that the best place to start is the beginning, and two, that the Heliopolitan Cosmogony is accurate—then we ought to start with an androgynous figure masturbating. That was how Atum created the universe, and it makes sense, after all; if one's cosmogony relies upon a single creator deity, then what more ready way to do the job? So let's start, then, with the mound of creation, a dark wet pile of earth emerging from the chaos waters. On top of this mound Atum has come into being and he is taking care of what he has to do.

First all the universe is contained inside one being, and then it's splattered all over the place, like the mirror-glass mosaics of Isaiah Zagar. All over South Street, walls explode out at the sun in glittering fragments, and yet stay intact. Covered in reflections of the city and the sky as seen from every angle, the wall is revealed, after all, to contain both the city and the sky.

We're all sitting in fractured, glittering Philadelphia smoking a hookah in Leila's Café, and the smoke (apple mint, the tastiest of the flavors) provides a sort of glue sticking the fragments back together. How soft and curving that smoke is, like the women in the imagination of 19th-century Orientalists! But Sir Richard Burton[2] would truly have been unable to contain his urge to create a universe if he had heard the conversation, which focused on Gina and her fiancé's recent decision to become polyamorous. The hookah is certainly polyamorous, anyway, penetrating everyone's mouths with equal abandon (except for mine; I put one of those disposable tips on the nozzle; Orientalist pastimes are no more likely to protect one from colds than is Communion wine). Gina's friend Dave has taken her hand, while her fiancé's brother chats with me. The café owner's daughter, who wears tight jeans and a blue headscarf and has a California accent, seems equal parts happy and dismayed.

Gina doesn't want to change her Facebook status to "Open Relationship" because she hasn't told her sister yet. By the time you're thirty, your Facebook wall becomes a mosaic of friends' babies' faces, small round eager things that blur, at thumbnail size, into soft ash-colored blobs like smoke rings, and then dissolve away again. At a distance these walls that Zagar treated, these sun-sharp multifaceted mirrors, are revealed as the compound eyes they are. The buildings must have always had such eyes, but it was only after Zagar made them visually explicit that we could tell. At what time will these insect-eyed creatures buzz away, up into the air, into the sun from which they came? At what hour will the city fly away from us?

Broken glass both inside and outside the museum: inside, where they broke into the vitrines, and outside, where they burned the cars and beat the protestors in Tahrir Square. The Cyclops eyes of news cameras have, more or less, closed by now. The compound fly-eye of the glass still stares open on the ground, though, constantly assaulted by the substance of the sun (the Greeks thought: we see objects because they constantly emit thin films that physically hit our eyes) and throwing that white sun-stuff back again.

No one does polyamory like gods, except perhaps for Muammar Qaddafi, whose "voluptuous Ukrainian nurse" has gone back to Kiev, while Ajdabiya burns. Even Jesus has his many brides, like Sister James and Sister Anthony at St. Anne's Preschool, who used to read the same story to us every day, about a bat trying to escape from hunters. I don't remember why the hunters wanted the bat anyway (how much meat could be on it?) but it was a very suspenseful story and always made the hour after snack time unnecessarily stressful.

Almost Easter, now. The river bank is burning with cherry blossoms, and it's almost time to go back to St. Paul's to share that yearly Middle Eastern meal. In Taposiris Magna they're looking for Cleopatra VII's tomb, even though they won't find it there; the ancient sources are quite clear on the location of the Ptolemies' mortuary complex in Alexandria. "Zowie" Hawass, as my parents call him, announced with great enthusiasm the project plans, in a video in which he calls his impending revelation of Cleopatra's burial, "the greatest discovery of all time." Entombed at her side they expect to find her Ukrainian nurse, Mark Antony.

Elizabeth Taylor's grave is in Glendale, California, and Richard Burton (the Orientalist) and Richard Burton (Mark Antony) can meet up, if they like, to share a hookah in St. Paul's Café. *If you lose your one true love,* says the traditional Scottish song, *you will surely find another, / Where the wild mountain thyme / grows around the blooming heather.* The Egyptian gods are famous, of course, for their numerous forms. Semele asked to see the true form of god; and so she did. It was fire.

And as for Dionysus: he was born in blood, of course. Ah, well, who wasn't? With him it was merely a bit more obvious, torn from his father's raw thigh. I suppose we all feel somewhat out of place in all the substitute wombs we find.

Dionysus the wine god: and don't those Sufi poets praise god constantly by invoking drunkenness? Indeed, the linkage of intoxication and religious ecstasy would appear to be cross-cultural; has there ever been a society that eschewed intoxicants? None that I've found yet, and I've been looking for a while. If it isn't liquor, it's tobacco, or herbal substances, or God knows what. Beloved, Beloved, you surpass all wine.

One could square the circle if Mary were to be the one to destroy the body of her son, to rip it up, the way Agave does. But she doesn't do so—no. Wine in the cup, and that is blood; bread for flesh, like *sparagmos*. I never drank that wine, not even at my first communion. My mom was afraid that I would catch a cold from the other children, and after all, wasn't she right? I could have done. The mother knew better than the priest; but, after all, that's always true. It was true of Mary, wasn't it? And of Agave, too.

It seems like it must be nice to be a polyamorist. But then again, it also seems rather unpleasant. As for me, my Beloved is mine, and I am my Beloved's. Pass me more of that burning, iron-tasting wine. They say that Californian wines exceed the French; in fact, the Judgment of Paris[3] decided it. Does that then make the United States equivalent to Aphrodite? I like it, I like it; everyone's Beloved, why, the sacred whore. I like it, I like it. But all the same, it isn't fully true.

The old country laborer, passing me in Alexandria, grinned and asked, "How much?" I gave him the finger, only afterwards realizing that the gesture might not transfer cross-culturally; perhaps he was thinking, "Only one pound? Wallahi, what a deal!" But what's to be done? Many pretty girls in Cairo wear sparkly veils that only half-hide their hair. Most of my boyfriends prefer to wear a veil of words: each syllable glittering, like mirrored tesserae. Sometimes you see yourself in them, and sometimes you see the whole design. Sometimes you see both at once, but that's a rarity, much to be cherished, like simultaneous orgasm.

The first question I got at my interview for the Cornell professorship was, "How does your work engage with Edward Saïd?" In Luxor I was looking for a birthday present for my dad when I came upon a stuffed goldfish, modeled after the main character in *Finding Nemo*, which played Arabic pop songs when you pushed its stomach. Of course I bought it;

as the man at the souvenir shop said when I tried to bargain down the price, "But it's *Nemo!*"

Running along the Schuylkill River's mirrored glass in
spring, you pass numerous geese with half-grown babies. In
a New Kingdom love poem from Papyrus Harris 500, migra-
tory birds appear as images of the soul. A girl goes hunting
for birds down by the river, and accidentally catches her
own soul. As for me, I don't want to make them angry; when
they have young they are notoriously mean. The baby souls
ripple the water, swimming carefully in line. Drops of flying
water, each a tiny little magnifying glass—when I was a
small child I thought I was the first person who had ever
noticed the magnifying effect of water drops. Glittering river, mirror water, Zagar's walls dissolved—well, good then,
keep on at it, little fuzzy souls.

[1] *Sep Tepy*: "the first time" (Hieroglyphic Egyptian). In Egyptian
religious texts, *sep tepy* refers particularly to the moment of the creation
of the universe.

[2] Richard Francis Burton (1821–1890): British explorer, captain in
the East India Company, and translator of various Arabic and Sanskrit
texts, including the *Kama Sutra* and *The Perfumed Garden of the Shaykh
Nefzawi*.

[3] A wine competition held in Paris in 1976, at which Californian
wines swept all categories.

Thank You for Mixing with My Emotional Circuitry

CAConrad

rollercoasters are
my favorite form of
transportation

what is bribery
in poetry going
to prove?

pluck me out
of my gown
throw me
against your song

I claim a hundred feet of
air above
my head

a murmur of sparrows
flies in flies out keeping
me nauseous with love
making use
of tiny instruments
needing their
music absorbed

HOW DARE
the mayor of
Philadelphia refuse
our collective joy of
rollercoasters
over buses

tally your
math again
I love being a
statistic involving
spun sugar on a stick
and instability

counted upwards
of a thousand
drops of saliva

we can read
ANYTHING
go out and read
the engine's cold
throttle left over
night in one
position

love came
breathing
against me I did not
mind the captivity

elevating these
harmed avionics
of the brain
climbING the track
ROARing downhill
reborn through the S-curve

the extortion of poetry
an opera mounting
the bed sheets we
won't stop it when
we know we must

my critical review of
your little daisy staring
staring staring staring
STARING until it grows

Excerpts from Undeliverables: Prose poem postcards

Jacob A. Bennett

Little pinprick, little leaklight: so much dissipates in the wake; so much accumulates in a delay. A wink become a nova become just another patch of darkness. The wind was up a little today and I was watching a flake of mica vibrate, a loose tooth-filling aching to free from igneous pebble, and its little dance was brighter than the sun—if reflected, if minuscule—and I was watching a single iridescent insect wing flashing rainbows, veined and brittle, a little plastic smudge of oil—the greedy vestiges of little black bulges that spin webs and crystals and leave them.

The Drunkest Three-Year-Old in the Room

Amanda Erin Stopa

Here comes a school of them right now—
Just look at em! They are sooo wasted
they have to be strung along on a guide rope,
one walking like Frankenstein, another like he's on
    Broadway.
These addicts can't take two steps in the same direction
    without
falling all over the place. And it's only noon.
And that one's wearing a tutu, on a Monday.
I'm going to guess she's coming off a weekend long bender;
looking mighty sloppy. And look—
over by that fountain, those two kids are so hammered—
running, trying to climb over each other up the backside
of a copper goat. But oh, it looks like their little drunk
    girlfriend
is a bit of a downer, possibly cross faded the way she's
    kicking around
the grass, yelling at her Velcro shoes. Loose cannon.
But the drunk I love most is the one who is finding his legs
for the first time. Unashamed at how he wobbles, arms
    reaching
towards his intention, the blonde woman cooing through
picket fence teeth, he takes his first steps to sobriety.

At Night I Smoke

Dutch Godshalk

At night I stand in the street and smoke
among rows of dormant cars, and all dark
save for sporadic twitching television hues
in third floor windows like the last heavy
winks of eyelids fighting sleep. When rain
leaves dry spheres under uncut trees,

when the doors dead-bolted and the
street lamps wane a bit and the neighbors
upstairs stop pushing furniture around,

I stand in the street and spread my arms
wide and smoke facing the line of sky where
a far off forest's edge cuts into the horizon

and red lit radio towers pulse like postured
strings of Christmas bulbs and the stars all
strain and shoulder each other to be seen.

In the night as breath and smoke converge
and rise I stand centered amid arrested life
and say nothing, dreaming of sleep.

Naked and Hungry

Kelly George

The first time you saw me naked, I was standing in front of the refrigerator. I'd gotten up in the middle of the night to get something to eat. It was pitch black except for the refrigerator light glaring out at me, illuminating my naked body as I hunched into the fridge to see what was inside. It was in that tiny kitchen in West Philadelphia, with the cracked linoleum floors and the tin-topped kitchen table.

I thought you were sleeping, so I didn't bother putting my clothes back on. Sure, we'd already had sex, but not so many times that I'd let you get a good look at me. Always, there'd been partial clothing or sheets or fast getaways. You, on the other hand, you couldn't wait to be naked in front of me. I remember you stood next to our first pre-coital bed and tore off your underwear as you asked, "Is this OK?" You were naked and lying next to me before I could answer.

This was back when I still went to your apartment with legs and armpits clean-shaven. I still surveyed the six or so moles on my body that grow very long hairs and dutifully kept them plucked clean for you. I protected you from my sulfurous morning breath and always darted to the bathroom to brush my teeth before we'd go again.

This was back when you were a bachelor whose bathroom window was a broken pane of glass. Your front door wouldn't shut, much less lock. You dried oranges and other fruits in paper bags all around the apartment because there was no one there to object to the strangeness of it or the potential for mold.

When I heard your footsteps on that old wood floor in the hallway, I considered hiding behind the refrigerator door, but it seemed childish, and there wasn't enough time anyway. Suddenly you were there, leaning against the door jamb, watching me.

I tried to pretend I was not at all bothered by your seeing me this way, and I went about my business as if there was nothing at all wrong with midnight snacking. (The idea of hiding my body or my eating habits from you seems ridiculous to me now. My body has performed most of its basest functions in your presence. I have retched out sobs and vomit at your feet.) But then, you looked at my naked body, its unruly ripples, my bulbous inner thighs. You looked at me, naked and holding a carton of milk, scavenging in the darkness for a bite of old cheese or a jar of peanut butter I could dip a finger into. You looked at this thing, my body, lit strangely by a small, dirty light bulb, and you began to smile that upside down smile of yours, where the corners of your mouth are turning down, but somehow it's a smile anyway.

You looked at me as if I were the Pacific Ocean, or a newborn baby, or the goddamned pyramids in Egypt.

"You're such a pretty girl," you said. Like you could hardly believe it. Like you were somehow proud and thankful all at once to God and me and refrigerator lights.

I stood up straight to meet your eyes. And suddenly, I wasn't hungry anymore.

Dog People

Maxime D. McKenna

Because I no longer have a yard, at least not a yard that suits me (not like the one we had back in Wyndmoor), and because I am not the type, yard or no yard, to stay cooped up indoors—not on an evening where the summer heat has mellowed and the sun is orangeing—because of these things, I've been sitting out on the stoop these days, making it the place where I can undo my belt, slouch, and let my belly unfurl onto my knees. Where I can drink Bacardi and Diet Coke from the tiki glass that Lana abhors. Where I can stare down the cars creeping past, looking for precious street parking while my station wagon sits in the middle of two perfectly good spots.

At this time of day, little things happen all on their own: dirty rain water drips through a sagging awning, and the breeze scatters glass, wrappers, and other detritus to reveal skeletal forms in the filth. And the stray cat, the longest, thinnest cat I've ever seen, comes out from under my station wagon to rub shyly against my back before I let it climb into my lap.

"Hey you," I say to the cat, rubbing my hand across it. "Hey cat. Hey puss. Hey kitty."

The cat isn't all that grimy for a stray. I'm not sure what to call it: it has that quality between an it and a she.

"Are you a Catrina or a Catherine?" I ask it. "Or do you prefer to be called Mrs. Cat? Or even maybe Dr. Cat?"

The cat meows. I like to imagine she was once gainfully employed in the cat world, as a college professor or a medical doctor. When she fell on hard times, she became depressed, and rightfully so. Given how introverted a cat is to begin with, she must have been real unpleasant, so her family put her out on the street. But she's ready to turn a new leaf, so I give her the respect she needs to get back on her feet. I tell her about what I'm reading. We converse. After all, isn't this why people keep cats in the first place?

"Tough times, huh? You want a snack?" I ask. "Wait here."

Inside, Lana is preparing dinner. There aren't enough hallways, not enough alternate routes in this townhouse; to get to the kitchen, I have to walk through the living room where the three dogs lounge like a plague. Why even have a sofa? Why not just spread some hay in front of the television and let whoever wants lie in it?

I rattle the ice remaining in my cup until Charlie, the pit bull, shoots his head up and begins to whimper.

"Is that you, King of The Street?" Lana calls. "How does everything look out there?"

I answer her question with one of my own. It's not that I don't hear her. That's just how we talk nowadays.

"What's cooking, Lan?"

"Don't you want to guess?

"Steak?"

"Quinoa salad and baked fish," she replies.

"Aha."

I step into the kitchen, grab her bony hips, and watch her denude a ratty carrot over the compost bin. Then I go into the fridge and reach into the back corner for a slice of turkey.

"You're not feeding that cat, are you?" she asks.

"Nope," I say, putting the lunchmeat in my pocket and filling my glass with ice.

"Good. I don't want it to think it can come inside. We're dog people, now."

Lana likes to say that. But we aren't dog people by nature, and had never been when we lived in Wyndmoor. Dogs have conquered our new house, bit by bit. It all started when Lana adopted Charlie as a young pit bull from the animal shelter, where they'd told her that Charlie was the sweetest, most friendly dog, but good for protection too. And for the most part he was. But the day he was brought home, Charlie killed our cat, Bootsy, just killed her like there was nothing to it. He bee-lined for her, grabbed her in his jaws, and shook the life out of her like a plush toy. It was horrible. I had to wrestle Charlie to the ground, which got Charlie even more excited, and he started to lick my face with his bloody tongue.

"On second thought, there's no point in us losing two pets," Lana had said, after I had loaded Charlie into the trunk of the station wagon. The animal was circling around back there like an excited particle, pausing once in a while to look at us gleefully, his tail whacking alternately between seatback and windowpane. Not only did I blame Charlie for killing Bootsy, but somehow I blamed him for the fact that Lana, visibly, was not nearly as upset as I was. I started to hate Charlie that very day.

Charlie was soon followed by Megan the Weimaraner (a yuppie dog, gray, athletic, vacant—in other words, a yuppie herself) and George St. George, a shih tzu that I was allowed to name. I named him that way because he walked into the house the first day and stared down the bigger dogs into submission. George St. George is the one I dislike the least.

After dinner, we go for a walk. It's dark now, and the breeze is refreshing. Lana walks all three dogs at once, pulled along like a warrior on a chariot, driving through the night. She gets ahead of me instantly, so I sneak a glance under the station wagon. A pair of marbly eyes tells me that the cat is there.

"More turkey when I get back," I reassure it.

Lana pauses now and again to let one of the dogs shit. It's a shameless show that they take turns stoically performing while Lana and the other two dogs watch on. Once the dog has finished, everybody is reanimated, and while Lana stoops to clean up, the dogs gambol about as if nothing has happened.

"Good doggie," Lana says.

I lag behind on purpose, because I don't want to get

caught up in these chores of being a dog person. The up-
keep of my own life is hard enough. Lana is good at it
though—taking care of things, that is. We moved into the
city because she wanted to be closer to the yoga studio, the
farmers' market, and the animal shelter, and because she
was tired of taking care of our big old house. She wanted
something cozier, cuter; wanted to be more active in a community. She said being active might do me some good too.
But the only thing I was ever good at taking care of was the
yard.

Thinking about our old house, I get uneasy. My buzz
is wearing off and my belly starts to feel hollow. I start to
look around and see the cat slinking ten paces behind me
(you see, if dogs gambol, cats slink). I want to tell it to shoo,
but I like the idea of this unlikely parade making its way to
the park. Besides, I know that it won't follow us around the
corner.

We cross through the park. Up ahead, Charlie and Megan are barking at a Rottweiler that belongs to some va-
grant kids who smoke cigarette butts off the ground. George
St. George starts to bark at the whole lot of them and Lana
has to drag them away. I take this moment to turn around
and see if the cat is still there, but it's not.

"That's right, fuck off, lady," one of the kids says.

When I get up to where they are, the same kid asks,
"Hey man, spare some change?"

I reach into my wallet and pull out a five-dollar bill.

"Sorry," I say. I don't know why.

The next morning, while Lana is out at yoga, I make a
pot of coffee and go out onto the stoop. But the cat is nowhere in sight. So I go back inside, lift George St. George
from the couch, and leash him up, relishing the look of
disappointment on Charlie's face.

"I'll outlive you," I promise him. "You too," I say to Megan, who's done nothing other than to watch dumbly with
a plush toy in her mouth. It's her failure to understand me
that I can't stand. In Charlie, it's the opposite.

I walk George St. George to the park, where we throw

the ball around. This is my attempt at being active. The other morning dog walkers are there and another shih tzu runs up to George St. George. They start to sniff each other.

"How old is he?" its owner asks me. "Is it a he or a she?"

"A he," I say. "And I don't know at all how old he is. I have no idea."

She smiles behind her oversized sunglasses. She's in her twenties and very fit, yoga-fit, but not yet all ropey like Lana.

"They seem to be getting along," she remarks.

"Us or the dogs?"

She titters (women titter), and walks over to fetch her dog. Her pants cleave her ass like the cleft on a large peach, and while I know that I should find this arousing, I don't. Through my pocket, I check to make sure my testicles are intact.

Suddenly a big boxer comes running across the lawn and starts bouncing around the shih tzus in a circle, barking. The shih tzus start barking back and backing up a little bit. I see the owner of the other shih tzu swoop in to break it all up, and at the same time I see myself standing by doing nothing, George St. George's leash dangling in my fist like a lasso. *What kind of dog-person am I?* I wonder. *Do I rescue my dog or let him fend for himself? Isn't part of owning a dog having something that can fight and kill and die on your behalf?* I decide then that I'm really a cat person—that what dogs do is none of my business.

The young woman shoots a stern smile at the boxer owner, and one at me too. She picks her shih tzu up and cradles it. I try to apologize with my eyes, whatever that looks like. Then I walk over to George St. George and put his leash back on.

We stop off at the grocery store so I can pick up some breakfast, and I tie George St. George up as loosely as I can.

"Don't go anywhere," I dare him.

When I come out balancing milk and eggs and bread in my arms (Lana's on an eco-friendly kick, so I'm afraid to come back with a plastic bag), I see that George St. George's leash has come undone, though he doesn't seem to notice.

"Why didn't you run for it, son?" I say. "That ingrate Charlie would run. He would run and never look back."

There's no point in taking the leash—George St. George leads the way back to the house and I follow ten paces behind. Back home, Lana's just come out of the shower, and when she sees me with all the groceries she says, "How come you didn't bring a tote? It would have simplified your life."

"Sometimes I forget to do the things that simplify my life," I say, and head for the sputtering old shower, to let it lurch invectives of hot rust-tinged water on me.

That night, after Lana and the dogs have gone to bed, I lure the cat inside with lunchmeat. We go into the living room where I've set up a little spot for it under the bookcase with Bootsy's old food bowl and litter box. The dogs are all upstairs—sometimes they take my place in bed and I don't even bother to kick them out.

I sit down on the couch and watch the cat eating as if this food and being in this house were the most unremarkable thing, as if it were expected even. I'm reminded of Bootsy, and the way she stalked about the old house in Wyndmoor with utter nonchalance. Indifferent to the infestation we had, Bootsy used to stare blankly as we chased mice and roaches ourselves. It wasn't for a lack of eyesight, because she would chase a ball or well-aimed point of light. I once went so far as to capture a mouse and dangle it live and wriggling in front of Bootsy's face, only to prompt a lazy bath.

"OK, kitty," I say, kicking off my shoes and lying down now on the couch. "Time for bed."

I tap my belly, inviting the cat to come sit on me. But it just looks at me from across the room. I close my eyes and try to sleep. Ten minutes go by. Still the cat has not come to sleep with me. When I open my eyes, I've lost it.

I get up and walk the perimeter of the living room, and suddenly there it is in the corner, quietly watching. I'm getting frustrated and hot at the same time now, and I'm remembering a Poe story or two where the narrator is spooked again and again by the indifferent gaze of his cat. They can scare the hell out of you when they want to. And

once they've done it, you can't help but think that, even
when they're friendly, there's something removed and awful
about them. Maybe that's what Lana was glad to be rid of
the day Charlie mauled Bootsy. Maybe that's what she was
glad to be rid of when she sold the big old lonely house in
Wyndmoor. That indifference. Maybe I should have been
glad to be rid of it too.

I sit back on the couch and silently will the cat to come
over, maybe I even murmur a prayer. And finally it does,
but only to the edge—it doesn't jump up. I desperately want
to take off my shirt and pants and sleep now, with or without the cat, but I don't dare undress as long as it is in the
house, watching.

I wake up the next morning, fully dressed. The cat has
gone; I don't know where. I spend the day out on the stoop
and it doesn't show up, not once. Evening comes and Lana
charges out of the house with the herd and I watch them
disappear down the street to go perform their shitting and
playing spectacles in a more public place. The cars still
creep by and the ice melting in my tiki glass gives off a pop.
And I think, somebody is making these nice things for me.
Somebody is composing this world in a way that it hasn't
been all year, for my enjoyment and my enjoyment alone.

One in Ten Fish Are Afraid of Water

Che Yeun

The following story is the winner of the fifth annual Marguerite McGlinn Prize for Fiction.

1.

Riko finds you in the swimming pool, chest-deep in HELLO TODAY THE TEMPERATURE IS 26.5 DEGREES. This is how you get through swimming lessons: clutching onto the edge, bicycle-kicking your legs. Water overflows around you into skimmer drains. Your knuckles ache. Watch the clock.

Riko is unmistakable, even across an Olympic-regulation distance. For about a year now, acne has erupted into bright lesions across her jawline. You've heard other girls describe her scars as burning, bubbling plastic. Soon she'll be close to you, and her goggles will come off. Look into her famous right eye. Riko turns to the side to keep it far from you, but you will still see the eye twitch and tremble under a fluttering lid. Altogether it's a face that makes you feel grateful, even for your slitty eyes and moon cake cheeks.

She swims up to check the time on the clock. Touch her feet with yours. When she breathes, you smell hot air coming out of her mouth, so unlike sterile chlorine fumes. You like the sourness, the smell of something living.

"They tell me it's disappearing," she says, as if you two were in the middle of a conversation. A rough scratch runs down along her voice.

"What is?" you ask.

"My blemishes and discolorations." Riko dunks her head underwater and up again. Her hair clumps around her face like seaweed. She tells you diluted chlorine helps combat her outbreaks.

"What do you think?" she asks. "Do you think it's working?" She tilts her head left and right to give you a complete view.

What you assumed to be her scars in plain sight were actually several coats of make-up. What you see in the fluorescent light, with all the powder washed away, is much worse.

Riko looks at you. "I'm just kidding," she says finally. "I don't need to know what you think. I'm not blind."

2.

Your school stands on a hill, overlooking downtown Tokyo. Purchased for one American dollar by four nuns back in 1908, now your school is one of the most valuable slices of real estate in the world. Out back, the cathedral alone is worth ten billion yen. Every morning you bow hello to nuns in gray habits as they tend a garden. The ancient gates at the bottom of the hill are flanked by pungent camphor trees.

In 1944, the old school structure burned down when America firebombed Tokyo. The new structure, like the rest of this city, is prefabricated and fireproof and gray. From your biology lab you see Tokyo Tower and the red-light district of Roppongi and an old neon sign for Midori. In class you imagine how the sign looks lit up, a radioactive green. Imagine cold Midori sliding down your throat.

This is where all hapa girls come for their education. Most of them have Japanese mothers and white European fathers. This is the most ideal arrangement. From early on these girls dabble in modeling. High school brings contracts and record deals, thanks to round, neotenous eyes and European last names. If these girls aren't practicing dance moves or promoting albums on radio shows, they are sitting in the back of class, mouths covered, yawning at formulas and equations they will never need to know. Look around and lose your thoughts in the rows of symmetrical faces and sparrow brown hair. Here they are, the prized pooches of Eurasian breeding.

Your hapa blood is all wrong. You have your father's Japanese last name, Japanese black eyes and Japanese crooked teeth. Your legs fit regular Japanese jeans. Your white blood has sunk too far from the surface and can't get you anywhere. Without any contracts or record deals, you will have to learn grammar, vocabulary and the scientific method.

Riko, like you, is also the wrong mixture. After swimming lessons she often invites you over to her place. Her father is a famous composer often written up as the Brahms of this generation. When he moved away, Riko kept his tank of tropical fish in the drawing room. "I used to think he'd come back for them," she explains, "but now I'm pretty sure they're mine." When you first walk into her apartment, it's that blue aquarium glow that greets you from down the hall.

Riko has two different men come in to take care of her fish. One in charge of feeding, and another for cleaning and maintaining water levels. The tank is as wide as a road, and it makes you dizzy. Observe from a distance. Different fish occupy different depths, and once they reach one end of the tank they swish around and swim up the way they came before. Obedient little souls.

"Actually, some of them are monsters," Riko says, as if she's read your mind. "Look closer." She points out missing chunks of fins and tails, the injured specimens flicking their bodies in irregular, asymmetrical rhythms. "I had a piranha for a while."

"Why did you get a piranha?" you ask, still at a distance, not fogging up the glass with your breath the way Riko likes to.

"I wanted to see a live feeding. Can you imagine? It would have made quite a spectacle."

"But then what?"

She shrugs. "It didn't do much. Bite marks, that was fun to watch. But piranhas are mostly just timid and frantic.

Not as deadly as you hope." Blue tank light washes over her. You imagine the fish swimming around her neck, down her uniform collar, and disappearing into mossy shadows.

3.

You and Riko will meet the same fate of all minor hapa: an expensive education, followed by an expensive university, to book a quiet, expensive wedding in a hotel ballroom. No billboards at Shibuya Crossing, no famous boyfriends, no rock and roll. But you are still part white. You could have just as easily been part black, or part Indian, or part disabled. The corporate uses for you and your languages are endless. There are many ways to have your existence appreciated.

When you can't go over to Riko's apartment, spend your evenings with textbook problem sets. Take breaks with American movies. It's better than talking to your mother, who has given up on learning Japanese, or talking to your father, who has given up on your mother.

Smooth highways continue forever on flat Nevada deserts. Young insomniacs lock eyes and smile at the grocery checkout. COLLIDE WITH DESTINY. An apocalyptic bomb ticks down in New York. Mouth the names of important faces—Richard Gere, Keanu Reeves, Cameron Diaz—and watch as they act out lives of nameless, faceless strangers.

That is the America to plan for. You will be of use there as well, where universities seek you out for your contribution to ADVANCING THE FRONTIERS OF KNOWLEDGE WITH A GLOBAL SPIRIT. The land of excessive biodiversity, for fruit and cereal brands as well as people. COLLIDE with all kinds of climate, terrain, architecture. Stop wondering why beauty only comes to the same girls over and over again. Stop wondering why you look the way you do, how the same genetic recipe yielded such a different meal.

4.

America will prove you wrong. There, you will fall in love with a white boy who asks you to speak Japanese in bed, dirty phonemes you string into sentences with no concern for making sense. A Japanese boy who asks you to bleach your vagina into a petal pink. A black girl who, before you undress her, asks you to turn out the lights.

"It's nothing I haven't seen before," you'll say to persuade her otherwise, digging your fingers into her hair. "It's nothing I don't already enjoy."

She will squint against the light and gather her arms over her chest into a pretzel twist. "What about my enjoyment?"

You won't remember which one of you loses contact first. But by then you will have absorbed this trait of hers, and you will only touch another body in total darkness.

5.
Your plan gets you by. You learn to bargain with yourself.

For every hundred English words you memorize, you earn one year in America.

For every exam you ace, you earn two.

If you swim from one end of the pool to the other, you earn a lifetime.

You never make it from one end of the pool to the other. Just paddle to the edge, cough it out, try to unswallow the water you just swallowed. You check back to see how far you made it each time, but it's never even close.

Riko dismisses your plan for escape. "So many girls leave," she points out, "and then they can't help but come back."

It's true. Shiina, who left for England to please her grandparents, returned one summer with half of her face paralyzed. Jemma, who left for Sydney to find more drugs, came back just in time to die in her sister's bed. Sachiko, who used to be the wildest one of all, lives in a suburb of Yokohama with her plastic surgeon husband and gets unintelligible at alumni cocktail parties.

"What if I make it?" you ask Riko one day as she smokes behind the cathedral at school. She has only recently picked up smoking, along with punk rock and combat boots, but the new Riko suits her. Like her skin, the rest of her also looks better covered up, in layers of ripped shirts and studded leather.

You tell her if you left, you would never come back. "Maybe that's why we don't hear about the ones that get away, because they get away so clean."

"How does that work?" She stubs out her cigarette, stained black on one end by her lipstick. She throws it over the fence into the garden for nuns to find tomorrow. "You have to make sure everyone sees you do it. Make sure they talk about it. Otherwise you might as well be dead."

That summer, one of the J-pop girls in your class comes out with a song you can't get out of your head. No one can. It's in a Honda commercial that plays twice every hour, and it fills every subway train. Only Riko remains unaffected. Immunized by The Clash, headphones as big as dinner rolls shielding her ears.

6.

Final exams are coming up. National elections are coming up. You study harder than ever, and the fascist party protests louder than ever outside your school gates from eight in the morning. Climb out of your subway stop and onto the street, where the World War II songs greet you from loudspeakers. In between songs, the fascists shout bullhorn lectures on the glory of imperial Japan and the war crimes committed by the Allied forces.

Cloaked in wartime military flags, they explain to you that Asia will always belong to Japan and there is only one Dharma, only one true, pure Empire. Your mother is a whore, your father has betrayed his ancestors and in a perfect world, you would not exist.

Then the music starts up again. We are cherry blossoms, the singer warbles, we go in and out of bloom together in the garden.

Your headmistress orders everyone to stay home until final exams. Take the time to master chemistry. Picture molecular structures that you cannot see. Tear pages of the textbook and eat them, an ancient method you'd dismissed as a joke until now. Hold each crumpled ball of paper in your mouth. You have nothing to lose. Your saliva softens the ball into a cookie. Imagine all the exam answers seeping into your gastric juices, your pancreas, your bloodstream, your brain. For what this method promises, it doesn't taste so bad. Finish the year at the top of your class.

"All those nights studying with Riko are paying off," you say, and your mother is too pleased to question your absence.

On some nights, nightclub bouncers let you in without checking your IDs, as long as you are huddled with the white hapa girls. But most nights they don't. When this happens, stay in Roppongi anyway with Riko, smoking on the street outside a dirty bakery. She promises you the right group of boys will come along. They hook their fingers into the rips of her Ramones shirt and ask her for her name. Watch her follow their lead up an emergency stairwell. Wait on the sidewalk with a greasy kebab from a TURKISH DONER KEBAB 100% BEEF truck, and keep a tally of all the years of escape you've earned for yourself.

7.

Riko's mother doesn't mind having you around their apartment all the time. She opens the door in silk slippers, gives you three cheek kisses and says you look stunning. She leads you in with sedated steps, and then goes back to supping on wine and arranging flowers in a glass vase. Her words are always slurred, but her chignon on her nape has every strand swept into place. When Riko makes plans for the two of you to stay out late, her mother calls your mother and concocts another sleepover as your cover.

"What does your mother think you do when we go out?" you ask Riko one night. "What do you say to her?"

"I tell her the truth."

"She's OK with that?"

"She has to be." She shrugs and rubs black eyeliner under her eyes into thick smudges. "It's the least she can do after what she did to my dad."

"What did she do?"

Riko's reflection looks at you. Her right eye is moving again, and her gaze doesn't line up right. "It's a complicated history," she says, and then tells you to never ask about it. "But I'm glad she's messed up from it now. I'm glad she feels bad."

More often than not, you are at Riko's place when her fish handlers come by. The feeder comes every day, and stays long enough to make sure food hasn't sunk to the bottom to rot. The tank cleaner only comes twice a week. He is the one you like to see. Wrinkles are forming around his mouth, but you like his Kawasaki motorcycle helmet. He bows before coming inside and leaves his helmet on the floor next to his shoes. You and Riko watch for any reaction from her fish as he siphons in a fresh bucket of dechlorinated water.

"Can you get me another piranha?" Riko asks him one day.

"Why would I do that?" He sounds amused. "To get myself in trouble with your mother?"

"No." Riko watches his face. "To satisfy my curiosity."

He smiles but doesn't say anything. He touches the surface of the water with three fingertips. He explains that humans can detect up to a quarter of a degree difference in water temperature, then brings his wet fingertips to his mouth and licks them.

"What does that do?" Riko asks.

"Satisfies my curiosity."

You look away. Riko does not. Instead, she reaches out to dab some water on her hand as well. "Is that why you chose this line of work?" she asks him. To embarrass you further, she flicks droplets of water on your face.

"This isn't my line of work," he replies.

That weekend, Riko goes downtown to meet the tank cleaner at his real job. He manages a small S&M club in Shibuya. Pause the movie you're watching, and listen to her babble and laugh about his establishment. It's a place you've never heard of, even though she explains it's not far from other clubs you know, the ones where other girls from your school get VIP tables every weekend. Riko's definitely going back, and she wants you to come with her.

"It's a complete joke," she shouts. "He think it's crazy crazy S&M but it's not. His floors are cleaner than my house. Pathetic. They even have chandeliers."

Stare at your TV screen, where Julia Roberts and Mel Gibson are just about to open a refrigerator.

"Did he lie about your age?" you ask.

"Seriously?" You can tell she's smiling, maybe even happy. "Of all the things, that's what you want to know?"

8.

In America, you will wander through a street market fair and follow a fortune-teller into her tent. She won't take your name or scribble down characters to analyze your stellar alignments, like the fortune-tellers back in Japan. She won't even take your birthday. Instead, she'll ask for something that belongs to you, an object you have kept with you for many years.

Look through your wallet until you find Riko's nipple ring, the one she threw away when her left piercing got infected.

The fortune-teller will take the ring in one hand and wrap her other hand around that hand. She will whisper incantations into the dark cave of her hands. Try to ignore an orange price tag sticker on her crystal ball next to you. She'll ask you to close your eyes and transport yourself back to the time when you first found this object, so that's what you do:

Sometime between The Clash and The Dead Kennedys, Riko asks you to pierce her nipples for her. Get a safety pin and a bottle of alcohol solution. Get close and turn her naked shoulders towards the light. A Ziploc bag of ice melts on a marble vanity top. Hold one of her brown buds between your fingers. "Don't get scared," Riko coaches you, "it's just like an earlobe."

But her nipple feels nothing like an earlobe. It's even softer, like sponge cake, with the uneven cracks of elephant skin. Tell yourself you can always stop if it hurts her. But in practice, you can't even start.

Riko loses her patience and pierces it herself. She slides the safety pin through and then pulls it right back out to secure her new hole with a ring. You hear The Dead Kennedys through her headphones wrapped around her neck. She repeats the procedure on the other side. Afterwards the two of you sit in a Starbucks to kill more time. She keeps telling you that you have no idea how good it feels. A salaryman in the smoking section looks up.

The fortune teller will tell you the ring carries great pain. You will not be impressed. Of course, you'll think, of course a piercing carries pain. And shoes carry feet.

She will instruct you on some rituals to cleanse yourself of this pain—which crystals to wear around your neck, which direction to lay your head when you sleep, how to properly dispose of the ring without angering its spirit.

Give her the thirty dollars she wants. Keep the ring with you.

9.

The tank cleaner offers Riko a job at his club as a cocktail waitress. She finds it funny, and decides to accept. By the following month, she has completed his training program to work as a performer.

"Training program," she says. "Like I'm a pastry chef."

"Isn't some of that stuff dangerous?" her mother asks.

"Maybe there's a way," you think out loud, "to make it less dangerous. Like a magic trick."

Riko tells you you're missing the point.

Her mother listens calmly, only making encouraging sounds. "It's nice to see you happy," she says, and combs her daughter's hair with her fingers, careful not to rub any strands over her face and irritate her skin.

This is Riko's new work schedule: the tank cleaner picks her up from school and takes her downtown, where she works an early shift and makes it home before the subway lines stop running. Her bag grows every day with more and more things she needs for performing: PVC leather straps, chains, make-up, fake eyelashes, a shower kit, and a change of clothes.

The tank cleaner arrives at your school entrance on his motorcycle at three thirty sharp. You worry he will piss off the fascists in their trucks, since his bike drowns out their propaganda tapes. But the young boys are in awe of his Kawasaki. Whenever you and Riko make your way down the hill, he's handing out some glossy black and pink promotional postcards for his club to the boys, showing them free drink coupons attached to the back.

Riko takes her time saying good-bye to you. Her uneven eyes stare over your shoulder, towards the other girls passing under camphor trees. She makes sure they see her climb on the oil-black Kawasaki and wrap her arms around the tank cleaner's stomach. Once she puts on her helmet she will be anonymous, so she takes her time with that too. She sticks her hands into his jacket pockets, and they circle away.

10.

Deena. You remember Deena one day, the girl who ran away to Iowa with her US Marine boyfriend when she was halfway through her eighth-grade year. For a while, she was all anyone could talk about.

"What about her?" you ask Riko. "She never came back."

"Deena got pregnant and fat and boring and poor," Riko reminds you. "That doesn't count."

You're standing at the crossing in Shibuya, waiting for a green light. Riko and the tank cleaner have been arguing a lot lately, and she's asked you to be her escort to work and back instead. Most of her customers are sensible people, but alcohol changes everyone.

The light turns. Cross together, arm in arm. Even with all this noise around you, you can still hear the chains and buckles Riko has strapped on under her coat. They brush against each other and clink with every step.

11.

For every hundred English words you memorize, you earn one year in America.

For every exam you ace, you earn two.

12.

Neon wigs are the best way to stand out at work. It's easy for customers to remember Riko and request her again when they return. Riko's electric red bob unsettles you, as it does most people who stand close to her in trains. But you're more shocked by the men and women who don't flinch, who only give her a steady smile.

"It's working," she whispers when they pass. "They recognize me." She tells you everything she recalls about these men and women: who enjoys getting whipped on stage, who prefers to be quietly handcuffed in the back corner, who leaves their personal email addresses hoping to receive close-up photos of her uneven eyes. Listen. Don't be fooled by how normal they look in their business-casual blazers and conservative office shoes.

"Do you ever get anyone we know?" you ask. "Anybody's parents? What about our teachers?"

Riko turns slightly, from the one angle where her eyes line up dead square into yours. "I get everyone," she says. "I have a pretty good reputation."

You finally visit her club. You are surprised by the décor. You'd expected a lot of transparent plexiglass and metal, a place obsessed with the future like the rest of Tokyo. Instead, you see a wide ring of private booths, each with a thick wood slab serving as a tabletop. This could be a TGI Friday's.

You discover her reputation has been rightfully earned. Most nights she is so popular and behind schedule that she doesn't have time to talk. She struts from booth to booth, swinging her whip to the beat of each song. In the dark, with enough make-up on, her skin looks all right. The boots stop just a few centimeters below her crotch, plump and tight in leather shorts.

When Riko is busy, she puts you in a booth with the

newest hire, Suzume, who wears a neon blue wig. With only one week of experience, Suzume doesn't have any regulars yet and she spends most of her time gossiping with you about other performers.

"Do you see the lady with green hair?" she shouts in your ear. "She masturbated too much as a kid and now she needs incredible amounts of pain."

You study Suzume's face and the small bones of her shoulders. She looks even younger than you and Riko, maybe not even fifteen. "What's an incredible amount?"

"She always carries this special needle and thread," she explains. "You can pay to sew up and down her arms and legs. And Riko-san," she shouts when Riko passes by. "She's the craziest."

"How so?" you can't help asking.

Suzume turns even further. She shouts less into your ear and more at the wall behind you. "She really likes the smell of urine and feces. She just rubs it all over herself."

The song ends and mixes into another one. Think of something to say.

"That must bring in more money than anything else, right?" Look at the floor, which is just as clean as Riko had said it would be. "More loyal customers?"

Suzume clasps her hands between her knees. "I don't know if I should tell you this." She pauses. "But Riko-san doesn't need money. I think everyone can see that's not what she's doing it for. It's just for fun. Maybe that's why they like her."

Don't tell her she's mistaken. Suzume is too young to properly argue with. Accept that whatever Riko does is her freedom to do so. As long as her mother doesn't know, Riko can't be ashamed. As long as the tank cleaner does his job right, she can't be harmed. As long as you don't say anything, there is no one to say anything.

13.

Keep her mother company when Riko is at work. Sit together in the dining room and answer all her questions about school that Riko doesn't have time for. Sometimes there's silverware to polish, or a movie she'd like to see. Don't worry about the problem sets from school in your bag. Halfway through her second bottle, she will fall asleep. Finish your homework early and spend your leftover hours looking into the aquarium. Cratered rocks decorate the bottom of the tank. They remind you of Riko's scarred face.

Look for signs of Deena online. She hasn't logged into her MySpace since last year, but all of her pictures are publicly visible. Create an account to grant yourself access.

She hasn't aged well—the white half, you think. Her husband is so white he turns red in the sun, and he only wears shirts that show off his military tattoos. You can tell their child will not learn a word of Japanese. Click through Deena's pictures some more, until it's time to call a taxi and pick up Riko again.

The driver drops you off at Shibuya Crossing. With fewer people pushing into you at this hour, you look up at the buildings instead of down at your feet. Just as you cross, a new music video starts on a billboard screen. The singer, another classmate of yours, is one of the whitest hapas you've seen with naturally green eyes. It's as bad as any J-pop music video, orbs of light floating through senseless dream sequences, but you watch it until the end anyway.

14.

Graduation takes place in the cathedral, with a stained-glass Mary and Jesus casting their colors on the audience. Riko skipped out. Sit in your designated seat. Don't turn to anyone. In one month, you will be in America.

Some famous girls in your class have invited their pop star boyfriends, who spend the three-hour ceremony posing for photos in the pews. They cheer for their girlfriends, their friends' girlfriends, and their girlfriends' friends, but no one else. No cheers for you, just some polite golf claps. Teachers play with their cell phones, anxious to get done and hit their expat pubs. In one month minus three hours, you will be in America.

For your going-away present, Riko plans a special night for you at her club. "I don't know how much longer I'll be doing this," she says. "I might as well show off all my tricks." She instructs you to arrive at one in the morning, when the curious drunks have left and only familiar regulars are around.

Riko greets you at the door and blindfolds you. Don't tense up. Give her your hands so she can lead you to a booth and sit you down. A wood post presses on your spine. When your blindfolds are removed, examine how tightly your hands have been cuffed to the post, over your head.

"I don't like this," you tell her, tugging at your cuffs.

"It's OK," she reassures you. "No one's born liking this."

When she gets close to breathe on you, don't worry you'll smell urine or worse on her breath, her wig. Think of her mother's perfume. Relax and enjoy her company, even when the cold metal cuffs make it hard for you to breathe. Don't squirm and plead until sweat rolls down your back. Riko will do nothing. It's Suzume, walking by, who panics and snaps you free.

Run outside. Have a greasy 100% BEEF kebab. Have a smoke and take a stroll through the deserted back streets of Shibuya. You will feel calm enough to make a big circle back to her club and wait for her shift to end. She eventually pushes through the metal doors, half of an electric red bob dangling out from her purse. She smiles at your punctuality. She walks towards you, scratching away at her scalp like a crazy person.

For every drunk backpacker she whips

For every CEO she puts out cigarettes on

For every cup of human waste she consumes

You never finish these thoughts. Before you can decide on anything, she's made it down the alley back to you, and she reaches out to link arms. Her hair is wet as always from her end-of-shift shower. Still you breathe in deep, searching for any unpleasant smells that might tell you the truth.

15.

The month you get to America, your father is hospitalized for an obscure liver condition. Your mother phones you every detail, mostly to convince herself there's still hope.

Even though you don't need your five years of etymology
drills to know liver must come from lifer.

When you talk to your father, only nod and answer with
hai and *wakannai*. His voice grows so unrecognizable and
small that you have to press your burning cell phone to your
ear to catch his words, but don't ever promise to go back.

16.

"I'll treat you big before I move," you say to Riko. "Maybe we can go on a trip somewhere before then."

But Riko is too busy, planning her final days at the club.
She is done with that lifestyle which, she now realizes, held
her back from finding likable qualities in other people. "But
it was funny for a while," she says, "I guess that's something."

She agrees to move in with her new boyfriend, one of the
Nigerian bouncers from the club next door to hers. She says
nothing about the tank cleaner, who hasn't come by the
house in a while, maybe weeks. A green film of algae now
coats the aquarium glass.

You recall a joke you once heard your Biology teacher
say to your English teacher. Something about rich Japanese girls rebelling against their families in a predictable
sequence of actions. Fucking black guys is the final phase,
the dangling head-first over the cliff, just before they crawl
back home to settle down with a law student.

Do not repeat this joke to her. Watch her stuff all her
PVC straps and gags into a separate suitcase, to be dropped
off at her club for Suzume. Help her pack her own suitcases
and line them up by the elevator. Riko's mother sends her
off with three cheek kisses. You offer to go with Riko to her
new place and help unpack them all, but she declines.

"Don't bother. This will be better." She holds up one
hand as the elevator doors close, whether to wave good-bye
or to say stand back, you can't be sure.

Riko's mother stands next to you with a glass of wine as
the elevator takes her daughter downstairs. She invites you
over for lunch the next day, and you don't know what to do

but accept and say thank you, although this will be the last time you see either of them.

Leave Japan. The eggplant tastes like cucumber, and the cucumber tastes like eggplant. Household items come in unfamiliar shapes. Develop new habits of eating and talking and sleeping, and wait for Japan to leave you.

Poem in the Freezer Section

Wes Ward

I would have remembered the grocery list
but the smell of the coffee spoon this morning,
just, well, the way it entered membranes
I didn't know existed, the way it swirled with a sign
above its head that read "This is the best smell
a Tuesday has ever known" made me forget.
And yet I'm doing okay in the aisles
at Super Fresh, not as disjointed as you might expect,
listless and all. The cart is almost full
and the bananas, bread, and peaches are cradled
in the seat where a child might sit, a child
with clever eyes who's buying "this, this"
in every aisle with the point of a small finger.
And I would buy him something in every aisle:
a stringed box of Animal Crackers,
a pack of fluorescent straws, a box of cereal
with a robot inside, an air horn.
But until I remember what it was you wanted,
I'll be in the freezer section, writing
lines to a poem on twenty foggy doors.

Is It Better to Sleep

Luke Bauerlein

I am trying, I am trying
to be right with my mind again.
For what else should I be trying
and to what end
when all the night around me
rises to my room
like the waters of a lake?
I want to make the call
the nightblind hours
refuse to make
and patiently distill—
the sky mercurial,
 slick as a kill.
Again, the dead have come full soon
to shed themselves
thin as a moon.
Thin as the horizon's
cold, blue arc.
Every season
is their season.
Every evening, their mark.

Atop the Camel's Hump

Casey Otto

Island is a word that calls to mind countless pictures. Common images, ones we all share through vacations, photographs, or what we see on television: azure waves, pristine white beaches, palm fronds sighing in a humid breeze. Islands are places of peace, sanctums of serenity.

Well, not *my* island.

My island is ugly. Bare and bleak. It rises from the earth, fifteen feet high and dimpled like a camel's hump, ringed by acres and acres of corn; an ocean of sweet Indian gold. Its muddy slopes are sharp and steep, treacherous in the rain. No soft carpet of grass adorns my island, no bed of furry moss. Instead, jagged thorns tear at flesh and snag on clothes. The island's only thriving flora, an ancient white oak, watches the world and casts a long black shadow.

It is a truly unwelcoming place, and not very lovely to behold.

Yet I love it.

The Camel's Hump I named it, upon staking my claim, believing I was the one person in the world to acknowledge this little plot of land, this poor wretched isle.

In the summer, when the country steams and sweats, the corn circling the Camel's Hump grows tall enough to scratch the sky. Miles of corn, all green and gold in the haze of morning, the stalks glittering like diamonds under a layer of dew. Mice feast on kernels until they are too fat to flee the foxes, and foxes feast on mice until they are nearly too fat to flee the farmer. (I think he lets them get away.)

Several signs along the road that divides the farm and the adjacent neighborhood read "No Trespassing," but for the moment I am blissfully illiterate. I'm only visiting, after all. The farmer will not fault one girl just for exploring. Corn swallows me like a gaping yellow maw. I run through it eagerly, losing myself among the stalks, the blonde hairs of the corn tangling with my brown hair. There is no north or south, no east or west; only corn, yellow and bright, rising up against a blue sky.

The earth trembles.

From somewhere out of sight comes a roar, followed by a great mechanical groan. The harvester coughing to life. For a moment I see myself racing through rows and rows of corn, desperate to find the road, but I am lost in the maze and the farmer's tractor hunts me down before I can escape. My bones are ground to dust, my blood and organs and sinew squeezed out of me as out of a tube of toothpaste as the farmer drives on, oblivious that his bountiful summer harvest is now two ears richer...and two eyes richer, and ten toes richer, and a nose richer, too.

But then I see my island. The Camel's Hump.

I can just make out the peak; the rest is obscured by towering stalks. The old oak stands sure and still, my lighthouse in the yellow sea. Its bark is ash-gray and splintered, its leaves fiercely green. I make it my target, throwing myself up the island's steep banks, clinging to roots and rocks while the tractor wheezes by, flattening the yellow sea in its wake. Well, thank God I'm not down *there*.

I am the tallest girl on the planet—emerald meadows and farms and dusty roads unfold before me. I am in the heart of the Garden State. I wait for the farmer to finish reaping his field, with only the splintered old oak for company. Its roots, as thick around as one of my thighs, erupt from the dirt as though the tree tried to break free of the earth and walk the world. Ants travel up and down its bark, which is scarred by time's passing. The lowest-hanging branches are still too high for a girl to climb, but the birds make good use of them. A red-tailed hawk, sharp of eye and sharper of talon, scrutinizes me from the safety of his perch. His tongue flutters from his beak like a trembling pink worm.

"It's hot today," I agree, and the hawk wheels away toward the summer sun. I wonder, when the black canvas of night descends, will he return to the oak? Or will some slow-witted owl claim the tree in his absence?

Around me, the earth rumbles.

Puffy white clouds fashion the shapes of fantastic creatures, dragons and dwarves and dinosaurs.

I love this place. Despite the rocky soil and vicious brambles (and my near brush with death) I am at peace, sheltered by the old oak. No one knows I'm here. Not the farmer or the drivers racing past on the nearby road. Only the red-tailed hawk—and who would he tell?

When the tractor sputters to a stop, spewing oily black smoke from its rusty exhaust pipe, I bid farewell to my island, carefully slide down to solid ground, and cross the flattened field of corn. Crushed vegetation cushions my feet and softens my footsteps. I feel exposed and naked—the wonder of the yellow sea trampled to a bitter green pulp. There's a shout behind me, likely the farmer, and I'm spurred to a sprint.

Over the field, across the road, and into my car.

The Camel's Hump looks bigger when not flanked by so much corn, yet somehow more vulnerable, a secret revealed.

It is winter before I visit again.

Snow powders the earth and cruel winds sweep across the land. Branches, weakened by frost, splinter and snap, loud as a bullwhip in the eerie stillness of December. The animals have all gone: birds to warmer southern states, rabbits to their warrens. Humans venture into the world only once properly bundled up against the elements.

The oak looms in silent vigil, its naked arms reaching toward the blue-gray sky. The corn is a summer dream, but the Camel's Hump remains.

Before I cross the snowy field I wonder how many winters the old white oak has seen. Twenty? Fifty? Has it ever seen a winter free of people? A winter before Hartford Road trundled along its left or Centerton Road to its right? A winter before the homes and farms and businesses? A winter before time? What ancient wonders, I meditate. What stories it could tell had the little seedling sprouted a mouth instead of roots.

I study the island from across the road. It looks as though an enormous camel fell asleep in the middle of a snowstorm.

Every season has its scents, I reflect, trampling across the unbroken snow. Spring smells like wet earth, summer like salty surf. Autumn has pumpkins and spices and rotten leaves. But winter freezes in your nostrils until your snot dribbles down your chin.

The old oak looks bigger. A handful of stubborn red leaves still cling to its branches, and a few are tugged free in the frigid winter gusts.

Carefully I make my ascent, pulling myself upward with one of the oak's massive roots.

There are a few animal droppings here, but otherwise the Camel's Hump has been left undisturbed. White snow, frozen earth. The gunmetal superstructure of the *Cornfield Cruiser*, an old US Air Force Space Command site, is visible from atop the island. The building belches steam, hot steam. Suddenly I'm aware of shivers rocking my body. My skin is raw and red, my lips split.

I have to do this quickly.

I take the Swiss Army knife from my pocket, a relic of the days when my brother and I were kids. Where once the blade had flashed polished steel, it now glinted dully, the victim of rust and mud and many gutted fish. Yet it would serve my purpose.

Normally I am not one for defacing nature, but this oak struck something in me. I want this tree to be *mine*. The sharpest edge of the Swiss Army knife hacks through the bark with all the grace of a poacher chopping his way through the Amazon. Small slivers of wood peel away under the blade, pepper the ground.

In minutes I'm done. On one of the white oak's roots I've carved my name: CASEY 2008. The letters are shallow on the root's girth, a root like an anaconda with a tiny tattoo.

As I make the short walk back to my car, I wonder who would come along after me. Two lovers, perhaps, drawn by the solitude. Children who dream of monsters and adventures. Who would see my name? Would someone add his or her own? And in fifty years, when the world is all sterile and steel, will the white oak with my name still live?

So many will hurry by without a second glance. Who could be bothered to marvel at a gnarled old tree and an ugly hill plagued by thorns? Not many, truly. An island in the Bahamas would better serve them. But someday, someone will see the world as I did: from atop the Camel's Hump.

2014

The Worm of the Heart

Ilene Raymond Rush

On a Saturday morning in late September, while waiting for her estranged husband Del to arrive with the payment for their daughter Natalie's final semester of college tuition, Lily Manheim accidentally swallowed her giant Schnauzer's heartworm pill.

In the Chestnut Hill house she had once shared with her husband and daughter, Lily worked on hacking it back up. But even without water, the beige bullet, taken in place of her daily vitamin tablet, had slipped down her esophagus into her digestive tract, bent on sending out evil dog worm killing enzymes.

Or whatever it was that a heartworm pill did.

Despite her 27-year marriage to a molecular biologist at Penn, Lily, with her master's in psychology and social work, had never been much for biology. The vitamins, which she often forgot to take at all, had been Del's idea. Del, who spent his life studying zebra fish in the hopes of uncovering the cure for heart disease, embraced the many paths to post-twentieth-century immortality. Throughout their marriage, he had tried to stick to a diet of healthful greens and fruit and had encouraged Lily to join him on hikes, bikes, and mindfulness retreats. Despite his pleas, Lily often bowed out, content to watch Mother Nature's plan for her thighs. Del told her she feared taking charge of her life.

"Your right hand never knows what your left is up to," he said.

And here, in the swallowed heartworm pill, rested Del's ultimate proof: Lily mistaking the multi-purpose vitamin in her left hand for the square, meat-colored dog lozenge in her right. Were these to be the final thoughts of her life? Clutching what might turn out to be her Final Vitamin, Lily located her cell phone on the downstairs table and punched up Poison Control.

"Heartworm pills? Aren't those for dogs?"

"Hence my concern."

Cell phone pressed to one ear, Lily unclenched her left fist to reveal the damp violet vitamin that clung to her lifeline. For a moment, she considered feeding the pill to Britney Spears, the Schnauzer, a karmic trade-in that might stave off future bad luck, but then she dropped it into her own mouth and swallowed. Perhaps, she mused, the two might cancel one another out.

"Hmm," Poison Control mused. Fingers clacked across computer keys. "A real stumper."

"No one ever did this before?"

"I'm sure someone has. Can you hold?" A blast of Death Cab for Cutie, then the voice resurfaced. "You're not one of those urban legends?" the voice asked.

"I swallowed it five minutes ago," Lily said, trying not to panic. "Am I going to die?"

"Well," said Poison Control. "Let's not get dramatic. I'd anticipate a little nausea, maybe some itching, but I expect you'll be with us for a while longer."

"No licking in inappropriate spots?"

Silence.

"We provide a very, very serious and important service to the community," Poison Control lectured.

The flat sorrow of the dial tone filled Lily's ear. Relief swamped her. She was not going to die—not today, maybe not ever. This was immediately followed by annoyance. In this new century, the entire country appeared to have lost its collective sense of humor. You couldn't blame them, really. It had been a very long summer full of serious and important issues. People sitting in emergency rooms without insurance coverage, nut jobs carting automatic rifles at open air rallies, unemployment a persistent plague. Her own job as a counselor at a clinic at Einstein Hospital was not exactly sound. And yet, here she was, toying with the idea of phoning back Poison Control to bark into the receiver.

The cell phone in her palm vibrated; perhaps it was Poison Control. She stared at it, determined that if she were given the chance, she'd take any proffered advice, elaborate on her specific symptoms, explain more carefully how recently she had been becoming more and more forgetful. Taking the heartworm pill was not an isolated case. Little things, like getting Britney Spears her heartworm pill on the first of the month (it was already the fifteenth), eating regular meals, and arriving to work on time had become more optional than required. Not that she didn't recognize in some back part of her brain that all of these activities were important, even vital. But, since she had asked Del to leave the house three months ago, time had taken on a peculiar shape, shifting in a manner that left less and less space for what once passed as regular, normal, organized life. Hours slid by; but what filled them she could no longer precisely name.

It was not that she missed him, exactly.

Or maybe it was. She punched a number into the phone.

"Lily? Are you ill?"

Her mother Ruth. Lily swallowed, noting an oddly beefy taste in the back of her throat.

"Why would you think that?" Lily asked.

"Because you were supposed to drive me for my iron tests," her mother said.

On the Art Museum calendar before her, Lily stared at the boxes filled with scrawls beneath a very scary portrait of twin Frida Kahlos holding onto a single bloody heart. What had possessed her to buy this calendar? Why not puppies? On the square marked for the fifteenth she read: *Take M to tests. 8:15. Don't forget. Important!*

"I'm sorry," she told her mother. "Del's supposed to drop off Natalie's tuition check this morning." She shot a glance at the clock above the refrigerator. "He's late."

"In person?"

Lily imagined her mother's face, her slightly Oriental looking eyes crinkling at the corners with unconcealed hope. Like everyone who met him, her mother had loved Del from first sight of his curly hair and dimpled chin. She knew what had transpired with Joy, but she had all her chips placed on an eventual reconciliation. *Everyone deserves a second chance*, she preached.

"Are you eating?" her mother asked.

"Britney Spears and I take excellent care of ourselves," Lily said. She caught her reflection in the toaster oven; a little lipstick wouldn't hurt. She headed to dig it out of her purse. "We're stocked up on kibble and fruit."

"A dog is not a husband, Lily," her mother said.

Lily hesitated. "But a husband can be a dog." Immediately she was sorry, but it was too late.

"Lily, Lily, Lily," her mother said. "Stop." And then she hung up the phone.

Lily stared at her cell. The second frustrated hang-up of the day, and it was not yet noon. How could she stop? She wanted to cry. Wasn't she the injured party here? Who said that *everyone* deserved a second chance? She started to dial back her mother, ready to argue or apologize, but before she finished punching in her number the patter of footsteps sounded up the brick steps to the back door.

At once, Britney Spears' ears perked up and her tail transformed into a giddy metronome.

"Is a doggy in there?" Del sang. "I come bearing doggy gifts."

Lily swabbed on the lipstick and dropped it into a utensil drawer.

"Use your key."

"That seems a bit formal." A moment later she heard the scratch of the familiar key. She had consulted with a lawyer friend about Del's refusal to give up the house key, but until the separation was formalized Del apparently had his rights. "Some people are easier than others," instructed the lawyer. "This one not so much."

"Britney!" called Del as he bumped the door closed with his hip. His traditional bag of peace-making onion bagels in one hand, a rubber chicken dog toy in the other, Dr. Delmore Swann, the love of her life, sauntered into the kitchen.

Britney Spears, who spent most of her time indoors inert, nose pressed to the tile and staring at the back of the self-same door, possibly praying continuously for this very celestial revelation, rushed forward at once, trampling over Lily's bare feet and straight into her beloved's embrace.

"Baby!" yelled Del. "Oh, how I've missed you!"

An unexpected pang rose in Lily's chest, but it was Britney Spears who made the leap into Del's tender embrace, Britney's pink tongue that freely swiped Del's freshly shaven face. Del dropped the bag of bagels and the dog immediately went for the warm circles of dough, nosing into the bag, splitting the paper and sending them spiraling. Del bent to grab them, but before he reached a single one Britney Spears sprang to grab the bouncy rubber chicken and knocked Del to the floor.

"Jesus H. Christ!" Del swore. "Britney, calm down." He rubbed his neck. "Britney, calm the fuck down." He waved his arms to ward her off. "What's wrong with this animal?"

Lily swallowed.

"She misses you?"

Del pushed to standing. As usual, he looked good—casual and rumpled. That was Del—rumpled casual. A pale blue button-down shirt that matched his eyes, straight-legged jeans that advertised his 33-inch waist, bare feet in penny loafers that held their shine.

Britney followed him as he retrieved the bagels. Strictly speaking, Britney Spears belonged to Del. Del had rescued her from a suburban SPCA at the tail end of their marriage—in part, Lily suspected, because his then-girl-pal Joy lived within dog-walking distance of their house and perambulating Britney Spears gave Del the perfect forty-five minute cover to escape from the house for a quickie with minimal suspicion. The dog, to put it bluntly, had served as Del's beard. Del and the dog ran a mutual adoration society, but when Lily kicked him out he had chosen a no pet/no kid apartment to share with Joy (who had—oh, the delicious irony!—abandoned ship after six weeks) and unmanageable, half-trained Britney became *de facto* hers.

Bagels gathered and regrouped across the kitchen counter. Del knelt back on the floor.

"Britney, my darlink." Del talked to the dog in the voice of Natasha from old *Rocky and Bullwinkle* cartoons. "How do I live vithout you?"

Months ago, pre-Joy, Lily might have provided the companion voice for Britney Spears: "Darlink, do not vorry. You are my one and only lurve." In those days, lured by Del's love of the dog, and her love of Del, this dog and master act might have served as a kind of foreplay. Lily would lean over to rub Britney's taut belly, her own sloping hip accidentally hitting Del's roaming hand. At such a moment, the two hands stroking the dog might have found their way to somewhere decidedly more interesting, and Britney Spears, sent to follow a bouncy tennis ball cast by Del into a faraway room, would have been all but forgotten as the two of them dropped to the floor.

Now, elbows perched on the counter top, watching Del make goo-goo eyes at the dog he had so easily deserted, Lily's eyes welled. She knew that as long as Del focused on Britney Spears he didn't have to deal with anything else—such as their broken-hearted daughter Natalie, who didn't understand why he couldn't come home. Or his infidelity. Or Lily.

She straightened.

"Tuition check?" she interrupted.

Outside, someone started a leaf blower. Lily remembered the punch line to one of Del's favorite jokes: "Sorry, I must be leafing." But she could no longer recall the joke.

With a natural grace, Del delivered a final pat to Britney's head and then jumped to his feet, pulling a green check from the back pocket of his jeans. But when Lily stretched over the counter to reach for it, he leaned back, keeping it from her reach.

"No games," Lily said.

"But I like games."

Lily made a second stretch for the check; Del again evaded her grasp. More than once she had asked him to mail the check rather than carry it over, but he refused.

"It's more *haimish* this way," he said. "Down to earth."

"Idiot," she said. But for some reason she smiled.

Del grinned back. For the first time since he had entered the room, Lily's spine loosened. The truth was that no matter how much he had hurt her—and he had truly hurt her—she wasn't totally sorry to see him. She had her own job and friends and life, but in many ways Del had been her life's work. As he waved the check in the air, she thought about all she knew about the man. How he had held Natalie in the steamy shower when she had the croup, the surprise fortieth birthday trip to Peru he had given her. Where he bought his iconic argyle socks. The time that this doctor who regularly dissected miniscule zebra fish hearts had sliced open his own finger parting salty oysters in Cape May. The origin of the tiny white scar on his right temple where Natalie, two years old and perhaps alert to future betrayals, had pinched him.

"Del." Lily leaned towards him, her voice softening. "This morning I swallowed the dog's heartworm pill."

"Jesus." The check dipped in his hand. "How pathetic can you get?"

Lily's head snapped up. "You don't mean that."

"What would you call it?" he asked. "Reasonable behavior? Rational activity? The sign of a well-functioning, organized brain?"

"I don't know what I'd call it," she said. *Everyone deserves a second chance.* "Maybe it doesn't have a name."

"Sweetheart." Del stepped towards her and set a hand on her shoulder. "Face it. You're a wreck." He smiled and massaged her upper arm. "You're lucky I'm here."

For the first time since Poison Control had suggested it, the tiniest rise of nausea clogged Lily's throat. But before she could swallow, before Del had time to say another word, Lily leaned in. She drew in a deep lungful of his familiar smell: a blend of Crest mouthwash, spicy aftershave, and an indefinable medicinal odor that he'd carried from the lab for all of their 27 years of marriage. Beyond her lips stretched his smooth collarbone, his pinkish nostrils, and his delicate earlobe, pale and juicy as a kumquat.

Closing her eyes, she considered her options. And then, with a quick snatch of breath, she parted her lips, bared her teeth, and settled them into the curve of Dr. Del Swann's neck.

"Fuck!" Del tried to jump back, but nothing budged. She

held firm. Britney Spears stared, interested but strangely impassive.

"Lily!" Del cried. "What the fuck!"

Teeth locked, she stilled, unwilling to give up her place. She didn't release him until the check, dangling in his loosened fingers, dropped to the floor.

Del sprang away, his face contorted, one hand clamped over his neck to staunch the pain.

"You're certifiable," Del told her. "You should be committed." A dark bruise had blossomed beneath his fingers. From the floor, Britney Spears whined for his attention, but Del paid her no mind.

"Don't think you're going to get away with this," he said. He stumbled to the doorway.

"Drop the key."

Del turned. From here, her handiwork resembled a love bite, a high school hickey. Her incisors tingled; her lips burned. The meaty taste had fled, replaced by the damp sweetness of her estranged husband's flesh. The metal key hit the tile. For the first time in weeks, maybe months, as she watched Del ignore Britney Spears to push his way through the door and out of the house, she believed that for a second she had tasted the center of things, wormed her way into the very heart.

The slam of the door echoed. Britney ran to the door and started to bark.

Lily studied the back of the door, her thoughts whirling. How could a man who studied molecules, who parsed strands of DNA, who published papers on the magical regeneration of the hearts of tiny fish that no one except those who published such papers might ever have a hope of understanding, be such a goddamn fool? Fool enough to throw away a good marriage, a solid marriage that she believed had been built on trust and love? All those songs about why fools fall in love had it backwards. The question was, why do smart people fall in love? Why don't they know any better? Why do they refuse to see what inevitably comes next?

"He's so not worth it," she told the dog. For some reason she was crying. "He's not," she said again.

The dog didn't pay her any mind. She kept barking and barking, bereft and alone.

Lily didn't move. She went through everything she needed to do: catch up on her billing, give the dog a bath, and clean the kitchen, living room, and bathrooms. Think about her future. Get over Del. The dog howled and howled.

Hide and Seek

Rae Pagliarulo

The following poem is the winner of the 2014 Sandy Crimmins National Prize for Poetry.

I
cracked the lid of the black World War II chest, my
    fingertips
split by the aging brass hollows where locks used to fit.
rooted my nose in the cedar closet, kicking around mouse
    droppings
and the scent of cured wood in my hair.
lifted the false bottom of my mother's bureau, the drawer
    where she kept *The*
Joy of Sex and a picture of the one she lost it to.
exhumed the basement floor, the remnants of a darkroom
and a dirt crawlspace fit for ghosts.
pulled back the carpets, peeled the paper from the walls,
undid the stitching on every pillow, slept under the bed
    for weeks.
cored myself like an apple, said ten Hail Marys, lit a candle
    and said
your name in the mirror 'til my smile bled at the edge.
wore the clothes of another girl, played my thigh bone like a
    bell,
felt the noise pierce my ear drum and throw my balance for
    good.
did everything you asked of me, held up my end of the deal,
    am waiting,
am waiting, I

am waiting
for you to show yourself.

A Broken Arm, a Mended Heart

Gina DeMillo Wagner

From the get-go I thought, "this guy is dangerous." By day, Kris was the web geek at the first magazine I worked for. But in his free time, he was an adrenaline junkie. He climbed 14,000-foot-tall mountains, skateboarded in empty swimming pools and, on a fat-tired bicycle, careened down steep, rocky hillsides. Each Monday, he arrived at work with a new bruise or glistening red wound from the weekend's folly.

One winter, he took a six-week sabbatical from work so that he could bike across Siberia's Lake Baikal, the oldest, deepest lake in the world. Of course, in winter, it's not really a lake at all, but a 400-mile-long swath of ice sandwiched between jagged rocks. On his list of gear to pack were studded bicycle tires, a sleeping bag rated to −40F, and a screwdriver in case the ice broke and he fell into the churning, subfreezing water (he'd use the screwdriver to claw his way out). Another time, he nearly plunged 1,500 vertical feet off the face of Oregon's Mount Hood. By luck—or divine intervention—the tip of his mountaineer's axe caught in a fissure of ice and stopped him mid-slide. He went on to summit the mountain, triumphant.

Kris was also dangerous in the sense that he was fiercely attractive. At the office, he fastened his long, wild, curly hair into a ponytail. He wore short-sleeved button-down shirts that complemented his broad shoulders and climber's biceps. Behind his glasses shone ocean blue eyes that could slice through your soul.

Adventure was his lifeblood. He had grown up a free-range kid on 300 acres in central Wisconsin, where he'd learned to hunt, climb and ice fish. He loved the cold, and insisted he'd teach me—a timid girl from Atlanta—how to snowboard. One January night, after he hosted a happy hour for several coworkers, I lingered. He set me up with boots that were two sizes too big, strapped me to the waxed fiberglass board, gave me a few pointers, and nudged me down the hill behind his apartment building. I thought snowboarding was easy and fun...until we got to the *real* slope in Vermont a few days later. During my inaugural run on the bunny hill, I tumbled and broke my arm.

That was our first date.

I could have cut my losses and walked away right then. Bones heal, after all. I wasn't so sure about my heart.

Avoiding pain had been my personal mission since I was five. My childhood home was dominated by brokenness and heartache, beginning in the early 1970s with my older brother, who was born severely developmentally disabled. He had seizures and threw violent fits and had to be monitored around the clock. My brother couldn't help who he was, but that didn't stop my parents from grieving. Back then, having a disabled child was a disease, and my parents didn't have a cure. They had me, and later, a "normal" son. But we weren't enough. Dashed hopes had already metastasized into resentment, lies and fury.

Dad eventually moved out.

After that, my mother was on a quest to fill the emptiness in her heart and beat back the depression that was engulfing her (and us). The men she pursued—some married, others womanizers—had no interest in the mother-of-three package deal, especially when it included a special needs kid. Even so young, I knew there was no way for these relationships to end well. My role was to keep the peace, to buffer her pain by shouldering some of the parenting load while she disappeared into the night. When she collapsed on the bathroom floor sobbing after yet another breakup, I was also her therapist. I told her what she wanted to hear, that everything would be all right, that her Prince Charming was still out there, somewhere. Meanwhile, I vowed never to follow in her footsteps. I resolved not to treat my heart so recklessly.

When it came time for me to date, I chose buttoned-up, glowing Southern boys who vowed to keep me chaste until our wedding day. What these conservative gents lacked in passion and adventure, they made up for in piety. I was allured by how steadfast they were as much as by their stable, two-parent upbringings. In so many ways, I was still five years old and pining for a whole and happy family.

When the relationships ended (never dramatically, but more with a cartoonish *wah wah wah* of unreturned phone calls or *it's not you, it's me*), I was sad, but not heartbroken. A heart can't break when it's shuttered away. I was so determined to live in opposition to my mother that I discounted the most important element of romance: attraction.

Now here was Kris. I couldn't get enough of him, and it terrified me. His voice was infused with passion and kindness and a yearning for life, and I just wanted to be around him and hear him speak more. In the beginning, that's all we did. We talked, sometimes until three in the morning, sitting in the passenger seat of his Jeep with the heat cranked and my legs sweating. Or sprawled on the futon in my apartment after cooking elaborate, messy dinners together—me with my one good arm. We discussed books and travel and movies and music and all that we dreamed of doing, of being.

For all his risk taking, it was weeks before Kris ventured to kiss me. He waited until my arm had healed and we could properly embrace. The moment was like throwing gasoline on a smoldering coal.

It wasn't long before I started joining him on adventures. We flew to London on a whim one weekend because an airline was selling round-trip tickets for $199. He'd seen the advertisement and said, "I've never been. Wanna go?" His optimism and spontaneity were infectious. We went camping in three feet of snow just for the hell of it, and stayed up all night, cocooned in our down sleeping bags. The stars were so thick against the black winter sky, like nothing I'd ever seen before. I gazed up and saw for the first time a future that didn't have to be defined by my past.

Eventually, we moved into a 150-year-old farmhouse in eastern Pennsylvania. The house sat on eight acres and was bordered by an organic farm on one side, a tree farm on another, and a Mennonite family farm across the road. Kris continued to chase his next adrenaline fix—scaling mountains, adventure racing, backpacking—but now he had a home base, with me. We loved to bicycle, and from our front door we could piece together 50-mile undulating loops that toured the patchwork quilt of Dutch Country and never once crossed a busy street. On Sunday mornings, we awoke to the clip-clop of horse-drawn carriages, our neighbors heading off to church. We bought eggs, bread, and organic produce from the neighboring farms and cultivated our own salsa garden full of tomatoes, peppers, onions and cilantro.

Kris loved it because it reminded him of where he'd grown up. I loved it because it was the exact opposite of how I'd grown up. He begged me to sleep with the windows open. His body craved the smell of grass, trees, dirt. But I resisted. My childhood home had been burglarized several times, once in the middle of the night while we were home, cowering under our beds.

"Don't you know I'll protect you, city girl?" he asked me with a warm smile as he slid open the rickety old windows and let the cool breeze pour in. I looked into his face, so genuine and loving, and knew he'd do anything to keep me safe. It took a while, but I leaned into this man, and I began to see that risk does not equal recklessness. He took chances in life, but not with my heart.

Kris likened our relationship to a tandem mountain bike ride on a sinuous trail. A journey not without steep climbs and rocky patches. But the smooth parts? The white-knuckle downhill stretches of trail that make you giddy, that take your breath away? Pure bliss.

So it seemed fitting that one day, just as I was descending the rockiest trail I'd ever dared to ride, feeling the panic-thrill that comes from suspending caution and reaping the reward, I found Kris at the bottom of the hill by a mountain stream, down on one knee. He was caked in dirt and grinning ear-to-ear. My knight on a silver bicycle.

"You've been my adventure partner, my best friend, my anchor," he said. "I want you to be my wife."

My heart pounded from exertion and the realization that he was sincere, that I could have it all—safety, adventure, and passion—for the rest of my life. I peeled the sweaty leather glove off my left hand and let him slip a ring onto my finger.

We rode away and never looked back.

Contributors

Allison Alsup ("East of the Sierra") grew up in Oakland, CA; in 2000, she and her husband purchased a decrepit, century-old cottage in New Orleans. They have since redesigned and salvaged several old houses in the city. Their current house is a work in slow progress. In addition to receiving the Marguerite McGlinn Prize for Fiction from *Philadelphia Stories*, Allison's short fiction has placed first in contests sponsored by A Room of Her Own Foundation and *New Millennium Writings*. Her work will also appear in *The 2014 O'Henry Prize Stories*. She is currently writing a historical novel about the final expedition of plant explorer Frank Meyer.

Caitie Barrett ("*Sep Tepy* (The First Time)") is a classical archaeologist and Egyptologist. Her poems have been published in *Pressed Wafer Foldems, Can We Have Our Ball Back, Palimpsest,* and *The Gamut*; she was also a finalist in the first annual Bow and Arrow Poetry Contest. She lives in Ithaca, NY and works as an Assistant Professor of Classics at Cornell University.

Luke Bauerlein ("Is it Better to Sleep") has published his work in *The New York Times, Mid-America Poetry Review, Shot Glass Journal,* and elsewhere. He currently lives in West Philadelphia and writes songs and performs with the band The Late Greats.

Jacob A. Bennett ("Excerpts from Undeliverables: Prose poem postcards") lives and works in Philadelphia, where he teaches rhetoric, poetry, and literature. Links to CV, other poems, and various well-intentioned screeds published at antigloss.wordpress.com.

Sharon Black ("Gift") has published poems in *The South Carolina Review, Cimarron Review, Slipstream, Alaska Quarterly Review, Mudfish, Poet Lore, Painted Bride Quar-*

terly, *Rhino*, and many others. Her work was nominated for the Pushcart Prize in 2005 and 2007. She is a librarian at the University of Pennsylvania and lives in Wallingford, PA.

Randall Brown ("Little Magpie") has been published widely, both online and in print, and blogs regularly at FlashFiction.Net. He is the author of the award-winning flash collection *Mad to Live*, published by PS Books, and *A Pocket Guide to Flash Fiction*. He is also the founder and managing editor of Matter Press and its Journal of Compressed Creative Arts.

Maria Ceferatti ("Inheritance") is a writer and music teacher in the Philadelphia area. She teaches creative writing to elementary school students with the Young Writers' Day program, and she is the Music Director of Acting Without Boundaries, a theater group for performers with physical disabilities. Maria is pursuing her MFA in Creative Writing at Rosemont College, and she blogs at southphillystories.com.

CAConrad ("Thank You for Mixing with My Emotional Circuitry") is the author of seven books, including *Ecodevianc: (Soma)tics for the Future Wilderness* (Wave Books, 2014), *A Beautiful Marsupial Afternoon* (Wave Books, 2012) and *The Book of Frank* (Wave Books, 2010). A 2014 Lannan Fellow, a 2013 MacDowell Fellow, and a 2011 Pew Fellow, he also conducts workshops on (Soma)tic poetry and Ecopoetics. Visit him online at http://CAConrad.blogspot.com.

Sandy Crimmins ("Spring") served on the *Philadelphia Stories* board from 2005 to 2007 and her voice and vision have fundamentally shaped *Philadelphia Stories*. Sandy was a poet who performed with musicians, dancers, and fire-eaters, and one of her proudest accomplishments was celebrating the work of her vibrant poetry community.

Christina Delia ("The Robbery") received her BFA in Writing for Film and Television from The University of the

Arts in Philadelphia. Her work can be found in the anthologies *In One Year and Out the Other* (Pocket Books), *Random Acts of Malice: The Best of Happy Woman Magazine*, *The Woman I've Become*, and *Uncle John's Bathroom Reader Presents: Flush Fiction*, among others. Christina was most recently published in the *Edison Literary Review*. She resides in New Jersey with her husband Robert and their daughter, Juliet.

Penny Dickerson ("The Decade I Longed to Be Grown") is a Florida-based poet and independent journalist whose passion is a combined endeavor of utilizing language and experience to create lyrics, prose, and news features that speak to the human condition. She earned a BA in Journalism from Temple University and an MFA in Creative Writing from Lesley University. Her work can be found in *Mosaic Magazine*, *Arbus Magazine*, Ebony.com, *The Florida Courier*, *The Florida Times-Union*, *Azure and Amber Anthology*, and more. Her poetry collection *Lyrical Soul* is available via Amazon.com and she has also written *Cancer in the Raw*. Penny is an Adjunct Professor of Liberal Arts and Humanities at Florida State College at Jacksonville (Deerwood Campus).

Kathleen Donnelly ("How Is This My Story") works as a writer and teaching artist in Pittsburgh, Pennsylvania. In addition to fiction writing, Kathleen is also a produced playwright and recipient of a fellowship from the PA Council on the Arts. Her one-act play, "Upon a Sea of Dreams: A Journey on the Titanic," is published by Theatrefolk and has been performed throughout the US and Canada. She is currently working on more projects than she should be and needs to buckle down and choose just one.

B.G. Firmani ("To the Garden") has published fiction in the *Bellevue Literary Review*, *BOMB*, the *Brooklyner*, the *Kenyon Review*, and *Word Riot*. A graduate of Barnard College and Brown University, she has been a resident at the MacDowell Colony and Yaddo and is a 2012 Fellow in

Fiction from the New York Foundation for the Arts. She also (occasionally) writes a blog about Italian-American literature and folkways called *Forte e Gentile*. And she once again thanks Steve Almond for choosing "To the Garden" for *Philadelphia Stories'* Marguerite McGlinn Prize for Fiction in 2011.

Kelly George ("Naked and Hungry") is a writer and teacher living in Philadelphia. Her essays have appeared in the literary magazines *Brain, Child,* and *Literary Mama.* She is now married to the man who appeared unexpectedly to watch as she rummaged, nude, through his refrigerator.

Denise Gess ("Not Tony and Tina") was the author of two critically-acclaimed novels, *Good Deeds* (1984) and *Red Whiskey Blues* (1989), and co-authored the nonfiction book *Firestorm at Peshtigo: A Town, Its People and the Deadliest Fire in American History* (2002). Her short fiction appeared in the *North American Review* and has been anthologized in *The Horizon Reader.* She was an associate professor at Rowan University. Denise, a longtime *Philadelphia Stories* board member, died of lung cancer in 2009.

Dutch Godshalk ("At Night I Smoke") works as a news editor for Montgomery Media and *The Lansdale Reporter*; he also writes for Ticket Entertainment as a music beat reporter. He is the recipient of two 2014 Keystone Press Awards as well as a 2014 Philly DoGooder film award. His work has appeared in *Apiary, Philadelphia Stories, The Times Herald, The Ambler Gazette, The Springfield Sun, The Souderton Independent,* and *Main Line Media News.*

Alexandra Gold ("Water, Communion") received her BA in English, Creative Writing, and Political Science and her MA in English from the University of Pennsylvania. She is currently pursuing her PhD in English at Boston University with concentrations in modern and contemporary poetry and in women's, gender, and sexuality studies.

Ivy Goldstein ("Fortune") was born and raised in the Mount Airy section of Philadelphia. She now lives in Beijing, working and studying Chinese. She fondly misses her hometown.

Leonard Gontarek ("A.M.") has lived in Philadelphia for twenty years. He has taught and presented hundreds of poets through reading series in the area. He is the author of *St. Genevieve Watching Over Paris, Van Morrison Can't Find His Feet, Zen for Beginners, Deja Vu Diner,* and *He Looked Beyond My Faults and Saw My Needs.* His poems have appeared in *The Best American Poetry, Joyful Noise! An Anthology of American Spiritual Poetry, The Working Poet, American Poetry Review, Fence, Field, Verse, Poet Lore,* and as a tattoo. www.leafscape.org/LeonardGontarek

Brian Patrick Heston ("On Seeing Old Footage of Norman Snead Playing for the Philadelphia Eagles") grew up in Philadelphia. His poems have won awards from the Dorothy Sargent Rosenberg Foundation, the Robinson Jeffers Tor House Foundation, and the Lanier Library Association. His first book, *If You Find Yourself,* recently won the Main Street Rag Poetry Book Prize and is due out in November of 2014. His chapbook *Latchkey Kids* was recently published by Finishing Line Press. His poetry and fiction have appeared in such publications as *Many Mountains Moving, Rosebud, Lost Coast Review, West Branch, Harpur Palate, 5AM, The Spoon River Poetry Review, Poet Lore, South Carolina Review,* and his work is forthcoming in *Cider Press Review, Tampa Review,* and *Tupelo Quarterly.* He is a PhD candidate in Literature and Creative Writing at Georgia State University.

Kathryn Elisa Ionata ("A Supermarket in Pennsylvania") is a Pushcart Prize-nominated writer whose work has appeared most recently in *The Toast, Hawai'i Review, Wisconsin Review, Schuylkill Valley Journal, U.S. 1 Worksheets,* and *Aries.* She teaches writing at Temple University, where she completed her MFA in Creative Writing Fiction. She lives in Bucks County, PA. Learn more at www.kathrynionata.com.

Jonathan Kemmerer-Scovner ("Bunker") lives just beyond the reaches of Philadelphia, PA, with his beautiful wife and cool son. When he's not contemplating end-of-the-world scenarios, he writes and tells children's stories and posts long-winded reviews of picture books at www.PictureBooksReview.com.

DJ Kinney ("I-80") is currently completing his doctoral dissertation in the field of the history of science at Florida State University. Recent publications include scholarly work in *Centaurus* as well as *The Polar Journal*. His fiction has appeared over the years in *Eureka Literary Magazine, Eclipse, Puckerbrush Review, Allegheny Review, Vincent Brothers Review*, and others. DJ resides for much of the year at Nantasket Beach outside of Boston with his wife Annette and their family of small dogs.

Paul Lisicky ("The White Deer") is the author of four books: *Lawnboy, Famous Builder, The Burning House*, and U*nbuilt Projects*. His work has appeared in *Conjunctions, Fence, The Iowa Review, Ploughshares, Tin House, Unstuck*, and in many other publications. His awards include fellowships from the National Endowment for the Arts, the James Michener/Copernicus Society, and the Fine Arts Work Center in Provincetown, where he was twice a fellow. He teaches in the MFA Program at Rutgers-Camden and in the low-residency program at Sierra Nevada College. A memoir, *The Narrow Door*, is forthcoming from Graywolf Press in 2015.

Alexander Long ("Unfinished Love Poem") was born and raised in Sharon Hill, Pennsylvania. He has worked as a musician, obituary writer, and fry cook. With Christopher Buckley, he is co-editor of *A Condition of the Spirit: the Life & Work of Larry Levis* (Eastern Washington University).

Helen W. Mallon ("My Charlie Manson") draws on her Philadelphia Quaker background to explore the ground between tradition and change. Her book reviews appear in the *Philadelphia Inquirer, San Francisco Chronicle*, and *Fiction Writ-*

ers Review. Her short story chapbook is titled *The Beautiful Name.* www.helenwmallon.com

Marguerite McGlinn ("The Sphinx") was the nonfiction editor of *Philadelphia Stories* from 2004 to 2008. Her travel stories appeared in *The New York Times, The Sun-Sentinel, The Philadelphia Inquirer,* and *The Los Angeles Times.* She edited *The Trivium: The Liberal Arts of Logic, Grammar, and Rhetoric* (Paul Dry Books, 2002). Three of her short stories won places in "Writing Aloud," a program of dramatic readings that matches contemporary fiction with professional actors. She was an adjunct instructor at Saint Joseph University in Philadelphia.

Maxime D. McKenna ("Dog People") has published his fiction in *Philadelphia Stories, Apiary, Cartographer: A Literary Review,* and *First Stop Fiction,* and he has contributed essays to *The Millions, Full Stop,* the *Journal of Modern Literature,* and *Filament,* among others. He is currently pursuing his PhD in English at the University of Chicago.

Eileen Moeller ("At the Mutter Museum of Medical Oddities") has an MA in Creative Writing from Syracuse University and many years of experience as a teacher, workshop leader, and storyteller. She's had poems published in *Ars Medica, Umbrella, Sugar Mule, The Paterson Literary Review, Feminist Studies, Melusine, Kritya, Paterson: A Poet's City, Schuylkill Valley Journal,* and *Fox Chase Review.* Her poem "Milk Time" won the 2011 Allen Ginsberg Award, and her blog—And So I Sing: Poems and Iconography—can be accessed at http://www.eileenmoeller.blogspot.com.

James W. Morris ("Richard the Third, the Second") grew up in Philadelphia and graduated from Central High School and LaSalle University, where he was awarded a scholarship for creative writing. He has published dozens of short stories, humor pieces, and essays in various literary magazines, and he worked for a time as a monologue writer for Jay Leno. He has just completed the manuscript for his first novel, called "Rude Baby."

Vincent Natale ("Aged," cover), a South Philadelphia native, is also a sometime actor, screenwriter, and stand-up comedian. Chiefly a self-taught artist, his interests and influences range widely but his primary focus is on the abstract representation of landscapes and everyday objects. As a young person, he studied at Fleisher Art Memorial and later at The Pennsylvania Academy of Fine Arts and The Hussian School. His belief is that art is the catharsis of nature and the blueprint of life.

Pat O'Brien ("Devon Drive") teaches creative writing at Penn State Brandywine. Her poems have appeared in *Philadelphia Poets*, *Mad Poets Review*, and *Schuylkill Valley Journal of the Arts*. She lives in West Chester with her husband and two daughters.

Casey Otto ("Atop the Camel's Hump") is a Rowan University graduate with a degree in Writing Arts. As she's something of an outdoorswoman, many of Casey's stories are inspired by the secret worlds she's found hidden in forests and fields, and in the songs sung by water and wind. This story won Rowan's 2012 Denise Gess Literary Award for Creative Nonfiction. Casey lives in Lumberton, New Jersey and is currently writing a novel for young people.

Rae Pagliarulo ("Hide and Seek") is a proud Philadelphia native currently working in the nonprofit development field. Her work has been featured on the Huffington Post Blog, as well as in West Chester University's *Daedalus: A Magazine of the Arts*. She served as the magazine's assistant editor and was awarded its "Best Short Work" award in 2003. She holds a BA from West Chester University and is happily working towards her MFA in Creative Writing at Rosemont College.

Ilene Raymond Rush ("The Worm of the Heart") has published her fiction, nonfiction, and essays in a wide variety of national publications. Her short fiction has been awarded an O. Henry Prize and a James Michener Fellowship from the University of Iowa.

Jacob Russell ("Like Nothing in the World") is a visual artist, poet, and activist living in West Philly. You can find links to his published writing and photos of his art on his blog, www.jacobrussellsbarkingdog.blogspot.com.

Adam Schwartz ("The Rest of the World") received an MFA from Washington University in St. Louis in 1995. His stories have appeared in *Arkansas Review/Kansas Quarterly*, and in 1999 he won first place in the *Baltimore City Paper*'s short story contest. In 2011, "The Rest of the World" received an Honorable Mention in *New Letters*' Alexander Cappon story contest and in 2012 it won the *Poets & Writers* 2012 Maureen Egen Writers Exchange Award. Adam teaches high school English in Baltimore City. The experiences he has with young people in the classroom sometimes find their way into his work.

Noel Sloboda ("Advice from an Opossum") is the author of the poetry collections *Our Rarer Monsters* (sunnyoutside, 2013) and *Shell Games* (sunnyoutside, 2008) as well as several chapbooks, most recently *Circle Straight Back* (ervená Barva Press, 2012). His work has recently appeared in *Fourteen Hills*, *Gigantic*, *Modern Language Studies*, and *Sentence*. Sloboda has also published a book about Edith Wharton and Gertrude Stein. He teaches at Penn State York.

Stories and essays by **Curtis Smith** ("The Prettiest Lie") have appeared in over seventy-five literary journals. His work has been cited by The Best American Short Stories, The Best American Mystery Stories, and The Best American Spiritual Writing. He is the author of the novels *An Unadorned Life*, *Sound and Noise*, and *Truth or Something Like It*. His story collections include *In the Jukebox Light*, *The Species Crown*, and *Bad Monkey*. His essay collection *Witness* was released in late 2011. This past spring, Press 53 published his most recent story collection, *Beasts and Men*. His next book, *Communion*, an essay collection from Dock Street Press, will be published in early 2015. His novel *Lovepain* will be put out by Aqueous Books in 2016.

Laura Spagnoli ("Waiting for Test Results in the Kitchen") is the author of the chapbook *My Dazzledent Days* (ixnay press). Her poems can be found in *Jupiter 88, ONandOnScreen, Apiary*, and *Bedfellows*, and her story "A Cut Above" was published in *Philadelphia Noir*. She lives in Philadelphia and teaches French at Temple University.

Justin St. Germain ("Atlantic City") is the author of the memoir *Son of a Gun*, which won the 2013 Barnes & Noble Discover Award in Nonfiction and was named a best book of the year by Amazon, *Library Journal, BookPage, Salon*, and *Publishers Weekly*. He lives in the Twin Cities and teaches at Hamline University.

Bringing a hardy compendium of voices—from the poem to the bass clarinet to the alchemy of hat-making—poet **Toussaint St. Negritude** ("Northern Liberties") is a well-hatted resident of Northern New England and has recently become a fond member of the Belfast, Maine poets' community. From San Francisco to Haiti to Philadelphia, and now to Maine, Toussaint St. Negritude is deeply informed by an expansive wealth of this globe's enlightening sources of wonder. Recent publications: PoemCity, the I've Known Rivers Project, *SOMA Magazine, The San Francisco Bay Guardian, Philadelphia Stories*, and *PenBay Pilot*. toussaintstnegritude.tumblr.com

Amanda Stopa ("The Drunkest Three-Year-Old in the Room") is a nomadic poet who spent a good amount of time in Philadelphia earning her MFA. Recent work has appeared in *Bearers of Distance Anthology: Poems by Runners* and *Spry Literary Journal*.

Eric Thurschwell ("Housemates"), a partially employed high school math tutor, lives in Ardmore, Pennsylvania. Eric bitterly regrets using "masturbation" instead of "onanism" in the second sentence of this story.

Sean Finucane Toner ("Night Diving") is a Pushcart Prize nominee and Best of the Net finalist whose creative nonfiction has found homes in *The Best of Hippocampus, Ardor, Brevity, The MacGuffin, Opium, Apiary, Referential, Word Riot, The Monarch Review, Perigee, Writers on the Job,* and *The Book of Worst Meals,* as well as at a Literary Death Match at the World Cafe in Philadelphia. He has served as vice president of the Philadelphia Writers' Conference and is the Editor-in-Chief/Nonfiction editor of *Referential Magazine* (www.referentialmagazine.org). Sean has been sightless since 1995. www.seantoner.com

Gina DeMillo Wagner ("A Broken Arm, a Mended Heart") began her career as an editor for Rodale Inc. in Emmaus, Pennsylvania. She now writes for magazines including *Forbes Travel Guide, Backpacker, Outside, Wired,* and *Experience Life.* Her personal essays have appeared in *Role/Reboot, Elephant Journal, Mama Moderne,* and more. She is at work on a memoir and lives with her husband Kris and their two children in Arizona.

Wes Ward ("Poem in the Freezer Section") holds an MA in writing from Johns Hopkins University. His work has appeared in various magazines and journals, including *North American Review, Sewanee Theological Review,* and *Birmingham Poetry Review.* Wes teaches high school English in York, PA and lives with his wife Karen and his children, Ethan and Isley, in Newville, PA.

Pediatrician **Kelley White** ("Called") worked in inner-city Philadelphia and now works in rural New Hampshire. Her poems have appeared in journals including *Exquisite Corpse, Rattle,* and *JAMA.* Her most recent books are *Toxic Environment* (Boston Poet Press) and *Two Birds in Flame* (Beech River Books.) She received a 2008 Pennsylvania Council on the Arts grant.

Che Yeun ("One in Ten Fish Are Afraid of Water") was born in Seoul, Korea. Her writing can also be found in *The Pinch, Enizagam, Kartika Review,* and *Trop.* She lives in Cambridge, England, where she is working on a collection of stories and studying the history of medicine.

Tim Zatzariny, Jr. ("Are you Ready for the Country?") is a lifelong resident of South Jersey. He teaches writing at his alma mater, Rowan University. His work has appeared in *Philadelphia Stories, Thieves Jargon*, and elsewhere. He is at work on his first novel, set in his hometown of Vineland, NJ.

www.ingramcontent.com/pod-product-compliance
Lightning Source LLC
Chambersburg PA
CBHW060905250626
47159CB00008B/2882